'Nicola Rayner has written the new *The Girl on the Train*, with note-perfect prose and an ending that will leave you gasping'
Observer

'Nicola Rayner writes like a dream. An engrossing and emotionally honest thriller'
Emma Curtis, author of *The Night You Left*

'A tantalising and suspenseful mystery. Absolutely brilliant!'
Lauren North, author of *The Perfect Betrayal*

'A haunting mystery with beautifully written characters'
Jenny Quintana, author of *The Missing Girl*

'Superbly written . . . An author to watch with the greatest of excitement'
The Chap

YOU AND ME

Nicola Rayner was born in Abergavenny, South Wales, and works as a freelance journalist. *The Girl Before You*, her first novel, was picked by the *Observer* as a debut to look out for in 2019. It has been translated into multiple languages and has also been optioned for television. She lives in London with her husband and Jack Russell.

NICOLA RAYNER

YOU AND ME

avon.

Published by AVON
A division of HarperCollins*Publishers* Ltd
1 London Bridge Street
London SE1 9GF

www.harpercollins.co.uk

A Paperback Original 2020

First published in Great Britain by HarperCollins*Publishers* 2020

A catalogue copy of this book is available from the British Library.

ISBN: 978-0-00-837459-4

This novel is entirely a work of fiction. The names, characters and incidents
portrayed in it are the work of the author's imagination. Any resemblance
to actual persons, living or dead, events or localities is entirely coincidental.

Typeset in Sabon Lt Std by Palimpsest Book Production Limited,
Falkirk, Stirlingshire
Printed and bound in UK by CPI Group (UK) Ltd, Croydon CR0 4YY

MIX
Paper from
responsible sources
FSC
www.fsc.org FSC° C007454

This book is produced from independently certified FSC™ paper to ensure
responsible forest management.

For more information visit: www.harpercollins.co.uk/green

For my first friends in the world,
Lucy, Sophie and Mark

I've always been of a determined nature. Patient, they used to call me. I like to see a thing through to the end.

– Margaret Atwood, The Penelopiad

Prologue

In the winter, the lake outside his house ices over, and the birds – the ducks, moorhens and even a pair of swans, who come and go like royal visitors – huddle under the weeping willow. But it's May now, his birthday. When I made my trip this morning, there was a different texture to the air – something silky, springlike. A teasing breeze ruffles the surface of the water; it makes me feel hopeful that things might change.

I always sit on the same bench by the lake – I'm a creature of habit like that. Apart from the birds, I have the garden to myself. I wait for a long time, thinking about how it began between us all those years ago. His present sits in my lap. I haven't given it to him yet. I'm not sure I will.

At our school there was an award called the Back Prize – the winner was someone who excelled at sitting up straight and still and, I don't like to boast, but I won it three times. As Mrs Morgan, our housemistress, said:

'Some girls are pretty and some girls are sporty, but you're good at sitting up straight, Fran.' If you wait, something always happens eventually, but today I can't wait for much longer.

I get to my feet and begin to walk around the lake to the front of the house. I'm always struck by the beauty of it. As if someone created it to be admired. Making my way along the path, I nearly tread on a duck egg, still warm when I pick it up. It's a shade so delicate it could have been artificially created. The nest is easy to find in the hollow of a nearby tree. I put it back as carefully as I can and say a little prayer that its mum doesn't reject it when she returns. Babies should be with their mothers.

Glancing up, I see two small faces peeking out of the nursery window on the first floor. I'm not sure if they've seen me and I'm torn, for a moment, between delivering his present and scurrying quickly away.

1

It's merely coincidental I'm there the night Dickie Graham dies. That is what I shall say if they ask me. I never liked Dickie, so, on that matter, I may have to dissemble, but nobody deserves to die in that way. Not even the worst of us.

There's no sign, that morning, of what is to come. I wake with Branwell curled up on my bed licking himself and listen to the children next door through the thin walls. It's too porous, London living – there's no escaping other people's sounds and smells: the judder of a neighbour's washing machine on spin, the billows of marijuana travelling through the pipes from the flat below.

I have my daily rituals. After feeding Branwell, I say good morning to the photograph of Mother and Ellie. It's a picture I took of them myself. They're in Whitby, sitting on what we used to call the halfway bench, the midway point on the steps that run up from the town's cobbled streets to the Abbey. We grew up in a cottage on the North York Moors, and Mother never tired of our trips to Whitby, dropping in to see the Abbey like an old friend, or popping over to Scarborough to visit Anne Brontë's grave.

In the photo, Mother smiles, a faint sheen of sweat on her forehead from the climb, but Ellie looks restless, as if she can barely sit still long enough for the picture to be taken. Mother's arm is heavy on my sister's shoulders, holding her close while she can before Ellie darts off. She was a physical child who always needed to be moving, either running up the steps ahead of us or plunging into the sea, even when the weather was inclement. She'd shiver, wet hair dripping, in the car on the way back. That was before she gave up swimming.

The next thing I do each morning, if there's time, is check Ellie's Facebook page. Since yesterday she's posted a photograph of her and Rose perched on what strikes me as a perilously high wall for a two-year-old, looking up at the Eiffel Tower, with the caption: Another one off the list for Rose! Paris, je t'aime.

You can only see the backs of their heads, but the image fills me with longing. Ellie's hair is the same white-blonde cloud it always was, but Rose's is thick and brown like mine. Wherever they are, Ellie has a knack of framing the shot perfectly. But she doesn't post as often as I'd like, and as Rose's face has developed over the years, from baby to toddler, I've missed the tiny, incremental changes.

Sometimes I wake to find they've moved again – another country or even another continent. She never tells me

4

where she's going next. I just learn through Facebook like the rest of the world. I try not to get too cross about it as I move the bit of Blu Tack on my globe to the new location, to help me imagine where they are.

When I get to the bookshop, Ingrid and Liam are leaning against the bike railings outside the staff entrance, both smoking and admiring Ingrid's long legs crossed out in front of her. They barely look up at me as I type the code into the keypad and let myself in. Ingrid and Liam are in their twenties and think they're better than the job – she's an actress, though I've never known her to go to an audition, and he's a photographer. He's not her boyfriend, but he'd like to be. What I think of as the old guard – Gareth, the manager, Brenda and me – we're different. We're in our late thirties now. There are certain dreams we've given up on. I suppose that's just part of growing up. I once hoped to be an English teacher, like Mother, but it didn't turn out that way.

I still have the chance to talk about literature every day. One of the best parts of the job is introducing the right person to the right book. I like to imagine myself as the bookseller's answer to Jane Austen's Emma. Indeed, such is my aptitude for making matches, I flatter myself I'm more successful. Which is why when I overhear a tired-looking man asking Ingrid at the till if she can recommend any books about bullying, I step in. Ingrid has already fobbed him off with vague directions to the Mind, Body and Spirit section by the time I reach him, but I believe I can do better.

'Is the book for an adult or a child?'

'My daughter – she's nine.' He shoots me a grateful look, while Ingrid scowls.

'How about Roald Dahl's *Matilda*?' I begin. 'That's a good one to start with. Or there's *The Boy in the Dress* by David Walliams. I'm guessing it needs a happy ending?'

'Isn't that comedy?'

'It's funny, yes, but moving. It's about a child who misses his mother . . .'

'My daughter does too.' He says it so quietly I can barely make out the words.

I glance at him and notice how empty and sad his eyes look. I have the urge to reach out and touch his arm, which is unlike me.

'She's shrunk into herself,' he says.

I know what that feels like. Sometimes when I wake from a particularly vivid dream, I forget that she's gone for a moment. Until she became ill, Mother was such a substantial person physically. Solid, dependable, like me. Without her, with Ellie so far away, there are moments when I feel completely unmoored.

I know what the bullying feels like too.

We spend quite a long time in the children's section picking out a shortlist. I have to ignore the occasional ting of the bell as Ingrid tries to summon me to the till. I leave it for someone else to help her. At times like these, I see books as medicine and it's important to get the prescription right.

After I've made the sale, the man thanks me, raises a hand to his salt-and-pepper hair and hesitates. 'I suppose you're tired after your shifts here,' he says uncertainly.

'You probably don't feel like going out at the end of a long day.'

'Usually you'd be right,' I say, 'I like to go home and read, but tonight I have plans.' I smile to myself at the thought and turn to the next customer.

'He was hitting on you,' Ingrid says after he's gone. She pulls a face as if the idea appals her.

I hadn't realised. Things like that don't happen to me as often as they do to Ingrid and I'm not good at noticing them. Even if I have the faintest inkling, I'm not sure how to respond, what they expect of me. Anyway, it's true, I do have plans tonight.

At home, I get ready with care, choosing an old favourite I picked up from Oxfam – a navy Fifties-style dress that shows off my blue eyes and gives me something resembling a waistline. I dress, as I often do, in Mother's bedroom upstairs, where there's more space and a full-length mirror. My own cramped room is on the ground floor, but I've never thought to swap. This space will always be Mother's.

Ellie and I never got around to sorting it out after she died. We talked about it, especially when Ellie was pregnant with Rose – I suggested she use it as a nursery; Mother would have liked that – and we even went in to do it one rainy Saturday. Ellie opened a drawer in Mother's desk at random. We both glanced down at what it contained – a couple of batteries, three old notebooks and a packet of out-of-date paracetamol – looked at each other, then Ellie closed it. 'Do you want to go for a walk?' she asked and I nodded quickly.

When I'm ready, I check my reflection in the wardrobe

7

mirror. Not too bad. Still a bit on the large side. 'Looking *hot*,' says a mocking voice in my head as I assess myself. I still hear them sometimes – Dickie Graham or Juliet Bentley making fun of me after all these years. When I catch my reflection in shop windows, looking a little pudgy, or if I say something in a group situation that makes everyone else go quiet, I can hear them chuckling, making clever comments. As if they're always watching, always judging.

I close the wardrobe door and check the time. I hope it's not a late one tonight, but at least it's not far to go. I don't have to leave for another thirty minutes, so I choose a book of Romantic poetry from the shelf and sit in Mother's rocking chair reading it as I wait. I love this chair. When we were children, Ellie and I used to quarrel over it. I'd sit in it, gently rocking and reading, but when Ellie had her turn she would swing to and fro violently, causing it to fall backwards more than once.

I run my fingers along the scars in the wood as I read. I would give anything to fight over it with her now.

I manage to shake off my melancholic mood for the rest of the evening, to push away the thoughts of Ellie while I drink and chat and clink glasses like everybody else. I keep my loneliness well hidden. I've had lots of practice.

On my way home, I spot Charles's face through the crowd on the tube platform. He's still wearing his work suit. The charcoal one. He's loosened his burgundy tie a little. He still looks smart, if weary. His blond hair is cropped short now, not long enough to be pushed off his face, as it was at school. It sometimes takes me by surprise when I catch a glimpse of him these days – how much he has changed. I take a step towards him, pleased to have this opportunity, but then I see Dickie Graham is with him and I hesitate.

At school, Dickie always played the joker, with his broad freckled face and messy brown hair making him look like a *Just William* illustration. He was the sort of child a teacher dreads in their classroom, lurking in the back row, seeing his purpose there to make fun of everything and everyone.

Charles, of course, was always different, always kinder, but Dickie's presence makes me cautious about approaching. Circumstances are against us, in any case. Thursday evening at the time when the world heads home after drinks. It's twenty past eleven and the platform is crowded, the train delayed. I was about to give up before I saw Charles, on the cusp of elbowing through the wall of people and making my way home above ground.

The sight of his face makes me hesitate. Should I wait a little longer? The sign says the next train will arrive in two minutes, but it hasn't changed for so long that no one believes it. A few more people squeeze on to the platform, and then a few more. They keep coming and, just when you think we're at maximum capacity, more people filter through. The air down here is warm and stale. I'm not of a panicky disposition but I'm conscious there are too many bodies pushed together, blocking any way out.

As I give in and start to make my way slowly to the exit, I strain to keep my view of Charles. He always held his drink well. He's not one to overdo things. Dickie, on the other hand, is swaying gently. I'm far enough away for him not to see me, but in any case he looks distracted, as if his mind is somewhere else. He fishes in his pocket, searching for something, pulls out a packet of cigarettes and glances down at it absent-mindedly. Charles seems to remind him he can't smoke here and Dickie smiles and pushes it back into his pocket. But it's a wan, preoccupied smile. Marriage problems, perhaps. It's possible his wife has seen through him already.

A group of women begins to trickle in, all sparkly tops and pink lipstick, clutching their programmes for a Seventies singalong at the Royal Albert Hall – shrieking at each other in wine-fuelled tones. They push and shove their way onto the platform. Perhaps they're out-of-towners and don't know this sort of crush isn't normal; that there's a limit to the number of people the platform will take. Irritated, I continue shuffling my way to the exit, like a swimmer paddling against the tide. Now I'm nearer to him I can see Dickie is still swaying, standing too close to the edge of the platform. That's Dickie all over – seeing how far he can push something.

A breeze picks up then – the change in the air pressure warning of the arrival of the train at last. The crowd shifts like water, bodies pressing and pushing against each other towards the edge, where the train will be any second now.

There's a shriek of laughter and a hen party, dressed up for the concert with mullet wigs and oversized sunglasses, jostles its way between me and Charles. Close up they smell of alcohol and Chanel, hairspray and garlic breath. As the women push forward, Charles and Dickie hold their ground between the press of the crowd behind them and the rush of the train coming in.

At the sight of the train appearing from the tunnel, everyone squares up for the scrabble to get on. I catch another glimpse of Charles. We're not far away from each other but the scrum of women is wedged between us now. All I can see are the backs of their heads – some of them wearing those stupid wigs, others with hair neatly styled in bobs or worn loose to their shoulders. I fancy I see a cloud of white-blonde hair that makes me think of Ellie, alongside another, brown and unkempt like my own. There's a fierce energy to the movement of the crowd – a touch of malevolence that makes me think of the Furies demanding blood vengeance. They're not going to stop pushing.

The fear must be catching – there's a panicked shriek and someone calls, 'Watch out!' The words seem to pull Charles back from the yellow line. He draws away as the train rushes in. Next to him, Dickie glances back over his shoulder at the hen party and his expression changes. It's a half-smile as if he doesn't know whether to be happy or worried, and it could be that moment of recognition, or the fact he's not looking where he's going, that causes him to stumble sharply and fall in front of the train.

2

Later, I think of the famous photograph of the tightrope walker Philippe Petit on a high wire between the Twin Towers, the roar of the city below. That's how Dickie appears for a second: a small, fragile figure suspended in mid-air. Someone shrieks again. The driver squeezes her eyes shut and slams on the brakes, though it's too late, of course. We all know that.

All of us watching are bound together in that moment of terrible theatre. We wait as time seems to stretch and extend. Dickie is there and then he is not. There is a dreadful thud. No sound from him – no screech or yell. He slips away silently while noise rages around him.

I wonder later if he remembers Ellie in that moment, if he prays for forgiveness. But perhaps that's fanciful. If he thinks of anything, it's probably that pretty wife of his and their baby.

The driver is screaming, 'We have one under,' to her colleagues in the control room. A strange thing to say. A phrase you might hear at a cricket game. Too light for the circumstances. The crowd on the platform scoops away like a shoal from the incoming train, finding space where there was none before.

It's only then that I look at Charles. He has dropped to his knees and raised his hands to his face like shutters. He is the only still thing on a platform that is a blur of movement and noise. Dark uniforms begin to filter through – British Transport Police, Transport for London staff. I don't understand how they got here so quickly.

The driver is saying something over the system to the passengers about an incident but you can tell from the way they press against the glass to look for answers that they know something is very wrong. An old man next to me turns away and stares at the tube map, his lips moving as he whispers a prayer. Some people start to push, with urgency, through the crowd. I see a couple of the hen party scurry guiltily towards the exit, still wearing wigs and glasses.

Charles begins to weep, sobs shaking into his hands. It's a sight I can never unsee – as frightening as witnessing the tears of an adult when you're a child. A reminder that chaos is closer than we think and the people we love can be as fragile as paper. I want to go to him, but his grief looks so private, so intense, I can't bring myself to impose – or to risk his rejection. Someone from the Transport Police comes over and helps him to his feet. I tear myself away, but I promise myself it won't be for long.

When I get back to the estate, the dealer is standing at the main entrance, as usual. Ellie used to call him that, although we've never seen him deal anything, strictly speaking. He spends his time hovering at the entrance to the block of flats as if he's waiting for something or someone. He can't leave the premises because he's tagged, as he once showed us. He's a skinny man with a grey complexion and hair growing in patchy tufts across his face – not unfriendly, but I've noticed Branwell, my cat, always walks in a wide circle around him. Ellie said Branwell could smell trouble.

'All right, Franny,' he says. 'Been out on one of your secret jaunts?'

I stare at him for a moment, still shaking. I'm in shock, I realise. The reality of what I've witnessed is only just sinking in.

'Looks like you've got something on your face.'

He touches his left cheek and I mirror him, raising my right hand to mine. My first thought is: blood. I have Dickie's blood on me.

Then I remember that that's impossible. There wasn't any blood. Not that I could see.

Retrieving Mother's compact from my handbag, I inspect my face, but it's only a speck of vomit. I'd held off until I was out of the station and the fresh air hit me. Clusters of passengers were regrouping in the flickering blue light of the emergency vehicles. Friends rubbed each other's backs or called their families. One of the women wept, her make-up trailing down her face in glittery train tracks.

I wipe my cheek and put the compact away. I was too far away from Dickie to have been spattered by blood. It's just the shock. I'm not thinking straight.

'You OK?' the dealer asks.

'Yes,' I say. 'I witnessed an accident.'

'I'm sorry,' he says, fishing some tobacco paper from his pocket and starting to roll a cigarette.

'It's not your fault,' I say, watching him roll, grateful to have someone to talk to. 'Not mine, either – I just happened to be there.'

He glances up. 'What happened?'

'I saw a man fall under the tube. Someone I knew from school.'

I'd be more careful usually, but it's not as if the dealer and I have mutual friends. I don't know why, but I think of Charles and Dickie as schoolboys. Laughing as they walked back from the rugby pitch, their legs muddy, their faces pink after a match.

'Was he a mate of yours?' The dealer puts the cigarette to his lips and lights it.

'No,' I reply, ducking to pet his dog – a brute of a thing to look at, but as gentle as a lamb. 'Not a friend.'

In my flat, I strip down to my underwear and put everything in the washing machine. I know the noise at this time will annoy my neighbours, but I want to get rid of every trace of what happened tonight.

I put on a greying down-to-the floor nightgown and climb into bed. I check if the news has broken and there's already a story under the headline: 'Man hit by tube train at South Kensington.' They don't identify Dickie, nor do they confirm his death, but it doesn't look good. They're calling it an accident. I think of his wife and their daughter, of poor Charles having to make that phone call.

As I get up to put my laptop away, I retrieve an old photograph from my tuckbox at the bottom of the wardrobe. It's a photograph of the First XV at Chesterfield in 1997. The back row has its arms folded; the boys in the front sit with their legs splayed, hands on their knees. Only Charles is marked out as different – the captain, holding the ball neatly on his lap; his fair hair pushed back off his face, he looks confidently at the camera. He is flanked by the hulking figure of Tom Bates on one side and Dickie on the other. I close my eyes. *Who did you see on the platform, Dickie?*

That day, us girls had loitered nearby, pretending to be intrigued by the photographer at work, but really gazing at the boys, as usual. Juliet, standing behind the cameraman, had lifted her shirt just as the photograph was taken, revealing a red satin bra.

You can tell from the expressions. A couple of the boys are smirking at the sight of her, one is laughing out loud; Charles, ever the gentleman, looks ahead, ignoring her exhibitionism. I remember the hoots of laughter as the photos were laid out in the dining hall for us to see. Dickie's loudest of all. 'Slapper,' he said, digging Juliet in the ribs.

'I don't know what you're talking about,' she murmured. 'It was the wind.'

'Bullshit,' said Dickie. But I noticed he put his name down to buy a photo. His own personal keepsake.

In private, I asked Mother if I could buy one too. Not for Dickie, of course, but for Charles. 'Fran,' she sighed. 'Do you really need it?' It was a big request on her salary.

'Please,' I pleaded. 'I never ask for anything.' That was true, I was a thrifty child.

16

She conceded in the end – 'but not a framed one' – and was discreet enough not to let on to anyone else. Not even Mrs Morgan, her dearest friend. The only person I showed the photo to was Ellie, and it was her idea, later, to get a coin and scratch off Dickie's face.

3

It's Ellie, more than anyone else, I want to talk to the next day. By the time I wake, the news of Dickie's death is beginning to spread. Juliet has already posted on Facebook, Twitter and Instagram: Dreadful news about my old school friend, Dickie Graham. My heart is broken. There are no words.

She seems to have found a few though, as well as a proliferation of emojis. She's rebranded herself now as Jules – a minor celebrity with an interior design show on Channel 4. She always seems to be on social media these days, but I avoid her pages, unless I'm desperate for information.

I think, again, of Dickie's wife, Caroline, and try to imagine the kind of night she has had. She hasn't posted anything herself yet. Nor has Charles, though I wouldn't expect it – his Facebook page has been dormant since 2014. The last post I can see is still the one asking for sponsorship for the Blenheim Palace triathlon three years

18

ago. I'd made an anonymous donation of fifty pounds and written, I believe in you! Run like the wind! Almost immediately, scrolling through other people's three-figure sums and casual exhortations, I'd experienced a flash of regret. Thank goodness, I hadn't used my name. It's something Dickie would have picked up on and, even though I wouldn't have been able to hear his mocking words, I could well imagine. Why couldn't I learn to be more casual? Fit in more neatly.

Charles is only on Twitter in an official capacity for his work at the museum, which usually doesn't make for interesting reading, though I keep an eye on it for upcoming events. He hasn't mentioned Dickie there, of course, and, in fact, most of the tributes aren't by close friends, as far as I can tell, but acquaintances and colleagues. They all say how *fun* he was. It's a word that comes up a lot, but it didn't feel fun to be on the receiving end of his jokes. Dickie and Juliet could be a deadly combination. I took care passing the pair of them in the corridor at school the way you might tiptoe past a wasp nest. In more fragile moods, if I saw them heading towards me, I'd dart into a classroom or loo to escape the sting of their words as they walked by.

I want to tell Ellie, just in case she hasn't seen yet. I want to say, 'Dickie's gone.' I wonder if it would help. I don't think she will cry when she hears, but Ellie rarely does. 'So that's that,' she might say, drumming her fingers against her laptop. 'It's over.' Then I hope she gives Rose a big hug, squeezing her close, breathing her in, promising her that no one will ever hurt her.

I start an email to Ellie, but for now it remains in

limbo in my drafts folder. I need to gather my thoughts first, to decide how much to tell her. The memories of last night itch at me like sand in my clothes. I should have lingered longer, I realise now. I should have gone to Charles.

Most of all, I should have found out who Dickie had seen.

To distract myself I decide to take Charles a coffee at work before I start my own shift. It's not something I would usually do, but I can't stop thinking about the way he wept on the tube platform. The horror of what he saw last night. I buy him a coconut latte at Pret, hurrying to the museum so it's still warm when I deliver it. Charles discovered coconut lattes by accident when he was having a brief spell off dairy and then he found he liked the sweet taste. I hope it helps with the shock.

I love that he works in the V&A, the most beautiful museum in London. True, it's only on the finance side of things, but better, much better, than when he was in the City. I've always had a weakness for beauty.

A security guard waves me down at the main entrance.

'No hot drinks in the museum,' he says.

'But this is for Charles,' I say. 'Charles Fry. He's a director here.'

He folds his arms, standing firm.

'It won't take a second,' I persist.

He shakes his head. 'I can't let you through.'

I wait for a moment to see if he might budge, but he keeps his arms folded and looks at the door as if to suggest that's where I should be headed.

Disappointment weighs heavily on my chest as I walk to work. I take tiny sips of the latte, so as not to waste it, but coconut milk isn't my thing. Nor is coffee for that matter.

When I get to the shop, my spirits lift momentarily. Even after all this time, I still get a thrill out of the fact I work with books. The smell of them. Unloading a delivery and touching the Next Big Thing before anyone else can. A poster in the staffroom reminds us to think of our customers as fellow book lovers. It's something I try to keep in mind, even when they wander up to us, as they do every day, and say: 'I'm looking for a book.' To which we always have to resist replying: 'Well, you've come to the right place.'

If we're lucky they'll remember the title or the author's name or even, on occasion, both. At other times, we'll pause, our hands hovering over the keyboard of our search system, while they say helpful things like, 'The author's name begins with T – or was it V?' Or, 'I think it has a green cover.' Actually, one brilliant time, I knew just the book they were talking about – a bestseller in a lurid shade of green – and I bounded towards the two-for-one table with a spring in my step to fetch it.

As I reach the till, I can tell from the way Brenda and Gareth fall silent that they've already heard something.

'We were talking about the tube accident last night.' Brenda glances down at her phone. 'It's on the *Metro* website. He went to your school, didn't he?'

I fish out my own phone and start to read. The report says Dickie was out for a drink with an old school friend and links Charles to the V&A, identifying Dickie as an

21

advertising executive. There are a couple of quotes from witnesses. One complains about the crush on the platform; another describes watching Dickie fall. 'He wasn't looking where he was going,' she says. I realise she's referring to the way Dickie glanced over his shoulder. But at whom?

'How awful,' I murmur, realising that Brenda and Gareth are still waiting for me to say something.

'Was he one of the ones who bullied you?' asks Brenda sympathetically.

'No.' I wish I'd never told her. 'Nothing like that. I didn't really know him.'

I shove my phone into my pocket. 'We shouldn't really have these on the shop floor, should we?' I say pointedly.

'Didn't you say you were going out around here last night too?' asks Gareth, not looking me in the eye. I can't tell from his tone what he's suggesting.

'No,' I say again. 'I changed my mind and stayed at home.'

Making my way to unload a trolley, I try not to think about the fact that I've lied twice in less than two minutes. I pick up an armful of books, my mind preoccupied. The *Metro* report has nudged a memory of Dickie at school, spotting Ellie at a rugby match. The way he raised a hand to greet her. He was happy then, and nervous too. He didn't wave yesterday but his expression was the same – he'd seen someone he knew.

22

4

Dickie was so easy to read – that was his problem, I think, as I sort through the books on the trolley and put them on the shelves. He couldn't dissemble. That look of recognition would have been clear to anyone who knew him. His crush on Juliet had been just as transparent – the way he'd always rush to claim his usual desk in the back row, next to hers, but then try to act all casual, as if it was neither here nor there to him. My own favourite spot in English was the far corner, second from the back. It's no good being at the very back – you're in the firing line just as much as the front.

The day it started, the only remaining seat was the one next to me. We had been given an assignment to pick our favourite passage in *Wuthering Heights* and argue why it was important. I was first to speak and I'd decided on the pivotal 'I am Heathcliff' passage and marked it up in my book, underlining certain phrases and jotting down my arguments in the margin. It was a book I knew well – one I'd read with Mother the year before. Later, she'd played us the Kate Bush song and Ellie – never one for reading, or sitting still for that matter – made us laugh with her dancing.

Up until this point, three weeks into my first year at Chesterfield, nobody had actually spoken to me. The teachers talked to me, of course, but apart from asking for the salt at mealtimes or whispering 'bless you' when someone sneezed in the library, I hadn't exchanged much in the way of words with my peers.

I wasn't sure how to get started. It never seemed straightforward to me: the matter of making friends. I might make a comment about a book someone was reading in the prep room or attempt to amuse with some wordplay at supper – a good example being when Dickie Graham was mock-fighting with Tom Bates; they knocked into the fruit bowl and a lemon bounced out. 'There's no lime or reason to it,' I quipped, but the boys looked at me with blank faces. That was usual: blank looks, incomprehension or, worse, sniggers.

I might be out of my depth everywhere else, but in English I felt I had the advantage. Mother had raised us on books, particularly books and writers with a link to Yorkshire – the Brontës and Alan Bennett, *Dracula* and *The Secret Garden*. So I had an advantage when it came to *Wuthering Heights*, and I'd hoped it might be an opportunity; that people would realise I had something to say.

I arrived early for class that day, glancing over my notes one final time and leaving them inside my book on the desk, but a twinge in my belly made me dash for the loo. In the worst possible timing, my period had started and I returned to the classroom flustered and late.

Mrs Fyson was arranging herself at her desk. There was the usual low-level hum before a lesson began. My palms were slick in anticipation of having to read aloud in front of everyone but when I reached my desk, my copy of *Wuthering Heights* was no longer there. My heart jumped into my mouth. At the same time, Mrs Fyson cleared her throat. 'Francesca Knight,' she said. 'You're up first.'

I turned to the most likely culprit, Juliet, sitting behind me, and hissed: 'Did you take my book?'

Juliet, all wide-eyed innocence, asked: 'What book?'

'*Wuthering Heights*. With my notes in it. Did you take it?'

'Why would I, when I have my own copy here?' She waggled hers at me.

'But it's my turn *now*,' I said, utterly panicked.

Juliet gave a dainty little shrug as if to say it wasn't her problem.

'What's going on?' asked Mrs Fyson.

My face flushed hot as I stood up to explain. 'My copy of *Wuthering Heights* seems to be missing.'

'Did you forget it?'

'No,' I replied. 'It was on my desk.' I glanced around desperately. 'And now it's not.'

Mrs Fyson was more weary than angry. 'You'll just have to share with someone else then,' she said, checking a list on her desk. 'Which passage were you going to read?'

My cheeks were still very hot. 'But my notes,' I stuttered. I could feel tears building behind my eyes, the ache of humiliation at my throat.

'You'll just have to remember what you were going to say,' persisted Mrs Fyson.

My hatred for her, in that moment, was brief but intense.

'Fran can share with me,' a warm voice beside me said.

I glanced to my left. I hadn't noticed him enter; he must have slipped in late at some point during this exchange. A kind smile. Floppy blond hair. It was the era of Leonardo DiCaprio and that was the style back then.

I knew who he was, of course, in the way I knew who DiCaprio was, but he had about as much to do with my life. Charles Fry. Rugby star. Blue blood. The kind of person who, on paper, would have little in common with a shy bookworm like me. But I'd read the stories – Lizzy and Darcy, Jane and Rochester; it never looked like they would work on paper. Love could be surprising sometimes.

It was also at that moment I realised he was, quite simply, the most beautiful person I had ever seen in real life. It wasn't just his looks. It was his manners, his earnest way of speaking. His kindness. His rescue of me when all was nearly lost.

Mrs Fyson sighed in acquiescence and Charles dragged his desk closer to mine. He was so close that I could smell the peppermint-gum scent of his breath and his proximity made it hard to concentrate on the words. I stumbled and tripped over the sentences as I read and, when I lost my place, he ran his finger under the text to help me find where I was. With him next to me, I found the words to explain why the passage was so important. 'It's confirmation that they're soulmates,' I remember saying. Mrs Fyson looked as if she might

26

disagree with me but then Charles cut in with a question and rescued me again.

I think I knew, even then, how important Charles Fry would be to me.

As I took my time packing up, basking in the glow that lingered after Charles left, Meilin came up to my desk. She was always quiet in class and we hadn't spoken before. She was in another boarding house, close to the school, whereas mine was perched on the edge of Field, the huge green expanse where we played sports.

'I liked your talk,' she said politely.

I thanked her, but she hovered as if she had more to say.

'I don't think *Wuthering Heights* is about soulmates, though.' She wasn't as timid as I imagined.

'No?' I pushed my books into my satchel. I was out of adrenaline after the showdown at the beginning of class; I didn't have much fight left in me.

'Not in my mind,' she said. 'It's a book full of people hurting each other – floggings, humiliation, degradation, dog attacks.'

'Love can be fierce,' I said, thinking of the impression Charles had left on me just minutes earlier. The heat of it like a searing.

'We can talk about it over lunch,' said Meilin. 'Perhaps I can persuade you it's not about love at all.' She smiled. 'It's about survival.'

That was how I made my second friend at Chesterfield.

As for Charles, the next red-letter day I noted in my journal was when he ran out of ink just before a timed

27

essay and Mrs Fyson said, 'Well, Charles, it looks like you'll have to go and get some from the stationery cupboard, but we're not going to wait for you to start.'

I said, quick as you like, 'I've got a spare cartridge,' and Charles grinned at me as he took it and said, 'You're a legend.' Our hands touched as I gave it to him, just the lightest of brushes, but something passed between us. It was official then: we were a team. We would look out for each other. We would rescue each other. If it ever came to it.

Dickie never cared much for English in the way Charles and I did – he was the class clown; the one who made Juliet laugh. It was his need to entertain like this – to be in the spotlight – that made him such a gift on social media years later. You could always see where he was, from the moment he left the house. You could tell which airport he was at, and which terminal; you could see what he was eating and drinking there; you could read where he was flying to and with whom – Toulouse in the summer, where his parents had a holiday home, for bike rides and family time; Zermatt in the winter for skiing and boys' holidays.

Charles is cautious by nature, so it's much harder to discover where he might be of an evening, but Dickie, as his friend, was a gift.

On my forays between the trolley and the shelves, as I slot each book neatly into place, I am grateful that I have remembered something positive about Dickie to dwell on.

I don't know what I'm going to do without him.

5

Another gift from Dickie, though I feel guilty for thinking it, is that he has offered me a reason to get back in touch with Charles. An excuse to visit him, to make an above-board trip. No more lingering in the shadows, keeping a safe distance, plucking up the courage as I decide what to say. I just need to consider how much to reveal: whether I can tell Charles I was there too. On the one hand, the shared experience might bring us closer – and would make a compelling reason for my visit – but, on the other, I'll need to convince him my presence was coincidental.

Are my acting skills up to that? I imagine how, when I see him, I might tilt my head to one side. 'Charles, I'm so very sorry,' I'll say. 'Poor Dickie.' I'll bite my lip, as if holding back tears. 'We didn't always see eye to eye, but I can't believe he's gone.'

Charles will have a faraway look on his face and he won't be able to talk for a moment or two, while he fights back emotion.

'I hear you were there when it happened,' I'll say, omitting any mention of my own presence. 'Oh, Charles. How dreadful.'

He'll soften then, at the memory of that night. He won't cry, but his eyes will turn dewy. 'A terrible thing,' he'll say bravely. 'To see a life snuffed out like that.'

'It makes you realise,' I'll conclude, 'what the important things are.'

And I'll take his hand and, though we won't acknowledge it out loud, we'll both be grateful to Dickie for bringing us back together like this. That his death wasn't for nothing.

I've come to a standstill in the Biography section, staring at the book in my hand: O'Farrell – that should be shelved under O rather than F. Shaking myself from my reverie, I begin to refine my plan. I could go to the Cotswolds on my next day off with a little something to show he's in my thoughts. Something discreet would do. Something modest. This time I won't return the present undelivered to my tuckbox, as I usually do, with the rest of my Charles keepsakes. The moment has come to act.

'The morning comes quickly' – that was one of the things Mrs Morgan, our housemistress at Chesterfield, used to say. She had a whole set of aphorisms she used to share with Mother over a secret cigarette, or a less appreciative audience of girls at Lights Out as they lolled outside each other's cubicles in their nighties, reading the *Just Seventeen* problem page out loud or the folded-down bits of Judy Blume's *Forever*. I was usually in bed with a book by this time, having no one to loll with. Sometimes I'd put on my Walkman and listen to my old Gilbert and Sullivan tapes to block out the chatter of the other girls. It was never aimed at me. It's not always true that the morning comes quickly, though. Sometimes the nights creep by.

The birds are the first to wake in the Cotswolds. You can hear them in the way you don't in London. First, there's the silence of the sky and the lake below it, then the dawn chorus as they start to stir. It's one of my favourite things to watch his house sleep, the blinds drawn like closed eyelids.

My dawn visits to Honeybourne became a habit a few years ago – a brief respite from the noise of London when I could enjoy the garden alone and pretend it was mine: that this was my life, my house, my family. Just for a short time before I slipped off.

It seems utterly right he should live somewhere so beautiful. An unusual building for this part of the world, Honeybourne is more Brideshead than Pemberley, with its fairy-tale turret and glorious gables. An irregular, idiosyncratic dream mansion built by one of Charles's nineteenth-century ancestors. The only thing that's wrong is the woman he's living with.

'Fran,' Fiona says, when she opens the door. 'This is a surprise. Gosh, what a big fruit basket.'

We stand, regarding each other over the grapes. Even at this time of day, barefoot in jeans, Fiona looks well turned out. Her highlighted hair is exquisitely tousled, her toenails neatly painted. Her face has a slight horsiness to it, but that's probably the worst you could say about her and I've spent a lot of time looking at photos, trying to find fault.

31

I'm flattered she remembers my name; it's been a few years. It would be easier to hate her if she weren't so polite.

'I heard about Dickie,' I say. 'I'm so sorry. I know it's been a long time. I know I haven't . . . but I wanted to come.' My words rush out too quickly. None of it quite as I rehearsed, but then I'd practised my speech with Charles in mind. Flustered, I push the basket towards her. 'I brought this.'

She takes it from me, struggling for a moment under the weight of it. 'Thank you,' she says. 'How kind – quite unnecessary.' She touches her forehead. 'It's been so dreadful.'

'How is Charles?'

'He's just . . .' She stretches out the hand that's not holding the basket as if she can grasp the answer from thin air. 'Shocked,' she says eventually. 'So shocked. He was there, you know?'

Looking away, as if she might be able to read the guilt on my face, I realise this is my chance: to say I was there too. But then it wasn't her I wanted to tell.

'Is Charles around?' I strain to catch a glimpse of the house behind her. There's a child's truck in the hallway, two bouquets of flowers on the sideboard and another fruit basket, bigger than mine. My heart sinks.

Fiona takes a step to her right, barricading my way. 'He's in the shower,' she begins, 'and he's not exactly . . .' She shakes her head to convey that Charles's state is beyond words.

We stand, staring at each other again. I keep my feet firmly planted on the ground. I don't want to leave so soon. Not after travelling all this way. Not without seeing Charles.

'I heard,' I begin, 'that they're not sure it was an accident?' That's not strictly true. It's my own interpretation of the witness's statement, of that expression on Dickie's face. But, as I say it, I realise I believe it.

Fiona's eyes widen ever so slightly. She shifts the basket in her arms from one side to the other. 'Where did you read that? One of the tabloids?'

There's a slight edge to her voice, something you could nick yourself on. It was the wrong time to say anything, and certainly not the right person.

I shake my head. 'I must have got the wrong end of the stick.'

'It was a terrible accident,' says Fiona. 'I think he . . . I mean . . .' She bites her lip. 'Who'd want to hurt Dickie?'

I can think of more than one answer to that question, but not one that would find favour with Fiona. She didn't go to Chesterfield like the rest of us. There are some things she wouldn't understand. Charles should have married one of us. Which is to say: he should have married me.

I try to think of something else to say, something that will make her want to invite me in, offer me a meal in their sunny-yellow kitchen, in the way she did when I visited with Ellie four years ago. I long to return to that day – sitting next to Charles as he flicked through the books I'd brought, touching me occasionally on the hand or the shoulder as we reminisced. I rack my brains for a solution – a way to make her call Charles out of his shower, so he joins us, his hair still damp, the scent of his Molton Brown shower gel on his warm skin.

A child's shriek from the playroom makes her glance over her shoulder.

'I'd better go.' She smiles. 'Do you need a lift to the station?' Without waiting for an answer, she waves at her gardener digging in a nearby paddock.

He makes his way over to us slowly. A man my sort of age, in his late thirties, with a face ruddy from working outdoors.

'Thanks so much again for this,' says Fiona, lifting up the basket. 'Send our love to Ellie,' she adds, as her parting shot. 'When was she last back? March?'

'I don't really . . .' I say. 'I haven't . . .'

'Oh, I'm sorry.' She raises her hand to her mouth. 'I know you two aren't quite right at the moment. You mustn't lose each other, though, Fran.' She air-kisses me goodbye – awkward with the fruit basket between us. 'Family is everything.'

It's the sort of line you hear on *EastEnders*, I think, with sour satisfaction. She wouldn't be so smug if she knew what I knew.

The gardener is taciturn for most of the drive and I'm grateful for the silence, for being able to sit and stare out of the window, disappointment washing over me.

A couple of miles away from Charlbury station he glances at me in the passenger seat. 'I've seen you before, haven't I?'

'I don't think so.' I hold my hands neatly in my lap.

He nods, sure of himself. 'One morning, when I got to work early, you were on the bench by the lake.'

'No.' I look out of the window, so he won't see me blush. 'That wasn't me.'

'I was going to come and talk to you,' he says. 'Find out what you wanted, but you walked away before I could reach you.'

I turn to him then and fix him with a steely look. 'I really don't know what you're talking about.'

He shrugs, leaving the matter alone.

Silence settles between us for the rest of the journey through the winding country roads. As we pass through an estate, I spot a deer with her two fawns, still resting on the dewy grass. The beauty of it is too much, so that I have to close my eyes. The people who live here have everything, I think, but they don't want to share any of it.

6

Our parents met in a windswept pub on the Yorkshire moors. Mother used to go there for weekend breaks when she was doing her teacher training in Leeds. She first spotted our dad reading Keats behind the bar, with his Rochester forehead and Heathcliff hair. And that was it; I'm like her in that way.

After our father died, she brought us up on her own and taught at a local secondary school near home. I went there until I was thirteen. Chatting about the Brontës as if knew them personally, I didn't make many friends, but I never felt anguished in the way I did at Chesterfield either. I never wept into my pillow or comfort-ate chocolate biscuits in bed. I just spent breaktimes reading, while Ellie skittered around the playground with the younger children.

Ellie found it harder – not socially, that was never a problem for her – but her dyslexia meant she struggled with her studies. Mother would find her homework undone, hidden in the bottom of her satchel, or occasionally completed by me, though our deception was not sophisticated enough to go unnoticed by her teachers. She worried that Ellie would get left behind. And then one of her friends told her about Chesterfield – a public school in Derbyshire with excellent sports facilities that waived the fees for the children of staff. There wasn't a teaching vacancy at that time, so Mother accepted a role as matron in our boarding house instead. She was good at the job – waking all of us in the morning, dispensing medicine, reminding us about laundry. She never treated Ellie and me like we were her favourites.

At eleven, Ellie was too young for Chesterfield, which started at thirteen, so she shared Mother's tiny en-suite room and walked to the primary school in the village. I slept in a dormitory with eight other girls who were posher than anyone I'd come across, though like most posh people, I soon learned, they didn't like being called posh. They swore like troopers and were very concerned with sex, covering their noticeboards with posters of Christian Slater, River Phoenix and other pin-ups with bare chests and greasy hair. For a while I pinned up my own display – a handmade montage of cat pictures I'd collected from magazines – but after someone scrawled 'Nice pussies' across it in Magic Marker, I took it down. People can be so childish.

I missed it being just the three of us. I found I didn't know what to say to the other girls – who'd throw loud opinions over the thin cubicle walls to each other and sing along in mockney accents to Blur on their ghetto blasters. I'd lie there, pretending to be asleep, wondering if it was possible to be homesick with my family so close by. I missed my mother. I didn't like sharing her. I didn't like witnessing other girls roll their eyes after she told them off, seeing another version of her through their perspective.

Worse, there was the inescapable fact of everyone knowing that she was my mother, with her broad Yorkshire accent and her broad behind. There was no getting away from that. If you'd asked me where this divide between us and the other pupils might lead, I wouldn't have predicted how sour it would turn, but, even then, before things went so wrong, it didn't feel good.

Back in London, I check to see if there's any news yet of when Dickie's funeral might be. Funerals are often public, after all, and Dickie's might present an opportunity for me to speak to Charles. There's no news, but Dickie's wife has posted a black and white photograph of the pair of them with their daughter. She's written: My Dickie. I can't believe it. Thank you all for your love and support at this terrible time.

I stare at the photograph for ages. It's one of those classic family portraits – the three of them sitting on a picnic rug in the garden. Dickie and his wife look tired and happy. His wife, Caroline, has a kind face – freckled and unthreateningly pretty.

Juliet, meanwhile, has dug out an old photograph from Chesterfield of Dickie and her at a Halloween social. Dickie's dressed as Juliet with a long brunette wig, sucking in his cheeks and pouting for the camera, Juliet's wearing a First XV rugby shirt, her hair in a backwards cap. She's written: I miss you, Dickie Graham, my dear old pal. One of the good ones.

That was a stretch, even for her.

There's nothing new on Ellie's pages, and I look again at the email I started to her. I have another go at it, but I can't concentrate.

What I really want is to speak to Charles. To get him on his own, without Fiona, to talk to him properly. Charles might have seen who Dickie spotted on the platform. Or he might be able to reassure me that it was nothing but a horrible accident, like Fiona said. Either way, I need to see him.

I remember that tomorrow's Friday: the museum will be open late. There's a chance he might be there. He sometimes is, surveying the crowd from the atrium with his colleagues. Smiling benignly at the visitors, with a paper cup of warm wine in his hand. It's worth a try, I think, as I get ready for bed. I'll feel so much better once I've spoken to him. He might be able to put my mind at rest.

7

When I get there, the following evening after work, a guide pushes a Friday Lates leaflet into my hand and I'm surrounded by faces, thrumming music – the museum masquerading as a party host. I do a circuit of the atrium, trying to fit in with the other revellers, looking for Charles.

There's no sign of him, though, and after twenty minutes I'm about to give up when I spot a colleague of his I recognise. I'm not sure of her name, but I've seen them chatting before. She wears her hair in victory rolls and her mouth is painted scarlet.

'Hello,' I say, smiling broadly as I approach her. 'I think we've met before. I was wondering if Charles was here tonight.'

The music is so loud she can barely hear me. She points at her ear and I take a step closer.

'Where is Charles?' I bellow the second time round, quite close to her face. 'I wanted to see him.'

'He's not in,' she shouts. She's close enough that I can

smell cheese and onion crisps on her breath. 'He's on compassionate leave.'

I nod vigorously. 'I read about the accident in the paper,' I yell back. 'Dreadful. I was at school with Dickie.'

She smiles vaguely, so that I'm not sure she's heard me, and pats me on the arm. We're rudely interrupted by a brassy blonde with chunky earrings that almost brush her shoulders. 'Victoria,' she shrieks. 'It's been ages.'

I make a mental note of her name for future use – Victoria, how fitting – and leave them to it, wandering around the museum as I think about what to do next. I go and see my favourite sculpture – Canova's Three Graces, which reminds me of a mother comforting her two daughters. I always try to remember the names of the pieces here, so I can impress Charles when I bump into him. One that sticks is the Rape of Proserpina – a terrifying statue with Pluto's strong arms hooked around Proserpina's waist, his fingernails digging into her thigh, their bodies joined in that act of violence.

Physical passions have always been a mystery to me. I sometimes catch a glimpse of a couple kissing in the street – grasping and groping at each other – and I wonder what that might feel like. 'I love with my *heart*,' I used to say to Ellie.

'Well, don't knock loving with the other bits until you've tried it,' she'd laugh.

It's been another wasted trip, I consider, as I visit the Ladies' before heading home. I had hoped Dickie's death might bring Charles and me closer, but it's just been dead end after dead end.

I feel guilty for the thought immediately after having

41

it and sit on the lavatory seat berating myself for being so callous: Mother would be ashamed of what I've become.

In the midst of my self-flagellation I hear a voice in the next cubicle, cool and crisp over the background hum of the music.

'Who was that funny-looking woman, Vic?'

'What?' calls another voice from a further cubicle.

'That woman you were talking to, dressed like my grandmother. Plump. Intense-looking.'

'Oh,' says the second voice. 'We call her Freaky Fran.'

The first woman guffaws at this. There's the flush of the loo further down and the click of heels against the tiles.

'She hangs around here a lot, asking for Charles Fry,' Victoria continues over the cubicle as she waits. 'She went to school with him – I asked him about her once. I don't think they're friends, but he told me to be kind to her.'

'That's a bit creepy,' says the woman in the cubicle next to me. There's another flush and I don't catch what she says next as they return to the party.

I sit very still, looking at the wad of loo roll in my hand, listening to the revelry in the next room. Freaky Fran. The name has clung to me throughout the years. Like a curse I can't shake off.

8

The first person I heard use that uninspired alliteration was Dickie. I'd been watching the boys play rugby, waiting at the edge of the pitch and it so happened that Charles found the excuse to run right by me. We locked eyes and had one of our special moments, when so much was communicated without saying a word. Dickie ruined it, saying loudly: 'What's that freak doing here?' To which Charles said: 'Leave her alone,' and Dickie replied: 'Ooh, Charles wants to get off with Freaky Fran.' Charles punched him and ran away. That night, I couldn't sleep for hugging myself and thinking: 'Charles Fry wants to get off with me.'

I move from place to place and still the name finds me. I've heard Ingrid and Liam say it in the staffroom before Brenda or Gareth upbraids them. Once, years ago, when I first started at the shop, I slipped quietly back from the loo at a rare social gathering in the pub and interrupted a flamboyant impression of me. Only a bit of fun, said the actor in question.

'There's nothing wrong with being different,' Mother said. 'It doesn't make you any less special. "*To thine own self be true*" – that can be one of the hardest things in life – and you're already there, Fran. Your friends haven't learned that yet.'

It was kind of her to say. But I didn't really have friends.

Juliet was thrilled with the nickname and shortened it to FF, like the bra size, when I was in earshot – as if I wouldn't be able to work *that* out. I think it was around the time she started to find it funny to put things in my hair while I leaned close into my books. Once it was pencil shavings – she and Dickie managed to pile them in, piece by piece. I pretended to laugh it off. Next it was bits of cheese that got stuck, went off and made me smell. The worst was a piece of used chewing gum. I cried that night as Mother had to hack chunks of my hair away over the sink.

'I hate them,' Ellie said, sitting on the edge of the bath. 'I hate them so much.' She took my hand and looked at me fiercely. Ellie's small but she's not a person to cross. 'I'll find a way to get them back,' she promised.

For a week or two, things go quiet. I check on social media every day before work, but there's no news of Dickie's funeral. I wonder if they're planning to hold one privately but I can't ask his wife. It might seem strange – Caroline will know who Dickie's friends are – and I don't want her asking questions about me. Imagining that the manner of his death might present complications, I download some information from the British Transport Police website and read up about the procedure when someone dies in front of a train. Apparently eyewitnesses can be called to give evidence at the inquest. Guilt prickles at me when I learn this. But I reassure myself it could be months before one is held – I'll have the chance to speak to Charles beforehand: at the funeral or memorial. I'm sure there will be an opportunity. He'll help me decide what to do – if I should share my suspicions with the police.

There is only one occasion that stands out in my memory during this quiet period. One night, close to Halloween, I spend a couple of happy hours arranging our seasonal picks in the shop window. Ingrid and Liam have had their fun playing with the pumpkins and fake cobwebs, but I have the more important task of selecting and displaying the books. To prepare for the job, I've been revisiting a few of my favourites – *The Turn of the Screw, The Woman in Black* and so on, which, in view of recent events, was perhaps a mistake.

Maybe the ghost stories put ideas in my head. Dickie appears in my dreams, running down the rugby pitch at Chesterfield, bloody and bruised like something from a zombie film. At one point, always when I don't expect it, he stops suddenly in his tracks and whips his head around. 'It's *you*,' he says, looking straight at me. 'I thought it was.' His words chill me to the bone and I never know if he means me or someone else. Someone out of sight. I wake up, cold and sweating, longing for my mother's hand to smooth the hair from my sticky forehead, to tell me there's nothing to fear.

Perhaps it's the dreams, or the books I've been reading, but working in the shop window I start to feel someone watching me. I stop what I'm doing for a moment and glance over my shoulder. It's a particularly dreary afternoon, the rain bucketing down, but I can see, across the street, a woman with a pushchair outside Marks and Spencer. She has a rain hat pulled down low, so I can't see her face, but she stands like a statue, staring at me as I work. When I return her gaze, she springs into life and begins to walk swiftly down the Kings Road towards Sloane Square, her head down, shoulders hunched against the rain.

It leaves me unsettled, playing on my mind as I do my social media checks that evening. Dickie's wife hasn't posted again since just after his death – perhaps because of the mountain of tasks facing the bereaved. It seems unfair at a point in your life when you're at your lowest that you'll be faced with more mundane, but important, administrative tasks than you'll ever again encounter – death certificates, undertakers, cancelling bank accounts, standing orders and driving licences. The deconstruction of a life.

When Mother died, Ellie left the paperwork to me. She was good at the more practical things – talking to undertakers, getting in touch with Mother's friends and relatives, shifting things around in the flat and so on. Mother was fastidious about the lists she made before she died. She was ill for many years before she went and, ever the schoolteacher, she had time to gather her instructions in a ring-binder.

Despite Mother's best efforts, her paperwork went awry. Her life insurance certificate – the most crucial piece of paper; the one, when she became anxious and confused,

46

she demanded we get from the folder and show her again and again – was declared null and void when her medical records revealed she'd found the lump before starting to pay the premiums. It was a matter of days. But that's all it took.

I sat in her rocking chair and wept when I found out. My sobs were so loud that Ellie dashed from her bedroom to find out what was wrong.

'It's only money, Fran,' she said, kneeling at the foot of the chair, her warm hands in mine.

But it wasn't just the money I was weeping for – it was the idea of having to sell the flat, of Ellie and I perhaps moving on separately, of nothing feeling safe.

'We'll work it out,' Ellie promised me. 'It's you and me against the world.' She stayed there with me until I stopped sobbing.

The memory drives me to Ellie's Facebook page but nothing's changed since last time I looked. Out of habit, I check Dickie's wife's account one last time before going to bed. My heart jumps when I see she's posted: Please come to celebrate Dickie's life at a memorial service in the Empress Hall at Chesterfield on Thursday 9 November.

She adds a website with more on how to get there and some information on Dickie's time at school, his starring role as scrum half in the First XV and so on, and why they've picked the school as a meeting point between his family in Scotland and friends in London. I skim through all of that, smiling, despite myself, at a plan coming together. Chesterfield and Charles. Where it all began.

Buoyed by this thought, I return to the email to Ellie in my drafts folder. I delete it and begin again, keeping

47

things simple: Did you hear about Dickie Graham? You must have done. His memorial's at Chesterfield on the 9th. I thought you would like to know. How is Rose? Are you still in Paris? Come back soon.

I look at the last three words for a long time before deleting them and sending it.

9

On the morning of Dickie's memorial, I wake early with a fizz of excitement in my belly. My dark suit hangs on my wardrobe, pristine beneath the dry-cleaning wrapping. 'We love our customers,' says the logo. I'm always touched by those words of affection; it's one of the reasons I keep going back. My Mary Janes are sitting beneath the suit, polished and ready to go. I squint at my alarm clock – it's just after six. There's plenty of time – the service isn't until three o'clock this afternoon. Still, it's difficult to allay the Christmas-morning feeling in my limbs. It's important to get this right. Not only seeing Charles but my return to Chesterfield – the setting for some of the darkest but also the happiest moments of my life.

If I were to be honest with myself, I would say I never got over Chesterfield, how it made me feel, with its Gothic hall and oak-clad library. When I first arrived, I wanted to live a life worthy of these lofty new surroundings – not merely scuttling from classroom to classroom, books clutched to my chest, eyes cast to the ground. Not everyone was so daunted by Chesterfield's grandeur. Charles and Dickie could dawdle along the marble corridor or dash across the pristine quad, as if they'd grown up in buildings like this, which they probably had.

I could never quite work out Charles and Dickie's relationship – why someone as kind and noble as Charles, with such manners, such breeding, would be friends with someone as rough and mean as Dickie. And, after everything, how quickly he forgave him.

But I've never truly understood men, after growing up in an all-female household. Just the three of us almost from the beginning – my mother, Ellie and me. The presence of our father, who died when I was six, lingered at first on the edges of things – the texture of his corduroys when I sat on his lap, the bonfire smell of his jumpers when he kissed us goodnight, the way you could hurl yourself at him and he'd catch you, fling you in the air. Ellie used to love that. But, over the years, those memories wore out like newspaper print left in the sun. I'd take them out and look at them, but they'd feel less real, and my sense of him grew fainter.

The smell of Chesterfield is just the same. The same floor polish and sweaty cloakrooms, rugby boots and gym kits, the same coffee-soaked air billowing from the staffroom. An eclectic mixture of people gathers at reception. A few of us from school, as well as family and plenty of friends I don't recognise. Dickie was the youngest of four brothers – the slightest and sharpest of the lot. His siblings are here today, each one bigger than the next, like a set of Russian dolls. There are others I recognise from the rugby team; his parents, of course, much older and more fragile-looking than I remember from school. His father wears his hair in the same side-parting that Dickie did. His face has almost folded in on itself in sadness.

Juliet is there, dressed more for a fashion shoot than a memorial service in her tightly cut trouser suit. When she moves, bracelets jangle against her thin wrist, where the scars are still visible. As I arrive, she pretends she hasn't seen me and I return the favour, thrilled to spot my old friend Meilin, who, like me, is dressed smartly in matching jacket and skirt. She greets me warmly and we stand catching up quietly, while I keep an eye on the entrance for Charles.

He and Fiona don't appear until the last moment when we're about to proceed to the Empress Hall, led by the school chaplain, David Raven – known to generations of students as Dave the Rave. Charles looks immaculate, as always, in his charcoal suit, but his face has a Valium glaze to it, a beautiful sad vagueness. Fiona, with sleek hair and kohled eyes, sticks close to him, guarding him like a whippet. The pair of them seem to know everyone. They get swallowed up by greetings, pats on the arm and gravely delivered air-kisses. I shall have to wait for my chance to speak to Charles.

We proceed to the Empress Hall, walking behind the chaplain and Dickie's widow, whom I recognise from Facebook. Caroline is slight and sparrow-like, similar in build to Ellie. Dickie clearly had a type. Her hair is sandy, her face pale and freckled as an egg. Her baby isn't with her today. Occasionally, she glances behind her as if to weigh up the rest of us.

Everyone seems to know their place, as they always did, lining up to go into prayers. Meilin and I sit as far towards the back as we decently can and do justice to a rousing version of 'Cwm Rhondda'. Reverend Raven – his hair white now, his face craggy and tired – speaks in praise of Dickie's sporting prowess, his artistic talent, his popularity, his creative flair in the world of advertising. But there is a hesitancy there, I notice, a coolness in the delivery of the words. Perhaps he can remember the real Dickie. But it could be just wishful thinking on my part.

After the service, which is mercifully short, we file out to a neighbouring room for wine and a buffet. Meilin and I stand next to each other, eating quiche and murmuring observations about the gathered assembly.

'She looks nice, doesn't she?' Meilin nods at Dickie's wife, Caroline.

'She does,' I agree.

I've been in two minds about saying anything to Caroline. On the one hand, I'm interested to see what she's like up close; on the other, I don't have anything particularly kind to say about Dickie.

Meilin takes a gulp of wine. 'Why are you here?' she asks.

'To pay my respects,' I say primly, pushing salad around my plate.

'Oh, come on,' she says. 'It's not like you were close.'

I spear a cherry tomato and pop it in my mouth.

She laughs darkly. 'To check he's definitely dead?'

I swallow back my own laughter, but I realise, in that

moment, how much I have missed her and feel a touch of sorrow that we have drifted apart over the years.

'That's why I'm here,' she says. 'My only wish is that Tom Bates were in a coffin next to him.' She drains her glass.

She goes to fetch more wine, without looking back to see how I react to Tom's name. It brings on the cold sweat of a nightmare. I glance around the room again to confirm his absence. I'd scanned the congregation in the Empress Hall for his balding head earlier, but I couldn't spot him – and it would have been easy. He still stands head and shoulders above everyone else from what I can see on Facebook. A taciturn giant. The First XV's secret weapon. Another face scratched out on that team photograph.

10

Meilin returns with two large glasses of wine. 'Well, you can't just be here to catch up with me,' she says, pushing one into my hand. She's always been terrier-like. 'We don't need to return to this godforsaken dump to do that. I never visit the Peak District out of choice now. Too many memories.' She gives a dramatic shiver. 'You know they asked me to come back and give a talk about women in leadership. I said, "Over my dead body. Or at least not until you have a headmistress in place."' She sighs. 'It's like everywhere else – the women in the lowly caring roles – the matrons and teachers – and the men in the top jobs.'

Meilin has done well for herself and I'm pleased for her, but sometimes I wonder what she thinks of my own lowly job. Out of habit, my eyes skit to Charles as she rants and it occurs to me how strange it is – the way we see the people we've loved since childhood. As if they don't look any different. When I notice how Charles has aged around the eyes, or grown the slightest of bellies, well, it almost comes as a surprise that I'm looking at a man in his thirties. I still need to speak to him but it's going to be difficult with Fiona sticking to him so closely.

'Of course,' Meilin says in an aggravatingly knowing tone. '*That's* why you came.' She sighs into her wine glass. 'You're not going to start up all that again.'

She caught me once. I was sitting by his trunk, before they were all put into storage at the beginning of term, running my fingers along the letters CM Fry, daubed in white. Meilin liked Charles too – a lot of girls did – but she told me, 'Don't degrade yourself, Fran.' It was a choice of words I thought about from time to time over the years. It made me think of *Wuthering Heights*.

I blink away the memory. 'I wondered if Ellie might come,' I say. 'I thought there might be a chance.'

It was a daft hope, really, Ellie's relationship with Dickie being what it was.

'You two still not speaking?' Meilin's tone softens. She likes Ellie.

'It's been almost three years.'

'You should patch things up,' she says. 'She's the only family you have.'

I'm quiet, listening to the murmur of the room. The catering staff are beginning to tidy away the food, carrying in trays of teacups in its place. It was true: Tom's was not the only head I'd been looking for in the room. And Ellie's would have been easy to see, too, with her distinctive blonde curls. But I don't want to talk about Ellie – about her, or Tom, or any of it. A waitress carrying a large cafetière puts it down too sharply and a spurt of dark liquid shoots out, staining the pristine white table-cloth.

'I was there,' I whisper. 'The night Dickie died. I saw it happen.'

Meilin looks from the waitress back to me.

I'm as taken aback by this confession as she is. I haven't thought it through. It's a kneejerk reaction to being asked about Ellie. A distraction technique. And probably the wine.

'What did you see?' she asks.

I falter, unsure how much more to share, remembering the scrum of the crowd on the platform. The heat and the smell of so many human bodies packed up against each other. The flicker of panic as the train approached. The shift in the group of women. The way Dickie looked before he fell. I need to talk to Charles. My eyes return to him. Fiona remains at his side, her slim arm around his waist.

'The thing is,' I say to Meilin, my gaze still tugged to the other side of the room, 'I'm not sure it was an accident.'

'What do you mean?'

'I don't know – it's a hunch.' I look into my wine glass, deciding if I should say more. I realise I'm quite drunk.

Meilin takes a strangely long time to respond and when I glance up I see that Dickie's widow has come to join us. I stare at her, wondering how much she has heard.

'Hi,' she says. 'I'm Caroline. You must be Ellie's sister.' She places a small hand on my arm.

'Yes,' I say, puzzled. Ellie and Dickie weren't friends, after all. 'I was in Dickie's year,' I add. 'We were in the same English class.'

'I imagine he wasn't much good at that.' She smiles and takes a sip from the cup of tea she's holding.

'No,' I agree. 'Not really.'

'He was good at rugby, though,' adds Meilin tactfully.

'And art,' I say, remembering a picture of his in the summer exhibition in fifth year. A charcoal sketch of a life model – a skinny old man, his flesh slack and veiny. Everyone else got the giggles in life-drawing classes, but Dickie, in contrast with what one might expect, took it seriously, retreating into quiet concentration as he drew. I wonder if this was a side of him his wife knew too – a secret self kept hidden from the rest of us.

'Yes, he was,' she agrees. 'He sketched me when we first got together. It was very flattering.' She laughs. 'But I suppose it had to be.'

I realise I haven't offered my condolences, but already it feels too late. 'How did you and Dickie meet?'

She smiles benignly. 'At AA.'

It takes me by surprise. 'I didn't know,' I say. Though why would I? That was hardly something he'd have boasted about on social media. Remembering how unsteady he was on his feet before he went over the platform, it occurs to me he might have been keeping a secret from Caroline.

She nods. 'Dickie, well, he wanted to be better.'

'We all want to be better,' I say.

There's another silence. I'd forgotten this about funerals – the awkwardness, the standing around, thinking about what to say next.

'Do you want a tea?' Meilin asks me. 'I'm going to get one.'

I shake my head and, as she slips away, Caroline says softly, 'You work at that bookshop, don't you? On the Kings Road?'

I look at her dumbly, recalling the figure standing in the rain, staring.

'I saw on Facebook,' she says.

'I don't really put anything on there,' I reply.

'Oh, I'm sure I saw it somewhere.' She takes another sip of tea.

She's looked me up then. It shouldn't make me feel unsettled – I've looked her up too, after all – but it does.

'Could I come and see you there?' she asks.

My heart begins to thud faster. Did she hear what I said earlier? I rewind the conversation, trying to work out when she arrived, silently, next to us.

She returns the cup to the saucer carefully. 'There's something I wanted to talk to you about.' She seems to have taken my silence as consent.

It's at this juncture that Juliet joins us, dropping a jangling hand onto Caroline's shoulder.

'Caz, darling,' she drawls. 'How are you holding up?'

It gives me some satisfaction to watch Caroline step neatly away.

'Fran,' says Juliet. She tilts her glass at me. It looks like we're not the only ones making the most of the free-flowing Pinot.

'Juliet.' I nod, without smiling.

'It's Jules now,' she says.

I ignore this.

'I've got to catch the chaplain,' says Caroline.

Juliet shakes her head sadly as she watches her go. 'Poor woman. It can't have been easy with Dickie.'

'I thought he was your friend,' I say pointedly. 'One of the good ones.'

'Did I say that?' Juliet slurps her wine. 'Nice to know you've been keeping an eye on me. Mind you, you were always good at keeping an eye on things.'

A festering silence falls between us. I glance over to the table, hoping to transmit to Meilin the urgency of her return.

'Did you hear about the psychopath test, Fran?' asks Juliet, tracing her scars with her fingertips.

'The book?'

'No, the test,' she insists.

'It goes like this.' She gestures as if she's telling an anecdote on television. 'A woman goes to her mother's funeral and she meets a man she likes – a stranger, someone she hasn't met before. A few days later, she kills her sister. Why?'

There's an acidic taste in my mouth. All that wine, and being back at Chesterfield. It's too much. From the other side of the room, I can see Meilin start to chat to Fiona. That means Charles has been left unguarded. I have to speak to him, to escape Juliet. I don't know what she's getting at with her stupid story, but I've always felt, with Juliet, that she can see through to the darkest heart of me.

She is still looking at me, though I haven't given her an answer.

I wait for her to explain, knowing she won't be able to resist.

'She murders her sister in order to meet the man again,' she says triumphantly, taking a self-congratulatory gulp of wine.

'Interesting,' I say blandly, only half paying attention, straining to work out where Charles is.

'Her logic is: if she met him at a family funeral, he'll come to the next one,' Juliet persists. 'She kills someone just to bump into the man of her dreams again.'

I glimpse Charles then, saying goodbye to the chaplain. Fiona by his side again, the pair of them looking sombre and united. I feel a sudden flash of rage at being penned in like this by Juliet, at her stupid story, at how the afternoon has gone to waste speaking to everyone except the one person I came here for.

'I don't really know what you're getting at,' I snap.

Juliet smiles slowly. She has my attention at last. 'It's just strange that Dickie's death has brought you back into a room with Charles.' She looks down at her scars. 'Some people do psycho things for the ones they love, don't they?'

11

On the train, over an egg sandwich and KitKat, I tell Meilin about the psychopath test.

'Typical Juliet,' she says. 'Or *Jules*,' she adds, smirking. 'Just trying to make you feel as uncomfortable as she did. It's pretty clear Dickie's wife is no fan of hers. Charles's neither, I should imagine. I reckon she's lonelier than she lets on.'

'Do you think Caroline overheard me?' I pull the crust off my egg sandwich. 'About being there when Dickie died.'

'I don't think so,' says Meilin thoughtfully. 'But perhaps you should mention it to the police? As a witness.'

For all her dark humour, Meilin is a law-abiding citizen.

'I'll think about it.' I decide against sharing my plan to speak to Charles first. Meilin wouldn't approve. 'I really don't know what Juliet was driving at,' I add, unable to let it go. 'Trying to imply I'm psycho.'

Meilin snorts. 'She can talk.'

'Well, exactly.'

'She was always jealous of you.'

'Hardly,' I reply doubtfully, remembering school.

'I don't know.' Meilin peels the lid off her fruit salad. 'You had your little sessions with Charles. And were always so self-contained. You never seemed to need anyone else.' She licks the fruit juice off the lid. 'And then there was Ellie,' she adds. 'All the boys liked her.'

I couldn't disagree with that. Ellie's looks have always been her blessing. And her curse. She isn't vain, isn't a preening sort of person, but she knows the power she has. I remember leaving a drinks party with Mother when Ellie and I were children – one of the rare times we went out as a family. I clung to my mum's hand while Ellie was in her arms beaming toothy smiles at the guests as she passed them. 'She's going to be trouble, that one,' said a big, red man, with a cigarette in his hand. And our mother had smiled in a rather strained way and pulled Ellie close.

The memory worried at me.

'Where is she now?' asks Meilin.

'Paris, I think.' I nibble the chocolate from my KitKat as a distraction.

Ellie was always restless, even before we fell out. Unlike my steadfast years at the shop, she drifted from job to job in the years after school – dancing on podia at nightclubs or, when that got too exhausting, pressing UV stamps against the hands of partygoers, or mixing cocktails. She did a bit of everything and I struggled to keep up. Occasionally, I might happen to be passing a bar where I thought she was working and put my head around the door. 'Is Ellie here?' I'd ask and they'd say, no, she wasn't. Sometimes a man behind the bar, polishing a glass with a tea towel would look me up and down and twist his mouth in a certain way as if there was something he wasn't saying. It was the same with her friends. People came and went but she didn't seem to form permanent attachments. She'd get along with those in her immediate vicinity and then move on when her job changed again. Perhaps her dyslexia made it harder for her to keep on top of texts and emails. She is still a sporadic communicator these days, though her writing has improved now – automatic spellchecks must help.

Another trick of hers when we lived together was the way she'd suddenly vanish on trips abroad. One birthday I gave her a copy of the book *1,000 Places to See Before You Die* and she began to send us postcards from wherever she went saying, 'Another one off the list.'

'It's like she's looking for something,' I said to Mother once, when the latest missive had arrived.

'Of course she is.' She took it from me and stared sadly at the Taj Mahal. But she didn't tell me what it was Ellie was searching for.

At St Pancras, Meilin hugs me goodbye. 'It's been fun catching up,' she said. 'Let's do it again soon.'

I agree cheerfully enough, but, despite the warmth between us, I find myself doubting it will happen. As soon as Meilin returns to her sleek flat in Canary Wharf, with its smooth granite surfaces and views of the water, back to her women-in-management meetings, spinning classes and after-work cocktails, I suspect that this intention to stay in touch will flicker and dim, that I shall become another name on a list of people she feels guilty about.

And there's something else. If Meilin were ever to pay

a visit to my flat, with its sticky linoleum floor, flimsy walls and the smell of marijuana billowing up from the dealer's flat below; with Mother's room upstairs left just as it was when she died, and Ellie's next to it waiting for her to come back; and the dusty globe in the corner of the front room, keeping track of her movements, I would not be able to hide my loneliness. And I'm not sure I could bear for anyone else to witness it.

When I get back to the flat and switch on my laptop it's as if my thoughts of Ellie have summoned her up. An email. My heart is racing as I open it. I heard about Dickie, she writes. How was the memorial service? Were the 'gang' all there?

Her tone's sarcastic, and she's ignored my questions, I notice. Ellie never liked being interrogated, but this feels as if I have something to work with. It's the first time I've heard from her since Mother's birthday in September when she sent a bouquet of lilac roses, which were always Mother's favourite. A reminder of her Christian name, which my niece shares. The roses are our thing, marking the annual day of truce in our estrangement. Ellie's the only person who's ever sent me flowers.

In my email back to her, I pour my heart out in the way I once did in my journals – what it was like to catch up with Meilin, how Juliet baited me as always, my disappointment at not speaking to Charles. I just pull myself back from telling her that I witnessed Dickie's death. That I saw a jostling crowd of women cram up against him. That in that scrum, one could have easily pushed him. That I suspected it was someone he knew.

12

Before I go to sleep, I look through my Charles collection. A consolation for not catching him today. There's no need to keep it locked in my tuckbox now, but I still do. I get everything out, glancing at the team photograph, the rugby socks, the wrapped birthday presents I never delivered, the leather-bound journals from my school days – still among my most treasured possessions, though I don't write in them any more. I'm careful what I keep a record of now. I find the passage I'm looking for and read it a couple of times before climbing into bed and reliving it again as I drift off. Another red-letter day.

The first time he came to find me in the prep room, Charles was still in his rugby clothes, his thighs plastered in mud. I didn't know where to look. In my memory, it was the golden hour: the light soft through the windows, a glow surrounding him like a religious icon. It's possible those details may have been added later – it's hard to tell after all these years.

Even though I was used to sitting next to him in class, he seemed bigger somehow close up, outside of that formal setting.

'Fran!' he said at the doorway. 'Just the person I'm looking for.'

Meilin, who was visiting me from her boarding house that night, gawped as he made his way over.

Charles sighed, took a seat and threw his legs onto a chair. 'My legs ache,' he said.

I looked down at his mud-smeared thighs. 'Did you win?'

'Yeah.' Of course he won.

He smelled faintly of beer. How manly, I thought.

He smiled. 'Fran. Is that short for Frances?'

'Francesca.'

We'd never spoken for so long.

'That's a pretty name. It suits you.'

I heard a snuffling noise come from Meilin. I couldn't tell if it was admiration, or laughter.

'Francesca, this timed essay on *Henry IV, Part I* for Mrs Fyson tomorrow – I don't get it.'

That was it. My moment. A present handed to me out of the blue. I had just been preparing for this very essay. 'It's about acting versus acting,' I began proudly.

'Right,' he rubbed his chin. 'Crystal clear.'

'Let me explain. Hotspur'—I stabbed the text in front of me with my finger—'is a man of action, whereas Prince Hal is a man who can dissemble. Act. Get it?'

'Hm, so it's about the two meanings of acting?' He picked up the text and looked at it doubtfully.

'Yes.' I took the book off him, wondering at my boldness.

'You know that speech when Hal talks about how he is biding his time, messing around in the pub with Falstaff; how eventually he'll reveal his true self like the sun from behind the clouds?'

'I know that bit,' chirped up Meilin. '"*If all the year were playing holidays, To sport would be as tedious as to work . . .*"'

I shot her a look. It wasn't *her* moment. 'It means that his real nature is like the sun – that it will come out eventually,' I explained. 'Until then he's dissembling, biding his time. Slumming it. Acting, I suppose. Until he becomes a man of *action* – the warrior prince his father needs him to be.'

Charles took the book off me and was quiet for a moment as he read the passage.

'I like that,' he said eventually. 'What about the other characters? We have to write about them too, don't we?'

'Well,' I said, 'with Hotspur – he's a man of action. But it doesn't do him that much good.' I drew a little illustration on a piece of paper in front of me, of Hotspur with a sword, jumping up and down like a hothead.

'Why not?' Charles flicked through the book. We hadn't finished it in class yet, but I'd read ahead.

'He dies,' said Meilin breathlessly. 'Hal kills him.'

'Huh, thanks,' muttered Charles.

'It's Meilin,' she reminded him eagerly, though no one had asked her.

'And Falstaff,' I continued with my lesson, sketching out the fat bearded man, sitting on a chair with a tankard in his hand. 'He's a character who dissembles too much. Lies. Like when he says that he killed Hotspur, but he hasn't. So, in the end, Hal has to reject him, to leave him and all his lowlife buddies behind. I guess what it's about, really, is that too much of either kind of acting is a bad thing. The characters who do best are the ones who can do both.'

13

'Someone's asking for you,' says Gareth. I'm in the basement helping Ingrid and Liam sort through a large delivery. Outside, it's an uninspiring autumnal day, the kind of afternoon that barely gets light. The rain comes down in a steady drizzle, so it doesn't seem worth taking a break.

My heart does a small jump. A skip. It won't be Charles, of course. I don't know why I even let myself dream it might be.

'A woman. With a baby,' confirms Gareth.

Definitely not Charles then.

Gareth doesn't stop to say more. He's wary of me these days. I hurt him and I'm sorry for that. He's a kind man, a little tubby, with a sweet, boyish face. I always felt safe around him and enjoyed our conversations about books. We used to spend some time together outside of the shop, but that's all stopped now.

When he first asked me out, I told Ellie. 'It sounds like a *date* to me,' she said.

'What happens on dates?' I asked, partly teasing, partly curious. I'd seen dates on TV, of course, and sat on Ellie's bed watching her get ready for them. She was quick at it – a lick of this, a smear of that, fingers through her curls and then she'd be gone.

I remember how she pulled a naughty face and said, 'It's more about what you do *afterwards*.'

I'd never done the thing she was talking about – and I didn't think I'd be starting with Gareth – but I'd heard voices late at night upstairs in Ellie's room in the months after Mother died. Perhaps it was her way of dealing with the stress – not just the grief of losing Mother, but the money worries that plagued us afterwards; the calls from our mortgage lender; the bills with 'urgent' stamped on them that we were struggling to stay on top of.

By morning, there might be an empty wine bottle or two in the kitchen, the whiff of cigarette smoke or a condom wrapper in the bathroom bin, but there would be no sign of what we termed her gentleman callers.

'And what was the name of last night's visitor?' I'd ask her over breakfast.

'Oh, I don't give them *names*,' she'd tease. She'd just call them The French Man or The Banker or whatever. 'It's like pets,' she'd say, tickling Branwell's tummy. 'If you name them, you have to keep them.'

I'd enjoyed my time with Gareth – our author talks and cinema trips – but when Charles came back into my life four years ago, I found myself looking at Gareth with different, more critical eyes. I couldn't help comparing him with Charles. Like on our disastrous date, towards the end of our time together, in an Italian restaurant, when he got terribly flustered choosing a wine and spilled spaghetti in his lap. We couldn't think of anything to say to each other and by the point I asked him if he had any siblings for the third time, I knew we were lost.

These days he is polite but distant. Careful with me like someone near an item that could cut them. A tin opener. A sharp knife.

I walk up the stairs slowly, conscious of every step. If it is who I think it is, I'm going to have to be careful about what I say. I still haven't told anyone except Meilin that I was there the night Dickie died.

Caroline stands at the till upstairs in a dripping raincoat and hat. She has a pushchair with her. I peer through the transparent cover at Dickie's daughter.

'What's her name?' I ask, though I already know.

'Daisy,' she says.

Daisy, who has her mother's sandy hair and her father's dark eyes, blinks and puts her thumb in her mouth. She looks sleepy.

'We were wondering if you had time to join us for a coffee?' asks Caroline. 'Or tea. Whichever you like.' She speaks quickly, softly. It occurs to me that she's nervous too. She looks down at bitten fingernails.

My gaze lowers to where water is dripping off the bottom of the pushchair, staining the carpet. My heart thuds in my chest. I wonder again if she overheard me at the memorial.

I make a show of looking at my watch, but I already know how I'm going to answer. It's risky but it might be

71

a move that brings me closer to Charles. 'I don't drink coffee,' I say, 'but I could go for tea.'

In the café, we have trouble manoeuvring our way with the pushchair. Caroline takes off her rain hat and shakes her head. Her skin is almost translucent, the rings beneath her eyes a light violet.

'How are things?' I ask.

'You know,' she says quietly.

She looks down at the pushchair where Daisy is snoozing.

'Are you sleeping?'

When Mother died, sleep was the thing that really separated the wild days from the sane ones.

'Not really.'

The child wakes with a furious squall. Caroline picks her up and she wriggles on her mother's lap and nestles in to her. Her thumb returns to her mouth. Caroline strokes her daughter's hair absent-mindedly.

'Would you like a babycino?' she asks.

I've always thought that the daftest of names. It doesn't even scan right, but Daisy beams at the word. Caroline catches a passing waitress and orders our drinks.

'It still doesn't feel real.' She continues from where she left off. 'Your husband goes to meet a friend and he doesn't come home. You keep going back over the things you did before you got that phone call – the meal you made, the TV show you watched, every single detail – and you wonder: if I had done something else, something different, would that have saved him?'

I nod. 'I felt like that losing my mother.'

It's true. Even though she was terminally ill, I went

over the day she died obsessively in the months afterwards, reliving every point at which I could have changed what was about to happen. Picking at a spot on the table, I think of Dickie, too. When he'd glanced over his shoulder, could I have done anything to stop what happened next? Called out? Waved? I'll never know.

'I always worried about him going out anyway,' she says. 'Because of the chance he might drink again. And then this was so much worse . . .' Her voice cracks a little. 'He hadn't been sober as long as me, you see, and it was a risk at the beginning – our dating. You're not meant to see anyone for a while. Maybe it was my fault. Maybe we did everything too quickly for him – getting married, having a baby . . .'

I shake my head. 'You can't think like that.'

'It turns out he had been drinking that night, you see,' she says. 'Charles couldn't stop him – he feels so dreadful about that. I know he's worried that I blame him for it.'

'Was it Charles who called you?' I try to keep my voice as neutral as possible as I say his name, pushing away the memory of him on his knees on the platform. Poor Charles. I should have stayed; I should have been there to comfort him.

She nods, picking up a teaspoon. 'He didn't have to say the words . . . He just said, "It's Dickie." And I knew. From the way he said it; how it was him on the phone and not Dickie – I knew it was something very bad.' She shakes herself a little, as if to rid herself of the memory. 'Do you believe in premonitions?'

'Maybe.' I look down at a smattering of sugar granules on the table.

'Dickie was off in the days before he died.'

'Off?'

'Not himself.'

'In what way?'

'Jittery. Secretive. He'd started drawing again, but his sketches were so dark I couldn't look at them. They unsettled me. I didn't like them – I told him as much, but I wonder now if he'd had a glimpse of something – his death. I know it sounds ridiculous.'

The night before Mother died, I dreamed of Branwell at the door, scratching and scratching to be let in and then, when I opened it, part of his face was missing, his flesh starting to melt away. I woke to the rasp of Mother's breath filling the room and I could tell the end was coming.

I take a breath, unsure whether to share this with Caroline, but then our drinks arrive and the moment has passed. Daisy's face lights up at the sight of the babycino. A couple behind us smile indulgently at her; Caroline too.

Her delight is irresistible. It's as if we're warming ourselves on the glow of it. Her mother passes her a teaspoon and Daisy begins to ladle the white foam into her mouth, spreading it all over her face like the bubble beards Ellie and I used to make in the bath. I think of Rose and wonder if you can buy babycinos in Paris. Daisy goes to grab the cup with both hands and her mother intercepts.

'I wondered,' Caroline murmurs, as if she doesn't want anyone else to hear us, 'could you put me in touch with your sister?'

The change in subject takes me by surprise. I take a gulp of tea too quickly. It leaves an ache in my throat like a bruise.

'Why?'

Caroline curls her fingers around her daughter's foot. She doesn't look at me as she says, 'I don't know how much you know about the twelve steps?'

'Not much.'

'The ninth step is about making amends. Usually to people you've hurt from drinking but there was something from his past – something from further back – that Dickie couldn't let go of. To do with your sister. He wanted to apologise. He reached out to her on Facebook, but she didn't respond . . . And then he tried again when Daisy was born. Then again more recently. Three times. At least. And she's ignored him every time. And I don't know why but since his death I keep thinking about that – wanting to know more, to understand what happened. He never told me properly. You know how there are those things you can't move on from?'

I lift my cup to my lips and regard Caroline and her baby. A picture of uxorial compassion. She's lost weight, you can tell: her cardigan is loose around her shoulders. Still, my pity doesn't douse the spike of fury.

'Absolutely,' I agree in a clipped manner. 'My sister doesn't swim any more you know. She stopped. She was a wonderful swimmer. The best in the school. And she never does now. Ever. In fact, she is frightened of water.' I hear my voice speed up. 'The sea, swimming pools, rivers. It's a terrible phobia. So yes, I do know about the things you can't move on from.' I take another gulp of tea. I don't want to waste it before I go. 'I have things too,' I add, warming to my theme. 'Things I don't like: not as bad as my sister's, but certain fears. I don't like cheese,' I list the points off my fingers, 'because Dickie and Juliet put it in my hair and it made me smell for days. Or chewing gum. Or anyone sitting behind me. Because they're in a position to hurt you when you can't see them.' I stop to catch my breath.

Caroline's green eyes have filled with tears. 'I'm sorry,' she says.

Sensing the mood, Daisy begins to wail.

I drain the last of my tea. 'If you have anything you want to say to Ellie, you can say it through me,' I tell her. 'Send me any questions you have. Here's my email.' I fish out a receipt from my wallet and scrawl my address on the back. 'But I should probably warn you – my sister's not very talkative.' I scramble to my feet. 'She's barely spoken to me in years, so I wouldn't get your hopes up.'

'I've upset you,' Caroline says before she leaves me outside the shop. 'I'm sorry.'

A bus pulls past, sloshing through a puddle. I take a deep breath. 'It's OK,' I say. 'It's not you I'm angry with.'

'Anyway,' she says uneasily. 'Thank you for helping me with your sister.'

I shrug. 'I'll try.'

'One thing?' She hesitates, fussing over the pushchair's rain cover as it starts to drizzle again. 'Please could this be a secret.'

'A secret?'

'From the others.'

Glancing back at the shop, I feel a small flush of pride

at the display I created spotlit in the window. I don't answer straight away. I don't want to tell her how little I see of the *others* – but I've already considered how, when I finally have the chance to speak to Charles, I might let him know I've met with Dickie's widow. It could bring us closer. 'Poor Caroline,' I might say casually. 'She needs her friends right now.'

On the other hand, if Caroline and I share a secret, it might bind us together more tightly.

Caroline carries on fiddling with the rain cover. 'Dickie said you once had a soft spot for Charles.'

'A soft spot?' I repeat dumbly. The words make me feel exposed. I try to imagine the kind of thing Dickie might have said.

'It's OK.' She smiles. 'I know what addiction is like.'

She puts her hat back on and moves away, shoulders up against the rain just like when I spotted her watching me silently from a distance. I can't help but ask myself if she has her suspicions about Dickie's death, just as I do, and why she really wants to get hold of Ellie.

14

The worry nags at me as I return to the shop. It's strange that Caroline didn't mention that earlier approach, that she checked where I worked at the memorial when she already knew. It's the sort of thing I do.

There's something else that strikes me later, as I sort through the stock: if Caroline is in the habit of following other people – her husband, for example, when she worried about his drinking – are there other occasions she has spotted me watching Charles? The idea of this needles me – that I might have been watched even as I was watching.

'I feel low, too, after seeing friends with babies,' Brenda whispers to me at the till during a quiet moment. 'It's harder at our age, isn't it? Especially with Ellie and Rose living abroad.'

I don't want to correct her or tell her that Caroline isn't really a friend. That I'm not upset by Daisy's presence. Not really.

'It can be difficult,' I say vaguely.

'I avoid seeing them sometimes,' she says quietly. 'Too painful.'

Brenda doesn't have children, though she's been married for years – since I first started at the shop. I've wondered, from time to time, whether she might have been trying, during periods when she's had lots of doctor's appointments or given up caffeine or alcohol. It seems that she must have been, but I don't ask any more. We all carry our private sorrows and she's right: sometimes I also feel that longing, like a thread tugged inside me, when I think of Rose and how she has grown up so far away. Perhaps that's why Ellie moved. To punish me.

To cheer myself up after work, I decide to go and see Charles. I leave early and find my usual spot on the triangular patch of land opposite the museum. I only want to see him leave, watch him stride down the steps, pinching his coat at the neck as he makes his way to the tube station. I wouldn't follow him or say anything. Not today. It's just to see him, to reassure myself that he is still walking on this earth.

As I wait, I pick at a packet of Wotsits, dusting the orange crumbs from the pages of my book and glancing up at regular intervals. Tourists traipse out of the museum in herds in the direction of the tube. I'm worried I might miss him if I'm not careful. Then I see her. I can tell it's her from the strut. Fiona. Her hair tucked into her navy coat, her hands clutching the twins' hands, their heads, blonde like their father's, bobbing next to her at thigh height as they try to keep up. A surprise, perhaps. A family evening out.

She pauses outside the main door, glancing around her as she waits. I sink deep into the bench, wrapping my scarf around me, hoping the traffic on Cromwell Road stays heavy enough to keep me hidden. After a couple of minutes, she looks up, raises a hand and I see Caroline trotting towards her with the pushchair. The pair of them embrace quickly and Fiona makes a call. A few minutes later, Charles appears at the door in his dark winter coat and the six of them walk swiftly back towards the tube.

I wonder where they're going – an evening meal? A theatre trip? *Peter Pan* and hot chocolate. The kids are probably still too young.

I get up slowly, stiff from the cold. What had I thought? That my tea with Caroline might lead to something? A friendship? An invitation to a group outing? Witnessing their neat little family units, their togetherness, stirs my ancient longing to be included. To be part of the gang.

Walking home, I remember a rare school trip to Stratford-upon-Avon. We'd been going to see the Royal Shakespeare Company in *King Lear* – something I'd been very excited about. We wouldn't study the play until sixth form, but I'd read it with Mother.

School trips always made me nervous – the question of who I'd sit with on the bus there stressed me out, and Meilin wasn't going this time, so I'd ended up next to Emma Bellingham, one of Juliet's friends. Against the odds, we got on well. I was able to highlight a few moments to look out for – the blinding, the storm scene and so on – and she seemed grateful for, rather than amused by, my tips.

After the play, we chatted all the way back to

Chesterfield and I remember thinking, on that happy journey back to school, that I'd made a friend for life, that this was the point at Chesterfield where my fortunes had turned, when I could speak in class or at mealtimes and not hear the sound of stifled sniggering, that I would be able to queue up for lunch without the sickening prospect of having to dine alone, without the feeling that anytime something good happened to me, someone, somewhere, would be hovering not too far away, ready to take it from me.

Anyway, as it turns out, none of these fantasies came true. When the bus pulled up at Chesterfield, Emma got to her feet and said, 'See you.'

I, of course, took 'see you' to mean: I'll see you tomorrow at lunch, where we'll be sitting side by side.

But it didn't – it meant just that. That sometimes walking down the marble corridor, arm in arm with Juliet, she'd glance back and, quite literally, see me, and on a good day there would be the faintest shadow of a smile on her face but mostly, in truth, it was as if I were a pane of glass and she was simply looking through me.

15

To my surprise, Meilin is true to her word. It's her suggestion we go for sushi in Notting Hill – not a typical evening
out for me, though I don't let on when we make plans
on the phone. I walk there after work and arrive twenty
minutes early, which gives me time to decide what I would
like to eat and to begin the Charlotte Brontë biography
I've brought with me. I spend half an hour or so sipping
iced tap water and batting away waiting staff who keep
checking if I want anything more substantial. Then when
I look at my phone, I see a text from Meilin warning me
she's running late. By the time she arrives, I've been there
for almost an hour and I'm fed up. I'm good at waiting,
but everybody has their limits.

'Sorry, sorry,' she puffs as she comes through the door
and gives me a sweaty hug. 'Work! You know how it is.'

'The shop was quite busy too,' I say pointedly.

'How are things going?' asks Meilin. 'Do you ever think
about trying again with that Open University degree?'

I pick up the menu, though I chose my meal half an hour ago. I don't want to think about that time – trying to fit my studies around work in the shop. It had briefly seemed like the perfect option. Working during the day meant I could help Mother with the mortgage payments she always struggled with, while studying at night. The things I'd miss out on – the social side of student life: the pub visits; student union and karaoke nights – hadn't bothered me so much. The longer-term plan had been that I might follow my degree with teacher training, like Mother. But it wasn't long after I started that she fell ill and I began to struggle, to fall behind with my essays and deadlines.

'No, that ship has sailed,' I say. 'Anyway, I get to review the books and read stories to children sometimes,' I add as brightly as I can, 'so it's different jobs rolled into one.'

Meilin nods kindly and waves a waiter over. 'Shall we order some sharing dishes?'

'I was going to have chicken curry,' I begin.

'Sure,' she says. 'But let's get some starters and other bits.'

I stare glumly at the table as she orders, losing count after five or six dishes and trying not to worry about how much it will cost. Meilin always asks about my degree, even though it's been years. I don't like to think about it: the beginning of Mother's illness in the early Noughties and how long it lingered over the next decade or so, stealing her from us piece by piece.

After she's ordered, Meilin gazes at me over her reading glasses in the way teachers at school used to when they asked you to stay behind after class.

'Did you think any more about talking to the police?'

'Like I said, I wouldn't really have much to add.' I do my best to keep the irritation out of my voice. I wish I hadn't told her – that I'd shared my suspicions with Charles first.

'What *did* you see exactly?' she asks, holding my gaze.

'I can't be sure.' I hesitate, picking up a pair of conjoined chopsticks and snapping them apart. 'I just had the feeling he'd seen someone he knew on the platform, over his shoulder – but that he wasn't sure what to make of it.'

'Strange,' says Meilin. 'Could he have seen you?'

I place the chopsticks back on the table. I hadn't thought of that. 'I don't think so,' I say carefully. 'I was standing further away.'

'But it's possible,' she points out agreeably.

'Well,' I say, 'anything is possible. There was a big group of women on the platform,' I continue, not wanting to dwell on my own presence. 'Pushing and shoving. They'd just been to see a show. There were too many of us.'

'It's strange that Dickie died next to a huge group of angry women,' Meilin half-smiles.

'Divine retribution,' I say. 'I thought of the Furies.'

'Or just retribution,' Meilin says.

'Dickie's wife came to see me.' I lift the chopsticks again and turn them over in my hand. I imagine what sort of weapon they would make. I do that sometimes – an old habit I once learned in a self-defence class. It makes me feel safe.

'What did she want?'

'It's funny, really. She wanted to get in touch with Ellie.'

'Hasn't she heard of Facebook?' Meilin smiles.

'Apparently Dickie already tried. Ellie ignored him.'

'Well,' says Meilin conclusively, 'I don't blame her.'

We catch up a little about work and she tells me about a colleague of hers, someone she likes – a quiet man with neat dark hair, who was working his way through the Booker shortlist and swapped notes with her about the novels on coffee breaks. Then the food arrives, the steaming plates arranged on the table with a touch of theatre. Meilin begins to tuck in heartily, though I still feel unsettled.

After I last saw Caroline with Fiona and Charles, I went home and warmed up with a hot bath. When I checked Fiona's Instagram account later that night, I saw she'd posted a photograph: Keeping an eye on our darling @carolinegraham_82.

Caroline sat between Charles and Fiona in the photo, her cheeks flushed pink, her green eyes clouded, the other two pressed protectively either side of her. I remembered her words. 'Please don't tell the others,' with some bitterness then. She'd made out that she and I were in something together.

Fiona's make-up in the photograph was immaculate, her hair artfully tousled – she's always so careful with herself, as if she can smooth over the age difference between her and Charles with foundation and hair mousse. Charles still had that distant, vacant expression he's had since Dickie's death. If I could just speak to him, I think now; if I could just tell him I understand.

'She works for Haven, you know?' says Meilin, interrupting my reverie.

I chew my mouthful of salmon, trying to work out what she's talking about.

'Dickie's wife,' Meilin says impatiently. 'It's a women's refuge. She does their digital marketing.'

'Oh,' I swallow.

'What would a woman like that see in Dickie?'

I'm not sure what to say. Sometimes I sense I disappoint Meilin in not matching her fierceness about such things. It's not that I don't feel it – it's not that the memory of Dickie and what he did doesn't make me sick, but I don't want to talk about it all the time.

'Ellie said it'd be OK,' I murmur in the end. 'For Caroline to get in touch.'

After checking Fiona's Instagram late that night, I'd gone on Facebook and seen that Ellie was online. Something strange happened today, I typed quickly. Dickie's wife came to the shop. I paused to eat a chocolate biscuit in two hasty bites. She wants to get in touch with you.

There was no reaction for a moment, then the three dots began to dance.

With me?

Yes. Something to do with Dickie and school. I hesitated and typed, Making amends, knowing Ellie would understand.

Oh Christ, she writes. Can you tell her to sod off?

I did. Sort of. I said she could send any messages through me.

I thought then that the conversation was over, but the next day I saw Ellie had answered – It's fine, you can give her my email address. Easier that way. x

I'd done as she said and passed on her details to Caroline on Facebook.

Meilin helps herself to more black cod. 'I was wondering,' she begins carefully, 'was it just a coincidence you were there that night?'

I'd been thinking about a second helping but now the serving spoon hangs stupidly in my hand.

'Coincidence?'

'You know what I mean.' She gazes at me. 'I've been thinking about how you used to follow Charles around at school. You don't do that any more, do you? I know it's been years, but there was something about the way you kept looking at him at the memorial . . .'

Nothing gets past her. I make a show of helping myself to more food as nonchalantly as I can.

'School was years ago,' I say. 'Years and years.'

'Why were you there that night?'

'I was meeting a friend for a drink.'

'Which friend?'

'Christ.' I can feel my face burning. 'What is this? Why does it matter so much?'

'I just thought I should check,' Meilin says calmly.

'I wouldn't judge you,' I snap. 'You and that situation with your colleague.'

'It's . . .' She hesitates. 'It's not the same.'

'The same as what?'

'Hanging on to someone from school days.'

'Hanging on?' I repeat.

'I'm worried about you.' She rubs her face wearily. 'You witnessed the death, up close, of someone you knew, someone you *hated*. You've kept it a secret from everyone except me and I'm not even sure what you were doing there. It's . . .'

'What?' I demand, daring her to say it.

'It's fr—' She stops herself saying the word. 'It's *weird*, Fran. I know you've been through a lot – losing your mum, Ellie moving away. But following Charles around – if that's what you're doing – that sort of behaviour scares people.'

I glare at the array of plates in front of us, the sauces congealing now, the noodles glazed and cold. 'I didn't want all of this food.'

'It's OK,' says Meilin. 'I'll pay for it.'

'I'm not saying that. It's just I didn't want it.'

'What are you hoping will come from this situation?' she asks.

'This?' I say, gesturing crossly at the table.

'No,' she says. 'Charles. What are you imagining might happen?'

I keep my mouth shut tight, my lips clenched in an angry line.

'He's not as special as you think,' she continues quietly. 'He's just a guy. Just an ordinary guy. You're pinning too much on him. You always did.'

I pull my handbag angrily onto my lap and rummage through it for my wallet. I'm not going to tell her now, not in these circumstances, that I know it will happen. That one day Charles will look up at just the right time and I will be standing there and he will realise, *This is what I have been waiting for. This is what was waiting for me all this time.* A deeper kind of love. A love built on years and years of knowing someone. I know I'm a plump, ordinary sort of person, but Charles is my one chance at magic.

I don't say any of this to Meilin now. She doesn't deserve it. She signals to a passing waitress and we spend the rest of our time together in surly silence. I'd known in my gut that our meeting would be a mistake.

I replay the evening resentfully as I walk home and get ready for bed. How dare Meilin imply that I'm stalking Charles. How *dare* she. And why does she care so much that I was there that night? She's the only person I've told about my suspicions, and she seems extremely concerned that I saw what I saw.

I don't understand why.

16

The next time Caroline and Daisy come to see me I'm glad of the distraction. It's an unusually quiet morning in the shop. Everyone seems to be away at the moment. Charles is skiing in Zermatt and Fiona's Instagram feed is full of friends and family unrecognisable in goggles and ski helmets, or her and Charles enjoying an 'après glass of vino', as she puts it.

Fiona looks pretty on the slopes, dressing in cream to show off her tan. Behind his Ray-Bans, Charles doesn't give much away. I wonder how happy he is and if such a noisy holiday gives him any time for quiet reflection.

Ellie has moved east for the winter too, by the looks of her Facebook. She posts a photograph of Rose's small feet on skis. It worries me, the idea of her on the slopes, but then maybe she's good at sport, like her mum. I think, too, of where I might fit into this picture, sipping a hot chocolate in the sun, perhaps, watching Rose play in the snow while Ellie whizzes down the black runs. I don't know why I even think of it – it's not as if she's invited me or even told me exactly where she is.

'I'm not interrupting, am I?' Caroline asks, jiggling the pushchair. Daisy looks up at me, sucking on a toy. 'We were wondering if you fancied a tea? Our usual place?'

In the café, Caroline sighs. 'I'm sure you've seen on social media, but Juliet is organising a charity auction to raise money for families of people who've died on public transport.'

I nod. Juliet's many posts attracted my attention because of Charles's involvement. The auction is going to be held at the V&A. I've been weighing up whether it might be worth making peace with Meilin so I can go with her.

'Maybe you have something we could auction?' suggests Caroline.

'Me?' I ask incredulously.

'Juliet is offering an interior design session and Charles has suggested a private tour of the museum with an artist – someone terribly hip I haven't heard of.' She smiles apologetically.

'We might be able to offer book tokens.'

'How about a personal shopping trip with you as well? Advice on the year's biggest novels – that sort of thing?'

I pull a face. 'I don't know – who'd want that?'

'Please.' She smiles weakly. 'It would be nice to have you there – I find that crowd a bit intimidating.'

I look away, trying to hide my pleasure. The warmth of it spreads across my cheeks.

Caroline scrapes the foam off the top of her cappuccino. 'Dickie and I had been thinking of moving away from London.'

'Where?' I ask, unsure what to make of this non sequitur.

'Scotland, maybe? The Highlands. Somewhere wild. I wanted to get him away from everything.'

I frown, trying to imagine Dickie in the Highlands. It doesn't make sense. 'He would have missed his friends.'

'Yes, but his family are up in Scotland and it's just . . .' Caroline pauses. A teaspoon of foam hovers in the air for a moment. 'He'd been drinking again.' She stops to lick the spoon. 'And it wasn't just the night of the accident. There were other times, before he died.'

'Oh,' I say.

'I know.' She hesitates. 'The post-mortem showed he'd drunk a significant amount that evening. He was quiet, Charles said, but then alcohol could make Dickie morose. They found a hip flask in his pocket, what was left of it, almost empty. He was really struggling with something.'

'Are you angry with Charles?' I ask carefully. 'For not stopping him?'

'No.' Caroline is quiet for a moment. 'Sometimes,' she corrects herself. 'But then what could he have done? Dickie wasn't his responsibility. At other times, I wonder if I deserve this.' She waves away my protestations. 'When I wake in the middle of the night, with pins and needles in my hands, that cold sense of dread, I wonder if Dickie and I are being punished for our alcoholism. For the hurt we caused.'

I think of Dickie then, dancing alongside the pool in Chesterfield. The stink of chlorine on his clothes. His crocodile tears later.

'That's partly why I work for a charity,' she continues.

'It's like if I help enough people, it'll balance out the ones I've hurt,' she says. 'Do you ever think that? If I give a pound to this homeless person, it'll make up for that bad-taste joke I laughed at. As if there's a final reckoning.' She laughs. A short, dark exhalation.

I'm quiet for a moment. 'We all have thoughts like that,' I say. I don't know whether to go on, but something about Caroline's openness disarms me. 'I fought with Ellie,' I add. 'Before she went away. I said things. Unforgivable things.'

She leans down to Daisy, strokes her forehead as the child drifts off to sleep. 'Things that seem unforgivable can change,' she says. 'I forgot to mention – I heard back from Ellie. She said I shouldn't worry about her fallout with Dickie; that the past is the past.'

I snag on the word 'fallout'. It's not enough to describe what happened. 'If that's what she said . . .' I murmur.

'I wish she'd talk about it,' Caroline says. 'No one seems to want to.' She sighs, her eyes resting on her baby's face. 'Do you think she would come back?' she asks. 'For the auction.'

'For the auction?' I repeat, trying not to sound incredulous.

'Charles and Fiona say she comes back sometimes.'

There's a swell of emotion in my chest, a flutter of it in my wrists. 'She does come back sometimes,' I parrot like an idiot.

'What do you think?' Caroline asks. She licks her lips quickly. 'I could even fly her over, pay for her airfare.'

'Why?' I place my hands on the table to steady myself.

'It would be an excuse, really,' she says. 'I just want to understand why Dickie felt so bad about what happened.'

I'm quiet for a long time. 'I can't explain it,' I say in the end. 'It's up to Ellie.'

Caroline blinks away tears, runs a hand over her eyes. 'I sometimes think that if we'd moved, he'd still be alive. We should have got away. I can't help feeling that . . . Have you ever had that after an accident? That there might have been something you could do to stop it?'

Juliet. I think of her then. How could I not? With the usual combination of shame and fury.

'People like Juliet . . .' Caroline says, as if reading my mind. 'I reckon she was almost disappointed Dickie gave up booze. She used to be one of his drinking buddies. And the rest.' She laughs darkly. 'She'd touch him sometimes. I'd catch her with her hand resting on his knee . . . I couldn't always be sure of her motives.'

'Juliet's motives have always been consistent – to serve Juliet.'

'I know he had a thing for her at school, but she didn't want him then, did she? When she could have him?'

'What are you saying?' I ask.

'I'm not sure.' She shakes her head. 'But Dickie was upset about something before he died.'

'An affair, you think?'

'I don't know, but I'm trying to work out whether it was an accident . . .'

'Or?' A tiny pulse flutters at my temple as I wait for her to speak.

'Or whether my husband killed himself.'

94

17

I have to swallow back my words. I can't tell Caroline that I don't think Dickie killed himself – that that's not what it looked like to me – because I can hardly tell her I think someone pushed him. But a thought occurs to me as I walk back to the shop: I need to work out what happened that night. It's the one thing that will solve all of my problems – the distance between Meilin and me, the thoughts preoccupying Caroline. And Charles. What will it mean to him? Is he torturing himself too for not doing more? Replaying what he witnessed? Was he in a position to see something – or someone – I missed? The auction will offer the perfect opportunity to talk to him. If I can just get him away from Fiona.

My old jealousy had reared its head at the mention of Ellie's friendship with Fiona. They adored each other. It made me feel envious, but I wasn't sure of whom. When Ellie first bumped into Charles in 2013, she bounded into the flat with a spring in her step.

'Guess who I've just seen?'

My first thought – an indication of my state of mind at the time – was Mother. That she had come back somehow, or appeared to Ellie as a vision. She'd only been dead a matter of months. I was missing her terribly.

'Charles,' Ellie said cheerily when I didn't answer. 'Charles Fry. You remember.'

Of course I remembered, though by that stage my Charles collection had started to gather dust in the wardrobe. While I thought of him from time to time with fond yearning, the realities of my life in the bookshop, my burgeoning relationship with Gareth, had taken over.

'He's married,' Ellie continued evenly. 'His wife's lovely. They'd love to see you.'

I stared at her, taken aback by this development. Ellie and Charles hadn't been particularly close at school – not until our final weeks when he'd helped her in the way he did. As for Fiona, I wasn't happy to hear about her at *all* and I felt the first flicker of possessiveness. *He's mine,* I thought. *He always has been.* And Ellie was too.

I didn't want Fiona to have either of them.

I could see, though, what drew Fiona and Ellie to each other. They were both sporty and outdoorsy, not bookish and dreamy like me. Fiona had grown up on a stud farm in the Cotswolds I learned, trained as a midwife in London and worked her way up to management, which is what she was doing when she met Charles. After they married, she gave up work and settled in to their country life, firmly committed to her hobbies of skiing and riding and so on. That was before the twins came along.

When Ellie and I went to visit Honeybourne together,

the first and only time we did, the three of them were cheerfully intimate, sharing in-jokes, talking in shorthand. I didn't like it. I was quiet that day. I found I couldn't stop staring at Charles. How well he had aged. He was kind and courteous as always, asking me questions while Ellie and Fiona prepared the meal together. Falling for him was even quicker than the first time.

After the meal, as the three of them chatted over coffee, I asked if I could nip to the bathroom. Fiona directed me to the cloakroom downstairs, but I decided to explore further afield. I tiptoed upstairs to use their bathroom instead. It wasn't hard to find, next to the biggest bedroom on the first floor.

A standalone bath crouched in the centre on clawed feet. The floor was polished wood, with grand draping curtains and a huge bunch of tulips in a blue spherical vase. An enormous gilt mirror hung over the double sink, with lotions and potions in glass bottles and jars reflecting the sunshine.

I sat on the loo and, reaching down for a book to browse, as I always do, I picked up, from the top of a pile, *What To Expect When You're Expecting*. So that would be the next thing, I surmised glumly. Little Charles-and-Fionas running around. I thought of Gareth – I couldn't imagine having any of this with him. The book looked well-thumbed, second hand. Second-hand goods, I thought, remembering the pristine pile of books I'd brought for them downstairs. She likes second-hand goods. I spat in the middle of it. It made me feel a bit better.

Next, I had a closer look at their bedroom, at the

enormous four-poster bed with crisp white bedding and mounds and mounds of pillows. And more antique furniture – a huge old wardrobe, an Edwardian writing desk and a Louis XV dressing table, with yet more pots and potions. I wandered over and took the lids off a couple to have a smell. There was a black and white photograph of their wedding day amid her beauty accoutrements, which I could barely bring myself to look at.

I went to the window instead, admired the view of the lake and the sheep-spotted fields beyond, and I imagined what it would be like to live here with Charles. Suddenly I found I needed something of his. It was a visceral tug. A need to be physically close.

The only other person I've ever felt like that about is Ellie. When she was born and I was a toddler, I'd press so many kisses onto her cheek that our mother would have to hold me back so I wouldn't squash her. That feeling returned later when she was pregnant and I'd say good morning to her belly every day and keep it updated on all my news and promise I'd read it the best stories in the world when it came out.

We didn't know then that Rose was a girl.

Or that I'd never meet her.

I needed something that smelled of Charles, but I couldn't see anything lying around. I looked for the pyjamas under his pillow, but the thought occurred to me, as I picked them up, that those would definitely be missed, so instead I went to the laundry basket, which I'd spotted in the bathroom, and pulled out a navy cashmere jumper – so classy, so Charles – and buried my face in it, inhaling deeply.

Except, two unfortunate things happened: first, my deep inhalation revealed a distinctly feminine whiff. The kind of scent advertised by a girl in an evening gown running through the streets, dropping scarves and things behind her.

The second thing was Ellie walked in right at that point.

'What on *earth* are you doing?' she asked crossly.

'Nothing,' I said, dropping Fiona's jumper like a burning thing. 'It's nothing.'

She didn't speak to me for the rest of the afternoon, nor on the journey back to London. It was the first and last time she invited me with her to Honeybourne. And she was even crosser when I broke up with Gareth the following week.

'You finished with him?' she said, aghast. 'Oh, Fran. Why?'

'Because of Charles,' I said. My overwrought state didn't enhance my patience. 'Because of seeing *Charles*.'

'I think you're barmy.'

'You'll see,' I said.

I was right, I reflect now: events had conspired to bring me closer to Charles – to the moment when we could finally talk, when he would finally see what he'd been missing all these years. When he would realise what a mistake he had made with Fiona; when we could work out what happened to Dickie together. Like Sherlock and Watson, except more romantic.

On the run-up to the charity auction, Juliet keeps sharing on Instagram which of her famous friends will be attending. No one terribly impressive – a couple of middle-of-the-road presenters like herself, a reality TV star or two, a handful of soap actors. Making it all about her, as usual.

I send Meilin the new Mary Beard book as a peace offering and suggest she joins me at the auction. I receive a kind note back saying she would have loved to, but she's out that night, on a date with her colleague. Despite the prickle of jealousy, I wish her well.

As for Ellie, she laughs at Caroline's suggestion about flying her back for the auction, or at least she sends me the weeping-with-laughter emoji in a Facebook message, which is as close as I get to Ellie laughing these days. I miss her careless cackle. I don't think I've ever known how to make someone laugh in the way I can with Ellie.

I don't blame you, I reply. Caroline means well, but it's too late to make amends. I don't really understand what someone like her was doing with Dickie.

Have you told her anything?

No. I pause. My fingers hover above the keyboard. There's something else I haven't told her . . .

Branwell strolls in and winds himself around my ankles. I need this, I think. I need to be able to talk to her about it. I write, at last: I saw Dickie die. I was there on the platform.

Christ, Fran. Why didn't you say?

I wondered if he thought of you as he went.

Writing that makes me want to cry. I don't know if it's too much. If it'll make Ellie skitter away from me again.

I could do with seeing you, I continue. Do think about

100

her offer, if she's saying she'll fly you back. It's not far. I almost don't dare write the words, but then I force myself. I'd love to see you. You and Rose.

She is quiet again then. Ellie has always known the power of silence.

I'm not sure she'll even answer, but, after a minute or so, the three dots begin to bounce along again.

Her answer comes in two short words: I can't.

As I get ready for the auction, I'm nervous. It's not often that I get to socialise at black-tie events. The last time I got dressed up like this was as far back as Chesterfield. There was a Christmas barn dance every year and the fretting about what to wear would start as early as November. Usually Mother would help me pick something from a charity shop. Vintage pieces in creaking taffeta, which only needed a *little* airing to get rid of the fusty smell.

The other girls in my year would buy skimpy dresses from Topshop or Miss Selfridge. I remember Juliet in a particularly tiny silver dress with long black gloves that kept wrinkling on her skinny arms. One of the band members couldn't keep his eyes off her as she made her way around the room in a circle dance.

Some people would find ways to sneak in alcohol and Charles, in our fifth year, drank too much beer and passed out on the sofa. I went to sit next to him and, as he slumped onto me, I stroked his golden hair and said, 'There, there.'

And while we were sitting like that, one of the fourth years said: 'Do you go out with Charles Fry?'

And I smiled at her, because I could tell she was jealous, and I said, 'Yes. Yes, I do.' That was one of the happiest moments of my life. And then Dickie found us like that and woke Charles up.

I'm interested in the Dickie Caroline saw, because the way she talks about him, it doesn't feel like the boy I knew. The thing is, I like her. She seems gentle and sensitive, caring. Perhaps tonight I'll be brave enough to ask her about him.

I pick a dress out from Mother's wardrobe, a dark glittering gown that trails on the floor behind me as I walk. I take care getting ready, teasing my hair with curling tongs, borrowing a lipstick of Ellie's that is, perhaps, a touch too dark. The effect is dramatic.

'Big night out?' shouts the dealer at the door as I leave.

'That's right.'

'How's that gorgeous sister of yours?'

'Still gorgeous,' I say lightly. He always had a thing for Ellie.

'When's she coming back?' he calls plaintively after me.

I pretend I don't hear him as I walk away to hail a cab.

18

As the car pulls up on Cromwell Road, I spot the red carpet, the cluster of paparazzi waiting. Juliet is posing with a couple of men with mahogany tans and dazzling white teeth. I don't recognise them but the photographers do. I have the urge to tap the glass screen between the driver and me to ask him to keep going, move on somewhere else. I'm dressed all wrong, I realise immediately: the other women are in miniskirts and jumpsuits, bare legs on display with bold earrings that glint when the cameras flash. My dress is far too formal. Far too much. I am slow to pay the taxi driver, sad to see him go.

When I walk up the red carpet, the photographers lower their cameras and glance behind me. In the atrium, the waiting staff stand to attention holding trays of Prosecco lined up in rows. At a small table, a couple of bartenders are hard at work, preparing cocktails. I order a drink and loiter there as long as I can, asking lots of questions to put off the moment when I have to stand alone, drink in hand. One of them is kind to me, a tall man with dark hair and a warm smile. I realise, as I walk away, that he's actually very handsome. I notice quite late sometimes – that it's someone's beauty drawing me to them.

I start to compose an email to Ellie in my head. It was awful. You were right not to come – I don't know what I was thinking.

I haven't spotted Caroline yet, or Charles, or anyone I know apart from Juliet. Everyone around me has someone to talk to. The details of what they're saying get swallowed up by the high ceiling like the babble of the congregation in church. I miss my mother – I have the strange and sudden urge to call her, to ask her to come and pick me up – and it's perhaps this that makes me think I can hear someone call my name in a high, light voice, not dissimilar to Ellie's.

I swing around to see where the voice is coming from and my handbag – which is to say my day bag, packed with books and my umbrella, not a neat glittering clutch – knocks into a sylphlike woman with iron-straight hair behind me – so light that she goes flying. She drops her glass on the marble floor and it shatters into a million pieces. We both stand and stare at the mess. The crowd shifts around us and, as I look up in panic, I spot Charles and Fiona, standing on the other side of the atrium, watching.

Juliet appears, drawn, as always, to trouble, tinkling with laughter. She clicks her fingers at a waiter, who supplies her friend, the sylphlike woman, with another drink and begins to clean up the glass.

'Oh, Fran,' she says. 'You don't change.'

I smile thinly. 'Neither do you.'

104

'You know, I forgot to include you in the email circular,' she says. 'You've done well to get here.' She looks past me, scanning the room for someone else to talk to.

'Fran has contributed tonight,' says Fiona, appearing by my side. 'Didn't Caroline tell you? She's offered book tokens and a personal shopping session. So kind of you,' she says to me. 'Dickie would be so touched.' She rests a hand on my arm for a second.

In spite of everything, I'm so grateful I could hug her.

'Fran was so clever at English,' says Juliet. 'With her private coaching sessions.' She sniffs and takes a sip of her drink. 'Charles benefited mainly.'

Fiona nods. She's in leather trousers and a leopard-print silk shirt, looking sleek and capable. 'He's so grateful for that – he's mentioned it before.'

'Has he?' Juliet asks archly.

If Fiona has picked up on her tone, she ignores it, brushing a hair off her face. 'How's Ellie?' she asks me.

'Yes, where is she now?' asks Juliet, perking up at a subject that could sting.

'Tignes,' I say quickly, before Fiona can answer. 'Doing a season.'

'How she manages to work and travel with a small child,' says Juliet. 'But I suppose she's not exactly a career girl. And I imagine she's not short of *friends* to help her.'

She emphasises the word friends as if it were a bad thing. I know what she means, though. She means men. I don't like what she's insinuating.

'Such a shame she couldn't be here tonight,' says Fiona. 'Caroline was so keen to meet her.'

'I don't really understand that,' says Juliet, taking a

gulp of her Prosecco and waving away the offer of a canapé. 'Dickie and her weren't exactly friends.'

Fiona pauses to help herself to a crab cake. 'She has her reasons,' she says, popping the canapé into her mouth.

I want to ask her if she's heard from Ellie recently, but I daren't in front of Juliet. She'll only needle me about our estrangement. And I couldn't bear that.

Juliet yawns, as if she's had enough of the subject. 'I hear you had quite an eventful journey,' she says to Fiona. 'What a star you are.'

'It was nothing.' A slight flush on Fiona's tanned face betrays her discomfort. 'Just doing my job. My old job.'

'Fiona delivered a baby on the M40 on the way here,' Juliet tells me.

'Gosh,' I say. 'How did that happen?'

'The traffic was terrible.' Fiona shrugs. 'A man was flagging down cars to see if anyone could help his wife and, well, I could – or at least I remembered enough. I'm not registered as a midwife any more, but the woman in the car didn't care.'

'You haven't got a drink,' says Juliet. 'I'm sure you need one after that. Prosecco?'

Fiona shakes her head. 'I'm better with vodka these days. I've developed an awful allergy to wine.'

'I'll get it,' I say, thinking of the barman, keen to be away from Juliet.

I wait by the table as he prepares the drink, comforted by the confident way he works. I've always felt more of a kinship with people serving at events like this than the other guests. I almost want to offer to help, so I have something to occupy my hands – a lemon squeezer or ice pick, a chopping board and sharp knife.

19

When I return to Fiona, she is talking to a tall man with an elaborately sculpted beard. She smiles her thanks as I pass her the cocktail and I slip off before she can draw me in to the conversation. It has occurred to me that now would be an excellent time to find Charles. I walk slowly as I scan the crowd looking for him, sipping a fresh drink as I go. Climbing the stairs will give me a good vantage point, I decide, and a rest from the prying eyes of the likes of Juliet. I gather my gown to climb and slip into a quiet spot on the balcony.

From above I have a good view of the floor. It reminds me of the way the boys would gather on the balcony on the first day of the autumn term to assess the new girls that year. It was never the other way around, but the truth is: we liked looking at the boys too. They weren't flawless, of course, with all the imperfections of youth – spotty chins and foreheads, the braces on their teeth, their muddy legs, the light fuzz of stubble, their faces still creased from sleep in the mornings. Back then, I could look at Charles all I wanted and there was nothing to stop me.

I spot him, at last, standing with Caroline, stooping slightly to talk to her, his mouth close to her ear. At one stage, he gives her arm a consoling squeeze. How lucky she is to stand next to him like that, to be anchored by his kind presence, protected from the rest of the room. Caroline is staring at something and I follow her gaze to a small, blonde woman in a blue dress, standing on her own near the sculpture gallery. Something about her posture makes me think of Ellie. Her hair is like Ellie's too.

My sister was always so good at hiding when we were children, even in the tiny cottage we grew up in she'd find a place that hadn't occurred to me, curled up in the hollow of a window seat or a box in the cupboard beneath the stairs. Places I couldn't even fit.

I stare at the woman in the blue dress, willing her to look up, just to check it's not Ellie. I know it's a daft thought, a vain hope. Nor is it the first time that my longing for her has manifested itself in a sighting like this. More than once I think I've spotted her on a London train – the white-blonde of her hair resting against the door or a flash of her skinny calves going around the corner. She stands very still staring at the Rape of Proserpina, like a statue herself, and doesn't turn around.

The longer she is still, the stronger the spell becomes: my conviction that she might have come along to surprise us. To laugh at us, perhaps; that would be more like Ellie. *How ridiculous you all look,* she might say, *done up to the nines for Dickie Graham.* I have to check. I have to see if it's her. I pick up the train of Mother's dress and make my way back downstairs.

In the atrium, I can't see through the crowd to where she was standing. Breathless, I push my way through. Guests sigh at me as I squeeze past, or glance down with derision. I don't care. I must get to Ellie, but I'm walking too fast and my heel catches in the train of my dress so I trip and fall smack into a man. As large and immovable as a wall. He glances down at me for a second, mutters, 'Steady on,' and returns to his conversation.

It's his dismissiveness that does it. That takes me back to Chesterfield. I might not have recognised him from a distance. He's lost even more hair than his Facebook profile photo lets on. His rugby build has changed into middle-age heft.

Tom Bates. The presence of him like this, so close to me, the way he smells – not so different from school – makes me feel sick. I stumble for a couple more paces into the cool of the sculpture gallery where the woman in the blue dress is nowhere to be seen. I stand staring at the statues, as if they can tell me where she is. My palms are slick from the shock. Dashing to the loo, I dry-retch a couple of times and sit there waiting to calm down.

In the cubicle next to me, someone else is retching too, the splash of vomit hitting the water over and over again. 'Are you OK?' I call. But she doesn't answer.

I sit on the loo for a long time feeling sorry for myself and when I return to the atrium, most of the party has moved through to the marquee for the auction. I think then of making a run for it – what a dreadful evening it has been so far – but I give myself a little shake. I'm not leaving until I've spoken to Charles.

20

Eventually, I find my place at a table in the far corner of the marquee – about as far away from the stage as you could be. The equivalent of sitting with the band at a wedding, which happened to me at the only one I've attended. Juliet's doing, I'm sure. The only person I recognise at my table is Charles's colleague, Victoria, with whom I'm standoffish, remembering the conversation I overheard in the loos. The elderly lady next to me works at the museum too; she's one of the guides. Her face softens when I say I know Charles.

'Such a gentleman,' she says. 'He always makes time to find a kind word for everyone.'

'He was the same at school,' I say proudly, filling her glass and then my own with white wine.

The meal passes in a blur, sharing notes on our favourite items in the museum and on Charles. I realise for the first time tonight I'm starting to enjoy myself. After our main course of beef wellington, the auctioneer, a confident man with a keen ferrety face, takes to the stage and talks briefly about Dickie and the charity, and outlines the rules of the auction – the most serious being not to wave your flag in the air if you don't want to bid. I sit very still. The ticket cost almost two days' work for me. My flag will not be leaving my lap.

Juliet's is the first lot and the auctioneer makes a big fuss of her as she goes on stage. She stands with her hand on her hip like a teapot. I glance over to Caroline who is sitting on the same table as Charles, close to the stage, but I can't make out her expression as she watches Juliet. The lot starts at five thousand pounds and is in the twenties in no time at all; the auctioneer speaks faster and faster as if he's being sped up like a tape cassette. Juliet beams, her face shiny with sweat in the spotlight. I drain my glass of wine and fill it again. Next up is the tour of the V&A, which goes for a more modest amount; then there are a couple of small things – a giant teddy and a piece of jewellery handmade by one of Dickie's colleagues. Then we're given a break for pudding.

The first lot after pudding is mine. I've drunk quite a lot of wine by this stage and can feel the hot blush of it on my face. I go to the loo again and return to hear the auctioneer say my name. The whole room turns as one to face me.

'Is that her?' I hear him say. 'Francesca.' He beckons. 'Come up on stage.'

I blink. It hadn't occurred to me that this would happen, that they wouldn't just hold up the giant-sized book tokens. I shake my head to indicate my unwillingness but someone behind me gives me a little push. 'Go on.'

My feet are glued to the floor. Old Chesterfield feelings are fluttering in my chest – eyes everywhere in the dining room, the sensation of being judged, being found wanting. The beady-eyed auctioneer puffs out his cheeks with impatience.

As I make my way slowly to the stage, I look for Caroline's face. She gives me an apologetic shrug. A small smile. It feels like a trick has been played on me. Then I notice Juliet grinning as if the whole thing is a big joke. Heat flushes across my cheeks. I wish I hadn't eaten so much. Beef wellington and chocolate mousse curdle in my stomach.

Before I reach the stage, someone shoves the huge book tokens into my hands. I hold them in front of me, unsure of where to stand. The auctioneer has already started speaking, his words tripping over each other as if he's running late for something. I catch the odd phrase – my name, the shop. Something about my knowledge as a bookseller, my friendship with Dickie.

I'm sorry, Ellie. I will write that in my email to her tomorrow. It all got out of hand. I'm no friend of his.

He begins the bid at just two hundred pounds – the same price as the book tokens – and for a moment there is a horrifying quiet. A silence like a desert falls upon the room. I look out at the crowd – a blur of faces and hairstyles. I don't know how long it lasts but while we wait for that first bid it's as if my life flashes before my eyes and I'm waiting to be picked for netball at primary school, my legs goose-pimpled with cold, the grim inevitability now apparent that no one is going to pick me at all because I always get flustered and drop the ball and I will just be assigned to a team in the end.

Then I'm at Chesterfield, reading *A Midsummer Night's Dream* aloud and I say Titty-ana instead of Titania and there's an explosion of laughter from Juliet and Dickie, and then I'm standing, with my head over the sink, while Mother cuts the chewing gum out of my hair and tells me that I'll have a Twenties bob to show off the next day, but I can hear the crack in her voice, because no one in secondary school gives a shit about the Jazz Age, and Ellie grips my hand and promises revenge.

I don't want to do this any more. My own voice is very clear and strong in my head. *I have had enough,* it says. I don't know who it's addressing or what it wants me to do about it, but it feels then that a line has been drawn in the sand. That life cannot and must not go on as it has. That I must get off this stage as soon as possible.

And then, right in front of us, at the table closest to the stage, Charles's flag goes up and he makes a bid.

21

The auctioneer is squealing with delight, the room begins to murmur and my heart flutters like a kite. It all changed, I continue the imaginary email to Ellie in my head, the moment Charles raised his flag. I knew it would be all right, after that. A mini bidding war ensues – nothing outrageous but a modest battle between Charles and the old lady at my table. While the auction takes off, I notice Tom Bates sitting not far from Charles, his arms folded, and even though his face is expressionless, it's clear he knows who I am now. That he's remembered. If he feels any shame, there's no sign of it.

In the end the tokens go for five hundred and fifty pounds to Charles. He comes up on stage to receive them and kisses my cheek. 'Thank you,' I whisper. There's no one else in the room for a moment. Just the scent of him. His face in front of me. I pass the huge fake tokens over to him and a small envelope containing the real ones. I can't believe this is happening. It's the stuff of dreams. My legs are unsteady as I make my way back to the table, still glowing with pleasure. Everyone cheers and I think: this is what it must be like to be famous. Or, at least, happy.

My table is animated by my success. A couple of others introduce themselves and ask for reading recommendations. It occurs to me that this is one of the great evenings of my life.

Thank you, Dickie, I say in my head, as we file out of the museum, gathering in clusters on the pavement. *This is the beginning of everything.*

I am brave now. Invincible. I walk over to where Charles is standing with Caroline. There are things I want to say – private things – about how I'll never forget this moment, how there is so much we need to discuss, but for now I just thank him, touching the side of his face with my cold fingers.

'My pleasure,' he says.

'Dickie would be so proud,' says Caroline, embracing me, her face flushed. 'To have friends like you.'

I look down at the dead leaves mashed into the pavement at my feet. 'Tom Bates was here,' I blurt out, without meaning to. 'I didn't know he would be.'

Caroline looks confused. 'I don't know who you mean.'

'I invited him,' says Juliet. 'He was a good friend of Dickie's after all.'

'Who is he?' asks Caroline.

'He's . . .' I begin. I find I don't know how to explain him. 'Didn't Ellie say?' I ask instead. 'In her emails.'

'He was at Chesterfield with us,' says Juliet dismissively. 'Big rugby player. Got suspended in his final year.'

I feel briefly grateful to her for keeping it so succinct.

Juliet sighs as if the subject is boring her. 'Drinks at

115

mine, Caz?' she asks loudly. She fishes out a cigarette case and lights a long, white menthol. She offers the case to the others: Charles takes one, Caroline shakes her head.

'I shouldn't,' she murmurs. 'I must get back to the sitter.'

'I can't,' says Charles. 'I need to see to poor Fiona.'

It's only then, I notice guiltily, that Fiona isn't there.

'She was terribly sick,' Caroline explains. 'Couldn't stop vomiting. We think it was something she ate.'

'Or drank,' says Juliet, and she looks at me pointedly. 'What was in that cocktail you got her? Was there wine in it? She's allergic, you know. She told you.'

'It was just vodka and orange,' I say. '*I* didn't make it.'

'Anyway,' says Juliet, 'it wasn't long after that she had to dash to the loo.'

'It's hardly Fran's fault,' Caroline intercepts. 'As she said, she didn't make the cocktails. It was probably one of those crab cakes. You know what shellfish is like.'

Caroline is interrupted then by a guest in an oversized faux fur coat who pulls her into an embrace and begins talking animatedly to her and Charles, leaving Juliet and me standing awkwardly, side by side.

'It's funny though, isn't it?' says Juliet. 'That she was taken ill and had to go and, after that, Charles made a bid on you.'

She steps to the side, her sharp heel pinioning the train of my dress. She still enjoys it – taunting me. It's a game to her; she still hasn't learned.

'Do you think he would have done that with Fiona there?'

'Maybe,' I say. 'Perhaps. It was for a good cause.'

'The cause. Of course,' says Juliet, inhaling deeply. She blows out a thin plume of menthol smoke into the dank

116

night air. 'Is that why you're here? For Dickie? For the cause? What would Ellie think of this sudden show of support?' She grinds her heel into the train of Mother's dress.

Without thinking, I tug hard, claiming it back, and Juliet stumbles and trips. Her hands reach out to break her fall and her cigarette drops onto the damp pavement. I experience a flicker of pleasure, but I would never admit to that.

'Gosh, are you all right?' Caroline turns to help pick her up.

'Temper, temper,' says Juliet, dusting down her jumpsuit without looking at me.

'It was an accident,' I say, panicking. I don't want her to ruin tonight. Not after such a triumph.

'That's what you always say.' Her hand moves to her wrist, covers the scars as if to protect them. I don't know if she's doing it consciously, but I will her not to say anything. Not tonight. Not in front of Caroline. She hovers above me then, and I wonder what she will do next. Am I frightened of her after all these years? Maybe.

'Jules!'

Victoria from the museum joins us then, flinging her arms around Juliet. Of course the pair of them are friends.

'Poor darling Dickie,' says Victoria. 'I still haven't got my head around it.'

She looks as if she's overdone it. Her cheeks are pink; her eye make-up is creeping down her face.

'I know,' says Juliet, taking a step to ensure I'm shut out of the conversation. 'I think of it all the time.' She lights a fresh cigarette.

I glance at Caroline, who has returned to the woman in faux fur, and wonder if she can hear.

117

'And to think we were so *close* to where it happened that night,' exclaims Victoria. 'I can't bear it.'

Juliet looks over at me to check if I've heard, and taps the ash off her cigarette. I can tell she wants Victoria to stop talking.

'We could have been there on the platform ourselves,' Victoria continues. 'In fact, it was only because I'd drunk so bloody much that I took an Uber home.' She gives a dramatic shudder. 'It sounds dreadful – the way Charles describes it. The crush that night. It could have happened to any of us.'

It's clear she's enjoying the thrill of her brush with tragedy – far enough away to wallow in it. Juliet, on the other hand, has become very still, like a fox caught in the flash of a security light. I know her well enough to sense how uncomfortable she is. And she doesn't know I was there too. That I saw the crowd of women get so close to Dickie. That one of them could easily have been her.

Caroline returns to us. 'What are you all talking about?'

'Nothing,' Juliet says, shooting Victoria a warning look. 'Just reminiscing.'

'Are you going west, Fran?' Caroline turns to me. 'Shall we share a cab?'

As we drive away, I keep my eyes on Juliet, standing on the pavement, smoking. After a moment or two, she's joined by the figure of Tom Bates. The way they stand like that, side by side, without saying a word to each other, suggests a kind of intimacy. As if they were allies. Or accomplices.

22

I wonder if Tom is still married. Juliet always wanted something that belonged to someone else. She was jealous of my study sessions with Charles from the beginning. He aced his *Henry IV* essay, of course. Mrs Fyson praised him as she returned it to his desk. 'Well done, Charles. Your best work yet – you really got it.' To me, she said, 'Fran, there's so much passion, as always, but not enough order. You need more distance. Your writing is too hot-headed. Like Hotspur,' she said, making a little joke. 'As Charles points out in *his* essay, you need to be cool-headed as well as passionate. Like Charles said,' she repeated, a touch unnecessarily. 'To succeed you have to be both.'

Juliet and Dickie couldn't resist the temptation to tease Charles after that and, in Juliet's case, to win Charles's attention back. Certain rumours had started about him and me. Rumours I neither confirmed nor denied. But then one evening Ellie and I caught Juliet and Charles together, pushed up against an old horse chestnut on

Field, a place where she had done that very same dance with so many others.

Ellie was furious on my behalf, swearing vengeance again on Juliet. 'I promise you,' she said, taking my hand. 'We'll get that girl back one day.' She reminded me of a small terrier we'd known in Yorkshire, straining at the lead every time it saw a bigger dog, curling its dark lips to reveal sharp, pointy teeth.

'It's OK,' I reassured her, trying not to think about what it had been like studying with Charles, our heads bent over books together. The way he'd tap the table when he repeated a point I'd made or fold his hands behind his head when he was thinking. 'It's like Jane Austen. The hero always sees sense in the end.'

And I had been right all along, I reflect in the taxi, replaying the moment Charles raised the flag from his lap. It had happened just as I always imagined: he'd had his epiphany. I was the one. As Caroline is quiet, I rewind the moment over and over again until I feel almost nauseous from the repetition of it.

'Charles,' I say out loud, unsure if Caroline is awake or not. 'So kind of him.'

'He's a kind man.' She gives my hand a squeeze. 'He knew what it would mean to you.'

I dwell on her words for a while, allowing Caroline to think it was just charity on Charles's part. When he comes to claim his prize at the shop, I can finally talk to him about Dickie. The thought causes me to exhale with relief.

'I feel safe when Charles is around,' Caroline says. 'You have that quality too.'

'It's my figure,' I say mournfully, patting my thickening waist. 'It makes me look reliable.'

'No.' She laughs. 'It's your personality. You're not like other people. You don't try so hard.'

I don't correct her on this point.

'Do you fancy coming back for a nightcap?' Caroline asks suddenly. 'I don't like to be alone on a night like this, after thinking about Dickie so much.'

She glances out of the cab window; the Tesco at Earl's Court is lit up like a beacon. I wonder if they're living in the same place: it's been a couple of years since I waited outside their house in Ealing. That night, Charles was there for supper and Caroline cooked a lamb dish – Dickie posted pictures later on Facebook. I've never been inside, though. Perhaps there will be photographs of Charles around the place, intimate traces of his life I could store for the future.

'I'd love to,' I say.

'Good.' Caroline squeezes my hand and closes her eyes again. 'Daisy will be thrilled to see you.'

It's the same house, I notice, as the cab pulls up outside. The smell of the hallway is comforting – traces of floor polish and spaghetti bolognese. In the kitchen, a blonde babysitter, with her hair pulled back into a high ponytail, jiggles Daisy on her hip.

'She's just woken.'

Daisy's chubby arms rise at the sight of her mother and Caroline scoops her up, dropping kisses on her hair. The intimacy of it does something funny to me, and I ask for directions to the bathroom. The walls of the loo have been painted bright blue and there's a framed print

– 'Yesterday is history, tomorrow is a mystery, and today is a gift – that is why it is called the present.'

I look at it for a long time – it doesn't seem like the kind of quote Dickie might have appreciated. In fact, I can't imagine him in this house at all. It's too sleek, too grown up. The things I associate with Dickie – team photographs and sweaty trainers, teasing girls and ironic dancing at discos. None of them fit here.

When I return to the kitchen, the babysitter has gone and Caroline has a saucepan of milk on the hob.

'Look, Daisy, it's our friend Fran. Do you want some hot chocolate?' she calls over her shoulder to me. 'I'll put her down and then we'll have a cup in the sitting room.'

Caroline's hot chocolate is delicious – rich and sweet. After a couple of sips, I feel a wave of tiredness wash over me. Caroline perches on a pouffe, while I take the armchair.

'Please stay,' she says. 'I'm sure you're exhausted and the guest room is all made up.'

'Actually, I'd love that, thank you.'

I stare at a photograph of Dickie in his winter coat, propped up on the table behind Caroline. His face is heavier – not fatter, but more substantial than it was at school. I can't see any photos of Charles, at least not in this room.

'I'm not sleeping well,' says Caroline, looking into the fire. 'I keep reliving the moment Dickie died. Over and over again. Charles said it was quick – do you think it would have been?' She sighs. 'I hope so.'

Glancing at the photograph of Dickie behind her head,

I try not to think about the look on his face. That half-smile. The way he fell. I remember Juliet instead – her earlier discomfort. I wonder again what she is hiding. 'I'm sure it was,' I reply.

'I've been thinking more about the possibility of suicide,' Caroline says quietly. 'Looking back at everything, every stage of our relationship. When we were first dating, we used to chat late into the night. Dickie would talk sometimes about a relationship in his life. Something dark. That made him want to drink to escape it. It wasn't until much later, when I met Juliet, that I thought it might be her, though he never confirmed it. He was loyal like that. But I think she brought out the worst in him . . . I don't know why he couldn't have dropped her altogether but he was too soft in that way.'

Juliet brought out the worst in me, too. She always had – always knew how to taunt me until I snapped. Was she there on the platform too? But why would she hurt Dickie? Unless the relationship was as toxic for her as it was for him.

Holding the cup close to my chest, I'm aware of the beginnings of a terrible headache, like something crouching in wait for me.

Caroline sighs and gets to her feet. 'I suppose I should leave it to the professionals – we have a date for the inquest now, did I say?'

I shake my head and drain the dregs of my drink, unsure how to respond to the news.

'It's in January,' she says. 'I'm dreading it, but . . .'

'It'll give you answers,' I say, finishing the sentence for

123

her. I stand up too to shake off the guilt, to stop myself saying anything more.

The guest room is simply decorated and spotlessly clean. Caroline has left a T-shirt on the bed for me to sleep in, as well as a tracksuit for my journey home tomorrow – not the sort of thing I'd usually wear. I look around at the double bed – white linen, beige cushions – desk, cupboard and chest of drawers, as well as a neat en-suite bathroom.

Hearing the tinkle of music from Daisy's room, the sound of a mobile playing 'You Are My Sunshine', I wait until Caroline has gone to bed before having a more thorough search. First, I check the cupboards, but there's nothing terribly interesting: some formal clothes – winter coats and evening wear – in the main cupboard, with piles of bedding neatly folded in the alcove above. In the chest of drawers, there's more bedding and some towels. I'm about to give up when I decide to check the desk. Its drawers are stiff as they open. There's a modest pile of papers and an old sketchbook. I begin to flick through it casually but I find I can't look away. The images are horrifying – drowning women, with huge eyes and tiny limbs, scenes of violence and cruelty, dismembered body parts, and eyes. Eyes always watching. There's one image in particular – a girl with candyfloss blonde hair being sucked into the depths of a whirlpool. I shut the book and shove everything back into the desk drawer.

It takes me a long time to fall asleep – my head pounds; my thoughts spin from Juliet and the conversation I overheard to the menacing presence of Tom Bates and

124

the woman retching in the cubicle next to me. It had probably been Fiona. I hadn't caused that, had I? Or should I have mentioned her allergy to wine to the cocktail waiter? Had he splashed in some Prosecco when I wasn't paying attention? Had I deliberately looked away?

Your mind can play tricks on you. I know that much.

To cheer myself up, I return to Charles raising his flag in the auction, but every time I begin to drift off, it's Dickie's creepy drawings that come back to me, infecting the hinterland between waking and sleep, so that everything twists and corrupts. Each time I return to that moment on stage all I can see is Tom Bates and his eyes like dead fish. It feels as if I've only been asleep a matter of moments before I wake up abruptly, with Caroline standing at the end of my bed looking down at me.

'Why are you here?' she asks coldly.

I sit up, drawing my knees to my chest. Her eyes are open, but her tone and demeanour are different, as if someone else is occupying her body. She's sleepwalking. A girl at Chesterfield used to do that, walk into your cubicle and start talking utter rubbish.

'You should go back to bed,' I whisper, remembering you're not meant to wake sleepwalkers up.

'This *is* my bed,' she says. 'Get out! I don't want you here. Always creeping around.'

I glance guiltily over at the desk, seeing with relief that I've tidied away Dickie's sketchbook. Surely she didn't hear me rummaging through his things.

'Did you come for Daisy?' she asks. She takes my arm tightly, her nails digging in. 'Are you going to take her away?'

125

I struggle away from her grip and ease her off the bed to guide her back to her room.

'No,' she says, pushing me off. 'You can't have her. I don't trust you,' she adds darkly. 'I don't trust you at all.'

She strides for the door and pulls it firmly behind her. I stand for a moment or two, my teeth chattering, my arm still tingling from where she dug her nails into my flesh.

23

The next morning, I wake nauseous, badly rested. My eyes are gritty, my mouth dry.

In the kitchen, Caroline is cooking eggs. The smell causes me to swallow a couple of times.

'There she is,' she says pleasantly to Daisy, who's in her highchair, stirring mashed avocado into a pulp. 'How did you sleep?'

'Not so well,' I say, avoiding eye contact, gripping the kitchen counter. 'Do you remember coming into my room?'

'No.' She shakes her head.

'You were sleepwalking.'

She goes quiet for a moment, pushing the egg around the pan thoughtfully. 'Was I talking nonsense?'

'Well'—I try to smile reasonably—'a bit, but it doesn't matter.'

'I'm sorry,' she says, dolloping a ladleful of scrambled

eggs into Daisy's bowl. Her brow is unfurrowed, her green eyes clear. It's like looking at a different person from last night. 'What was I saying?'

I smile at Daisy waving her spoon in the air. 'It doesn't matter.'

After breakfast, the three of us go for a walk, splashing through puddles left by rain in the night. Caroline asks me again about her sleepwalking.

'You were being a little threatening,' I say in the end. I don't really want to go into it.

'Oh God.' She brings a hand to her mouth. 'I've always had this horrible side that comes out. I hosted a party once in my twenties and, after passing out, I sleepwalked into the kitchen and threatened to kill all my guests. Alcohol was the worst for it.'

'You didn't threaten to kill me.' I laugh. I don't add what she said about Daisy – I don't want to ruin our morning together. But the incident has left me with a fluttering sense of unease, like the feeling you have after a nightmare. I can't quite forget the version of Caroline I glimpsed. Is she really someone I can trust?

'Let me get you a hot drink before you go,' she says, taking my arm. 'It's the least I can do.'

We squeeze into a crowded café full of Ealing mothers and their offspring. The kind of place with posters on the wall about where to park your buggies (pushchairs, I correct mentally) and babycinos on the menu. The kind of place I usually give a wide berth.

Once we're settled with our drinks, Caroline fishes Daisy out of the pushchair. Daisy is in a good mood today, beaming happily.

'Why don't you give Auntie Fran a cuddle?' Her mother smiles and plonks her unceremoniously on my lap.

I don't think I've held a baby since Ellie was an infant – and I'm not sure if I'm doing it right – but I keep both hands firmly on her waist and she tips her head back at me and smiles.

'There you go,' says Caroline. 'You've made a friend. Actually'—she looks from me to the door—'there's a call I have to make for work. Will you two be all right if I pop out for a few minutes?'

'Of course.' I feel a swell of pride in my chest. 'We'll be fine.'

Daisy's eyes follow her mother to the door, her lip trembles for a moment and I remember something Ellie liked as a child. I begin to sing 'You Are My Sunshine' – the song I heard coming from her nursery. I whisper it quietly so the words are just for her and she thinks better of crying and tips her head back again to smile at me. I put my face to her hair. It's everything I imagined it would be: candyfloss, milk and biscuity sweetness. My earlier jitters melt away.

Ellie and I are too close in age for me to remember her being born, but I still have a photo of me as a toddler watching her sleep in her Moses basket, a lollipop in my mouth. 'You were so gentle with her,' Mother used to say. 'Your first friend in the world.' In all the early photographs of us, we're always holding hands. I'm taller, sturdier, darker. Ellie was bald until she was two. When her hair came, in white-blonde curls, strangers would come up to us in the street and comment on her angelic looks. But Mother was careful not to let me feel any less special. I

129

was still the older sister, the protector. The one who did things first.

Ellie was never far behind, though. By the time I was four and she was two, she insisted on doing everything I did – following me to the top of the climbing frame in the playground or on to the bouncy castle at the village fete, where the big boys hurled themselves at the walls. Her first words were 'me too', as she followed me around, before that phrase lost its innocence. Once, when Ellie was three and I was five, her shrieking on the see-saw brought Mother tearing from the cottage, mistaking my sister's exuberance for fear. 'My mum always said little girls were tougher,' she told me years later, at Chesterfield. 'It never made sense to her that they sent the boys to war.'

I didn't know what to say to that. I was of a genera-tion where none of us had been sent to war, and I was thankful. I'd long since ceded the physical advantage to Ellie and retreated to my books. I thought our roles had reversed at school; that she was the one who could protect me now. I didn't know that that pact between us could switch back again. That I'd always be her protector, just as she would always be mine.

Daisy wriggles in my lap. My singing has become dreary and I pick things up with a rendition of 'Under the Sea', regretting the choice when my mind returns to Dickie's drawings. Outside, Caroline is perched on a chair, her face animated as she chats on the phone. Daisy chuckles as I jiggle my lap in time to the music.

'Aren't you lovely?' An old lady, on her way to the counter, stops to admire Daisy, reaching out to touch her cheek. Daisy smiles coyly and nestles into my chest as if she belongs to me and I understand, in that moment, with the warm weight of her against me, a happiness I haven't experienced before: a door opening in my heart.

'Having a lovely time with Mummy, aren't you?' the woman continues kindly. Her white hair is curled and she's wearing pink lipstick for her trip to the café, a smattering of it stuck to her teeth. The sight of it makes my heart ache.

I'm going to correct her, to tell her I'm not the mother, just a friend, but Daisy drops her toy giraffe and I lean over instead to retrieve it. I think then that she'll move on, but she doesn't. Perhaps we're the first people she's spoken to all day.

'How old are you?' It's clear the question is for me to answer, not Daisy.

I open my mouth and shut it, trying to remember when she was born exactly. Earlier in the year. Spring maybe. Not the kind of thing a mother would forget.

'Thirty-three weeks today,' says Caroline's voice behind us.

The woman turns around to make way for her. 'She's beautiful,' she says.

My face flushes hot. Caroline has done nothing wrong, just helped me out of a sticky spot. Then why do I feel cross and ashamed?

'I'll let you all get to it,' the woman says kindly and makes her way to the counter, but she can't hide the look she gives me. It's not reproach, I realise: it's pity.

'You're an auntie, aren't you?' says Caroline, smiling as Daisy reaches her chubby hands out to her mother.

131

'Yes,' I say, but I don't want to talk about that: how I never see Rose. How I've never held her in my arms.

When I get back to the estate, my flat feels different. I stand in the dark hallway for a moment, listening. There's the tick of the clock, the burr of a plane passing overhead. Something feels unsettled. As if the air has been disturbed somehow. There's an unfamiliar scent. Something sweet. Floral.

The front room is exactly as I left it. The curtains open, the windows overlooking the white-grey sky and Great Western Road below. Crumbs on the counter, tissues blotted with lipstick on the coffee table. A hand mirror I borrowed from Mother's room left out. I tidy away the tissues and wipe down the counter. I return the mirror upstairs to Mother's room and hang up her dress, trying to decide if I need to take it to be dry-cleaned.

In Ellie's room, everything looks the same, too. It's as tidy and bleak as always. Even when Ellie lived here, there was a lack of permanence to the space, as if we were still at boarding school. Like mine, there's a double bed, a desk and cupboard. The only effort to decorate the place, or make it her own, is a poster of the ballerina Natalia Osipova on the wall – she loved Osipova, aspired to her steeliness and strength.

The bed is still made up as it was when she left. From time to time I wash the linen and replace it. I never tell her about that. I want it to be a surprise when she returns. The same duvet cover as when she left, clean and waiting for her.

Finally, I throw open the door of my bedroom and

there, on the bed, is a huge bunch of roses. As delicate as tissue and the shade of a dusky sky. They've been wrapped in brown paper and placed carefully on the duvet. Nothing else seems to be disturbed. Beside them Branwell is purring, smug, as if he'd brought them himself.

Lilac roses. Mother's favourite. Ellie has been here.

There is no trace of her in the flat, apart from the flowers. I kick off my shoes and get into bed next to them. I don't know whether to feel angry or sad. Mostly, I feel bewildered in the way I did when we were children and she would always find somewhere new to hide. Somewhere I could never guess. Maybe she's reminding me she cares. Or maybe she's still trying to punish me.

24

Defeated, I sink into the sofa, the roses still in my arms. Whatever game we're playing, my sister is definitely winning. Ellie never really had to try. She's a natural winner. She struggled with reading and writing, it's true, but some things were easy for her. Like Ratings.

On the first day of the new year, the most popular boys from school would gather on the balcony of the dining hall at lunchtime. Everyone knew it was going on, but, apart from Mrs Morgan and Mother, whom I heard grumble about it, none of the staff seemed to mind or want to stop it. The boys would mark all the new girls out of ten. In the old days, they used to actually hold up numbers, but that had been stamped out for being tasteless. Now the marks were generally kept private by the boys, but things leaked out.

One girl – who was pretty but a committed Christian – had been marked a nine early on, but, because of her chastity, her lack of interest in the boys, not many of them bothered to learn her name, so she was just Nine for the rest of her time at school. Juliet was a nine point five. Dickie used to tease her with what the half mark had been knocked off for – 'Your little finger is crooked,' he'd say flirtatiously, or, 'You hadn't plucked your eyebrows.' As far as we heard, no girl ever got a ten.

I privately hoped that Dickie hadn't heard about Ellie's toes. It was a silly thing – part of her charm, Mother always said – but the second and third toes on both Ellie's feet were webbed like Father's had been. One of those strange inherited traits in families like the way raw carrots cause Ellie and me to hiccup in the same way they did Mother, or body lotions make our legs itch.

Mother and I used to tease her about it a little at home, but really it was a point of pride to us – a sign that Ellie was destined to be an excellent swimmer. A teacher at her primary school had been the first to notice her talent when she was nine. A well-built woman with a short, no-nonsense haircut, she stopped Mother as we left the leisure centre. 'Has your daughter ever had any swimming coaching?' she asked, and Mother laughed. The idea of anyone in our family having any sort of sports coaching was incongruous. 'Well,' said the teacher, 'perhaps she should.'

Four years later, on Ellie's first day at Chesterfield, I was particularly nervous that someone – particularly someone with a big mouth, like Dickie – might find out about Ellie's webbed feet. I hated the idea of being watched, of being judged, and lunch was the worst time for it. In the evenings, we ate in our boarding house, but during the day the whole school would gather in the enormous dining hall. There was nowhere discreet to hide. In our houses, there was a seating plan, so we always knew where we were meant to be, but in the hall you could sit wherever you wanted. The sweat would start to prickle at my neck in the queue to go in. It exposed you, you see. If you had no one to sit with, there was no hiding it.

Unfortunately, I rarely did – Meilin often worked through lunch, or had her cello lessons – so I'd try to hide on my own in a corner. That wasn't always possible, so I'd have to find a place at the end of a table, where a bunch of friends might be sitting together. It wasn't enough that you were lonely – or alone – you had to advertise it in front of the whole school. But now Ellie had joined me, it would be different.

I glanced at her approvingly. She looked so tanned and pretty from our summer spent outside. Her skirt was a bit on the short side, as if she'd hitched it up, and her legs were bare – we didn't have to wear tights until later in the autumn term. She wore her wild hair down.

As we reached the front of the queue, I said to Ellie, 'Remember that the boys are doing that thing today, so don't do anything to draw their attention.'

'I don't give a shit about that,' Ellie said. She didn't so much as glance up at the boys on the balcony. 'And I don't know why you do, either.'

As we picked up our trays and slid them along the metal rungs, Tom Bates, who had been queuing behind us, started to get impatient. He was in a rush to join the other boys. Tom was in my year, silent and huge. He wasn't quick-witted like Dickie or classy like Charles –

but his physicality lent him a power. To the boys he was a kind of hero. He was the only fifth year to play in the First XV with the sixth-formers and just the week before, in a match against Eton, had knocked out their best player. He'd had to sit out for the rest of the match but it raised him, in the eyes of the other boys, to the level of a martyr. Tom's 'red mist' they called it – the fury that blinded him to everything but his aim. A secret weapon that could be utilised for the higher good. A few of the more suggestible girls in my year reacted to this change of status by batting their eyes at him.

It could be because of his raised profile that he was so cocksure that day, harassing us in the queue, as Ellie lingered at the salad bar. 'Why are you taking such a bloody long time?' he snapped.

'Got somewhere important to be?' Ellie said, slowing down to annoy him.

He didn't answer, but he glanced up at his friends on the balcony.

'Oh yeah, that,' said Ellie in a derogatory way, dawdling over making her choice. 'Comparing dick sizes, is it?'

Tom and I both looked at her. That kind of bravado was usually the domain of the sixth-form boys. No one expected a cherubic first year to talk like that.

He flipped a hand under Ellie's tray so quickly that by the time I realised what he'd done, her plate of lasagne had landed face down on the floor with a crash. The dining room went silent for a second. My face burned at the feeling of hundreds of eyes upon us. Somebody started a slow handclap. I couldn't help it then, I looked up to check if Charles had seen all this.

From his position on the side of the balcony, he was staring straight at us. I wished the ground would swallow us up. Ellie dropped to the floor to retrieve her plate but the broken fragments of it were mangled up with the lasagne. I gave Charles a despairing look and he smiled back warmly and right at that moment, without his having to say anything, I knew, I just *knew*, he was going to give Ellie a ten. I loved that he would do that for me.

I couldn't wait to tell her. Once her broken plate was all cleaned up, and we'd found her a new one, we sat down, though neither of us felt much like eating.

'I reckon Charles is going to give you a ten,' I said. 'I just have a hunch.'

Ellie played with her lasagne with a fork. 'Why do you care so much?'

I sighed, tried not to look at Charles again. 'People like you and Juliet never care because you've always had attention,' I said, spearing a carrot.

'And you shouldn't either,' she said. 'You're far too clever for all that shit.'

I didn't know what to say. She was right. 'None of them ever speak to me except Meilin and Charles,' I said quietly.

Ellie looked up at the balcony, where things had settled down a bit. 'You really like him, don't you?' She could always see through me.

'*Whatever our souls are made of, his and mine are the same*,' I said dramatically, adding, in response to her baffled look, '*Wuthering Heights*. That's how it all started.'

'Hmm,' said Ellie. 'I don't know about that.' But she turned around and gave Charles a cheery thumbs-up, which, when Tom Bates glanced down, she flipped to the finger instead.

It made me uneasy at the time – Tom was a bad person to make an enemy of; for all of her boldness, Ellie can be naïve. She sometimes seems to miss an essential ingredient necessary for survival in these situations: cowardice. In the years that followed I found myself wishing I could go back in time to apologise to Tom and smooth things over.

It might have changed everything.

25

In the end, I throw the flowers away. I usually keep Mother's birthday roses, but these carry with them the sting of disappointment. I can't believe I missed her – if indeed it was Ellie who delivered them. I drop them down the rubbish chute, with only the slight clamminess of guilt as I hear them land softly. They must have cost a lot, but I don't want roses, I say in my head to her again: *I want you to come home*. Not everything can be bought.

As I walk across the communal garden to my flat, there's the itch of someone's gaze on my back, but when I turn around it's only the dealer, standing there with a cigarette in his hand.

'Afternoon,' I say, wishing I could remember his name. 'I don't suppose you've seen my sister?' I ask as casually as I can, as if Ellie had only just left.

He shakes his head, looking faintly surprised. 'I haven't seen her for years.'

'It's just'—I stoop to pat his dog's head—'she left something for me.'

'No,' he says. 'I'd remember seeing her.'

'You didn't see anyone else come in holding flowers? A delivery guy?'

'Did you fall out?' he asks, a sly look passing over his face. 'Is that why she left?'

'It's complicated,' I say, straightening my back, regretting that I sound like a Facebook status.

I have the day off before returning to work on Saturday so I set up camp in Mother's room, sitting in her rocking chair. On Facebook, the last photograph Ellie posted is still Rose on her skis.

Thank you for the flowers, I begin in a Facebook message. I pause, remembering where they'd just ended up. Maybe I should have found them a better home. But I'd like to see you, if you're back in town. I thought I saw you last night at the auction. Was that you? Are you still here? I'll come to wherever you are.

I look at what I have written and, as usual, remove the last sentence before sending it. Deciding to follow the message with an email, I continue with my news more cheerfully . . .

I have so much to tell you. Last night at the auction, Charles made the winning bid on my lot – some book tokens. It's a personal shopping session and I get to advise him on what to buy. But, most of all, it's *time* with him again. Like the old days.

I know you won't approve – I know you'll tut in that way you do and say that I never learn, but, Ellie, this is all I ever wanted. I will do anything – I can forgive *everything* if this is possible. If you want a sign that it was meant to be, Fiona was ill. Purely by chance. And he didn't go home with her, he stayed on until the end of the evening. I spent the night at Caroline's house – it was strange. Remind me to tell you about it . . .

I want to give her something to come back for, so there are some details I save for my next email: my suspicions about Juliet, Caroline's sleepwalking and Dickie's sketches – but it will be so much easier if we can meet in person. If she's still in London.

While I'm waiting for her to get back to me, I check Juliet's Instagram account and see that she's already posted hundreds of photographs of last night – mostly of her on the red carpet, her hand resting on her hip, her feet in third position like a dancer. Her face looks sweatier as the night goes on.

She gushes about Dickie in the posts, using hashtags #RIPDickieGraham #DickieGrahamOneInAMillion #DickieGrahamGoneButNotForgottten

It's embarrassing. Over the top. *What are you trying to prove, Juliet?* I stare at a photograph taken later in the night, where her shiny face is pushed up next to Caroline's, making a show of how close they are. Would someone go to the lengths of organising a charity auction to cover up pushing a friend in front of a train? I wouldn't put anything past her.

She's picked a particularly unflattering one of me on stage, my face pink and glistening under the spotlight, staring out needily into the crowd. I look at it for a long time, reliving the magical moment when Charles raised

142

his flag. Then I go through all the photographs again, liking all the images with him in them.

Unlike Juliet and the rest of us, he doesn't look shinier and pinker as the evening wears on. At the end of the night he looks as calm and composed as he does at the beginning, so that if you were to take his hand, you just know it would still be warm and dry and firm.

26

When Caroline pops by the shop to pick up the tracksuit I borrowed, which I've taken care to wash and iron, there's a lightness to her. You wouldn't know, to look at her, that she might be the sort of woman to sleepwalk into your room and grab your arm so sharply the half-moon marks of her nails show the next day.

Daisy smiles at me from her pushchair and throws her toy giraffe on the floor for me to pick up.

'Do you want to come with us to BabyGap?' Caroline asks. 'Someone's growing out of all her clothes – and you could get something for Rose.'

'I don't know,' I say doubtfully.

Baby shops make me feel uncomfortable. Any place with a high concentration of small human beings, in fact. Or their mothers.

It's like the time I briefly joined a book club with Brenda. Apart from the pair of us, they were all mums. We were reading *The Hand that First Held Mine* and ended up getting into a disagreement that culminated in the smuggest of the mums in the club saying to me, with a hand on her pregnant belly – her third: 'I hate to say it, but that's something you can only understand as a mother.'

Do people realise how often you hear those three words as a childless woman? Or how the phrase can be used as a weapon in the way 'as a daughter' or 'as a sister' never could be. It is the trump card. As if the rest of us – who will always wonder what it's like, who, whatever our circumstances or choices, will feel the tugging of sadness from time to time at that absence, or occasionally touch our breasts or bellies and think about another life where our bodies might have had a different fate – needed to be reminded of it.

'I understand things,' I said quietly that day. 'As an aunt.'

I thought of Rose then, of how I felt the pull of her from hundreds of miles away, how I would do anything to protect her.

But my argument didn't have the power of hers. And I knew it. Brenda went quiet during all of this. She started putting her coat on, waited for me by the door.

'I don't want to go back to that book club,' she said as we left, though the whole thing had been her idea.

'Me neither,' I agreed.

I've always preferred reading on my own in any case.

BabyGap is very light and bright with inappropriately loud thrumming music – maybe to keep the sleep-deprived awake. Caroline and I drift away from each other once we're there. I pass a mother shuffling through packs of underwear, her son, a bored-looking child of around nine, kicking at the floor. Caroline goes to look at the baby stuff and I head for the girls' section.

There's too much pink – Ellie wouldn't like that – frilly princess costumes, glittered jelly shoes, unicorns. None of it looks right. I end up standing in front of a display of more muted denim – dresses and dungarees for three- to four-year-olds. She'll be three soon, so better to buy something she can grow into. I think of Ellie as a tomboy infant, jumping into puddles, climbing trees. I pick up a pair of red dungarees – the sort of thing she used to wear. I want to buy her something that reminds her of home.

Her email to me last night was probably the longest I've had from her since she went away and, despite my disappointment at missing her, it feels like something is changing:

I'm sorry I missed you this time. It was a flying visit – and no, I wasn't at the auction on the night, but I've seen lots about it on social media. Thanks, Juliet ;) Was it difficult keeping your secret about Dickie from Caroline? Be careful with that, sis.

As for Charles, I don't know what to say, but I hope whatever happens makes you happy. That's all I've ever wanted for you.

PS I'm glad you like the flowers – enjoy!

'Are you going to get them for her?' asks Caroline, interrupting my thoughts as she appears at my side with an armful of clothes.

'I think so.' I glance at the dungarees and run my hand along the fabric.

Usually, I get Rose books. Occasionally Ellie will post about them on Facebook or Instagram with the book on Rose's lap or placed artfully on the kitchen table, thanking me. I sometimes have to nudge her, though. She was always scatty and these days she's worse than ever. I wonder if Ellie starts sentences to her new friends, 'As a mother . . .' I hope not.

On the walk back to the shop, I find myself wondering if I can casually steer the conversation to Juliet and her presence in South Kensington the night Dickie died, but I can't think of how, not in any subtle way. I'm not making any progress, but perhaps it will be easier when Charles comes to spend his book tokens and he and I finally have the opportunity to talk.

'Where have you been?' asks Brenda as I return to the staffroom, my cheeks still flushed from the cold. She takes her ready-meal out of the microwave, pulls the cellophane back carefully.

'BabyGap,' I say. 'Of all places.'

'Ah,' says Brenda blandly. She turns back to the sink, and doesn't ask any more questions.

For years, Brenda used to run the Children's section in the shop. She'd hold storytelling sessions once a month, her face coming to life when she read. She's so dozy, normally, so placid, you wouldn't think she'd be capable of bringing so much animation to *The Tiger Who Came to Tea* or *We're Going on a Bear Hunt*.

Then, last year, she asked management if she could

change to Non-Fiction. They weren't keen for her to move, but she insisted. Now she works quietly in Travel, avoiding any contact with children, while Ingrid, who fancies herself as something of a globe-trotter, is always grumbling that she could do a better job.

I'm pleased with my purchase. On the way home, I keep slipping a hand into the plastic bag and stroking the soft fabric of the dungarees. For some silly reason, they make me feel hopeful, optimistic in a way I haven't felt in a while – as if they could herald the end of our estrangement.

27

I know what comes next. It's always the same – after something wonderful happens with Charles there is a period of waiting. I comfort myself by recalling the story of Penelope and how her waiting paid off: unpicking her weaving each night so that the shroud would never be finished, playing for time, delaying the suitors who hovered like vultures while her husband, Odysseus, journeyed home. If you wait long enough, something always happens eventually.

It happens on a bright November day. There's something about the cold, clear weather in winter that stirs the blood. The clean, pale potential of the sky, like a canvas, makes you believe anything is possible. I've always been a winter person. On days like these my spirit soars – the season of opaque tights and radiators, hot chocolate with cream, cashmere socks and reading in bed.

The feeling of wellbeing persists. I don't often feel good about myself but today when I glanced in the shop windows on the Kings Road my hair seemed to fall with a pretty wave and my cheeks looked naturally rosy. My interactions with the customers have an ease to them, a playfulness – 'What an excellent choice,' I say once or twice, at the till, because they love it when you say that and always flush with pride. It's a day, in short, on which I feel glad to be alive. Once or twice I look up and see Gareth watching me as I move with purpose around the shop and I know it's Charles's attention working its magic.

But all this is the prelude – the overture to what is to come. It's as if everything had to be right first – all the pieces of the puzzle had to come together with friends in my life – first Meilin and now Caroline – and Ellie communicating with me again. We were messaging just last night – a silly back-and-forth about Rose's dungarees, which I'd sent to an address she'd given me in Tignes.

Your parcel hasn't arrived, wrote Ellie, What was in it?

I want it to be a surprise for Rose.

I promise I won't tell, she typed, adding a winky face.

I looked for the dungarees online but only found them in blue. I sent her the link.

She sent me the heart-eyes emoji. Thanks, sis. You're the best.

I spot him before he comes to me, looking through a pile of gift books at the front of the shop. The emotion isn't so much the giddy elation of my teenage years, but tenderness. It feels as if everything has been leading up to this day. A certainty. That's what it is. That I wouldn't even have to go over to him. That this time, he would come to me. I wait by the till for him. It needs to be perfect.

'Fran,' Charles says, putting the book down on the counter and fishing out his tokens.

'Of all the shops,' I say. I'd practised that line in the mirror.

I glance at the book. It's *Henry IV, Part I*. A beautiful gift edition. My eyes fill with tears. It's a book that makes me think of him every time I pass it on the shelves. That and *Wuthering Heights*. A cover I have to stop myself from caressing at times. I hold it in my hands for a moment too long before scanning it.

'You remembered,' I say.

'It's for you,' he whispers. 'Do you have a pen?'

I pass him one from behind the till and wish they could see me now – the naysayers, Meilin, Ellie, Juliet. I always knew it would come to this. That it was inevitable. I glory for a moment in my rightness, longing to return to that teenage Fran and tell her: it's OK. It was always just a matter of waiting.

Charles smiles and hands me the book. He doesn't stay to see my reaction as I read it. He's too much of a gentleman for that. He simply wraps his scarf around his neck and strides off into the crisp November afternoon. As soon as he's gone, I open the book.

Dearest F, I've finally seen the importance of acting. Would you mind if our private study session took place at the Victoria Hotel tonight – just around the corner from here. I need to talk to you.

I stand staring at the words for a long time.

'What did he want?' asks Gareth grumpily.

I close the book hurriedly and push it into my handbag.

28

There's no obvious bar at the hotel Charles has chosen, but when I ask for him at reception, I'm told he'll meet me in the library. It's a good thing I haven't had too much time to worry about this appointment. If I'd had the chance to go home, no doubt I would have started trying on various outfits and getting into a pickle about whether I was overdressed or not, but, this way, I have no choice but to run a comb through my hair and come along in my work clothes, walking smartly through the streets to the hotel to outrun my nerves.

The library looks like something from a film. It couldn't be more perfect if I'd designed it myself. Antique brown volumes on the shelves, a pair of armchairs by the fire. Charles staring into the flames, lost in thought. As I enter, he gets to his feet and asks what I'd like to drink.

I glance around, but this place is too sophisticated for menus. 'How about a gin and tonic?'

'Slimline?'

I touch my waist self-consciously. That must be how Fiona takes it.

'No, thank you,' I say. 'I like proper tonic water.'

'Quite right,' he says and disappears to order.

While he's gone, I scan the volumes on the shelves, looking for a title I can say something insightful about, but there's nothing I recognise. They're all volumes of local history, borough by borough. Books as furniture.

I pop to the loo, check my flushed reflection for a final time and when I return someone has served our drinks on a table by the fireplace.

'It was good to see you at the auction,' Charles begins.

I smile and take a sip of my drink. I hope he doesn't notice the tremble in my hand as I raise the glass to my lips. We haven't spoken one-on-one for any length of time for years, since Ellie and I visited Honeybourne. We have conversations in my head, of course. But that's different.

'I find I want to spend time with people from school at the moment. People who knew Dickie when he was young.'

I wait for him to go on.

'I can't stop thinking about him. The guilt is terrible.' He takes a sip of his whisky. 'I never should have let him drink that night.'

I'm quiet for a moment, thinking of Caroline and Daisy. 'Could you really have stopped him?' I ask in the end.

He shrugs. 'Maybe not. But it's not just that. It's all of it. I keep looking back to see if there's something I could have done to prevent his death. Fiona tells me not to; that there's nothing I can do now.'

'You must miss him,' I say, keen to change the subject

from Fiona. My tone is honeyed, understanding. There is a touch of acting involved, it's true, but I don't feel too bad about it. I daren't say what I really feel about Dickie's death. That it has given me a new lease of life. That everything, for me, has improved.

Charles nods. 'He wasn't perfect,' he says. 'I know you, of all people, are aware of that.'

The fire crackles and spits.

'But I was there, you see, that night. I saw it happen – and that makes all the difference.'

'I can imagine,' I murmur, trying to push away my own memory, in case I give myself away.

'I had to ring Caroline.' Charles takes a gulp of his whisky. 'I had to tell her. It was the hardest thing I've ever done.'

His tears on the platform. Were they for Caroline as well as himself? It would be like Charles to think of others in that way. I'd wanted to go over to him, felt the pull of him in my limbs, but it was a private moment. Sometimes we need to cry alone. And perhaps I was scared, too, of exposing my presence. I didn't know how he would react. I still don't.

'Fiona thinks I'm going crazy,' Charles says softly. He pauses before continuing. 'But I sometimes think it might not have been an accident. That someone might have pushed him.'

I'm silent for a long time, remembering the jostling movement of the crowd near Dickie and Charles. The shriek of 'Watch out!' The way Dickie glanced over his shoulder and half-smiled. This is what I've been waiting for: my moment to say something. To share my fears with

154

Charles. I take a breath, unsure how to begin and, without warning, the words from Ellie's email pop into my head: *Be careful, sis.*

I hesitate. The moment passes. 'Who'd have any reason to kill Dickie?' I hear myself say instead.

The truth is, I can think of at least one person, and I'm sure Charles can too. I've done well to avoid the thought so far – to push the memory down as deep as I can – but in that moment it leaps back up like a repressed spring. One of the women on that platform had hair like my sister's.

'There was a strange vibe,' Charles says.

He doesn't seem to have noticed any change in me. I hold my glass to my cheek to cool it down.

'People were being aggressive,' he continues. 'Shoving each other. A group of women who'd just seen a show – they were quite drunk.' He rubs his eyes. 'It sounds stupid but you could feel the situation getting dangerous. I stepped back from the line just in time.' His voice cracks. 'I should have pulled him with me.'

It's a strange experience to listen to the description of a scene you witnessed yourself. How easy would it have been for an arm to push between the bodies and make contact with Dickie? To tip him over the edge. We were so tightly packed the CCTV cameras might not have picked it up.

'Have you ever doubted your own eyes?' Charles asks.

I remember the woman I saw at the V&A. Her blue dress, blonde curls so like Ellie's. Like the woman on the platform. But then there were so many of them – one of them had hair like mine, another like Juliet's. You can't tell anything from that.

155

'I made my statement to the police,' he continues. 'Saying he just fell – but now, thinking about it, I'm not so certain.'

I swallow a couple of times to gather myself. 'They've set a date for the inquest, haven't they? Caroline says it's in January. They'll look into it thoroughly, examine the CCTV footage. I'm sure they'll get to the bottom of it.'

'I imagine they'll speak to other witnesses.' He glances up, his grey eyes seeming to look straight through me. 'There were plenty of people on the platform – maybe one of them saw something significant? I could wait to see what they say before reviewing my story . . .'

'Reviewing?' I shift in my seat. 'I'm not sure what the police will make of that.' It suddenly seems unbearably hot by the fire. I'm aware of the prickle of sweat at my hairline, my belly like liquid. Is it possible Charles saw what I saw? Or can he mean something else? Is he insinuating he spotted *me*?

He touches his forehead anxiously. 'I know, I know.'

I begin to breathe more freely: he's as nervous as I am. It's nothing. That's not what he meant.

'I can't change my story just like that. It will look . . .' He doesn't finish the sentence.

I want to reach out and touch him. 'What does Fiona think?' I ask instead.

'That I shouldn't say anything unless I'm sure. And I *wasn't* initially. It wouldn't be fair on Caroline otherwise. It might stir things up from Dickie's past.'

'What sorts of things?'

He looks down at the table. 'His drinking. Enemies.'

'Enemies?'

156

Charles leans forward. 'Dickie wasn't good with women. He had a bad track record. Ellie was the first, but I think there were others.'

He's said her name. My heart begins to pound with the urgency of an alarm. I hold my hands tightly in my lap, trying to calm down.

'Caroline's so blind when it comes to Dickie,' Charles continues. 'I'm not sure how much she knows about his history.'

'Well, Ellie lives abroad . . .' The words slip out too quickly. 'If that's what you're saying.'

'I'm not saying . . .' He laughs nervously. 'Christ, I'm not *saying* . . . Ellie and I are friends – you know that. I think the world of her. I don't know.' He lifts his glass and puts it back down again. 'Maybe I'm worrying too much, but it's just that he was bad to women and then there was a group of women next to him when he died.' He shrugs. 'Possibly – *probably* – accidentally.'

A thought snags on the roses on my bed. Those had arrived much later. Weeks after Dickie's death. There was no chance Ellie had been in the country. No chance at all. And anyway, she wouldn't. Ellie *wouldn't*.

'I'm probably just winding myself up,' says Charles, his face lightening. 'As I say, Fiona thinks I'm barking. Obsessing about things after everything I've been through.'

'Juliet was there,' I say quickly, trying to make the words sound casual. 'In the area. The night he died.'

'Oh,' Charles says, sounding confused.

'She mentioned it at the auction,' I say, waiting for a twinge of guilt that doesn't come. 'It might be worth asking her.'

'OK.' He frowns. 'I will.'

I follow his gaze to the fire, wondering if he's torn by his old loyalty to Juliet. They were together for years, on and off.

He looks down at the table. 'It's funny – she never said.'

A waiter checks on us to see if we'd like another drink and we move on from the subject to talk about our days, our work. Charles is good at levity – a tease, a joke. His humour is gentler than someone like Dickie's – it's never needling or unkind, but he helps me to lighten up. That's something I struggle with. Something I've been told all my life. But when you've learned to be watchful, untrusting of other people's motives, it's easier said than done. We make a good team, I think. This is what it could have been like all these years.

Now we've changed subject, I can relax and enjoy myself too. I just need to avoid the subjects of Dickie, Ellie and Fiona, and I'm fine. It's completely normal. Like being in the prep room again. Nothing has changed.

As we get up to leave, Charles helps me with my coat and walks with me out of the hotel. He pauses for a moment under the awning and steps out of the light into the shadows.

'Night, Francesca,' he says, and he stoops to kiss me on the cheek.

The warm press of his mouth tingles on my skin as I make my way home through the frosty streets.

29

In the shop the next day, I find myself humming scraps of Gilbert and Sullivan – the sort of thing Mother used to play loud in the cottage when she was spring-cleaning, while Ellie and I would leap around, jumping from the sofa as we pretended to be the Pirate King. After all these years of longing, I don't feel the need to confide in anyone about my night with Charles. Even if I did, the telling might dilute it. The details are too rich, too potent, to be shared. I hug my secret tightly to myself.

On my lunch break, I return to the spot on the platform – exactly where I was standing when Dickie fell. I don't know why, but after my conversation with Charles perhaps I'm hoping that my return will shake out a new memory.

It doesn't. There is no trace of Dickie's death now – no X marking the spot or the wilted bunches of flowers you get in road accidents. They have to act so quickly, the British Transport Police, erasing every trace. I walk to the place where Dickie was standing and close my eyes. Was there anything I missed? A familiar face in the crowd I might have seen but not stored carefully at the time. I would have known if Ellie had been there, wouldn't I? The scent of her, perhaps. Some kind of sixth sense between sisters.

'Watch out,' says a voice nearby.

I open my eyes.

It's a man in late middle age, carrying a briefcase. 'You were close to the edge,' he says kindly. 'There was an accident here recently, you know?'

I should be more careful. It's probably not a good idea for me to be revisiting the spot. It might look suspicious. Anyway, there's absolutely no chance Ellie was there. She was in France at the time – so I don't know why I'm worried. Hopefully Charles has spoken to Juliet by now, made her squirm a bit. I try not to reflect on how I mentioned her name as a way of changing the subject from Ellie.

What happened between Juliet and Dickie? Had there been an affair, like Caroline suspected? Or was it something else? A rejection? Or some old Chesterfield injury? I always thought the pair of them were on the same side but, then, I suppose sides can change. One thing I know for sure: Juliet always had it in her to be cruel.

I thank the man with the briefcase and make my way out of the tube. As I walk up the escalator, a memory of Dickie returns to me, leaping exuberantly on the rugby pitch after scoring a try. But I won't feel sorry for him, I decide, sliding out of the tube station with my head tucked down. He doesn't deserve it.

In the evening, I spend my time on social media, scrolling through photographs of Charles. Gorging myself on his face, his smile. I'm unsure how things are going to develop now, with the complications of Fiona and the twins. From the little I can see of the children on social media, they resemble their father more than their mother – but that's often the case with infants, I've read. Fiona doesn't post much of their faces. I suppose you don't know what weirdos are out there, watching.

While I'm scrolling on Instagram, an alert pops up to say that Ellie has tagged me in a post – a photo of Rose on a tricycle. It's an artful composition with the red tricycle contrasting with the glittering white mountains on the horizon, the blue of the sky. You can't see Rose's face as she pedals away from the photographer, but her hair is a tawny cloud curling behind her.

Ellie has written: A menace on three wheels! Watch out, world! Thank you, Auntie Fran, for these amazing dungarees. #BestAunt #ThanksSis

I stare at the photograph for a long time. It's the first one I've seen for a while and I'm struck by how much longer Rose's hair is now. Her roly-poly baby legs are starting to stretch out into the limbs of a skinny child. I've missed the years of her infancy. I'll never know the scent of her baby head or feel the weight of her in my arms.

But mostly I stare because the dungarees in the photograph are bright blue.

I like the image and then, bewildered, unlike it again. I write underneath. Is she wearing the wrong dungarees? But, because that makes me sound deranged, I delete the

161

comment – I have to look up how – and write Ellie an email instead.

Did I send you the blue dungarees? I was sure I'd sent you the red.

It's a tiny thing, not even worth dwelling on, but it leaves me with a flickering anxiety for the rest of the night. In the end, I phone Caroline on the pretence of making a date for tea. I've missed a call or two from her recently, and I've been putting off getting back to her after my evening with Charles in case I blurt out something I shouldn't about his suspicions. We catch up briefly, making a date to meet soon, and I mention it as casually as I can before I say goodbye.

'You know the dungarees I bought Rose?'

'Mm-hmm.' She sounds distracted. Daisy begins to grumble in the background.

'They were red, weren't they?'

'I think so, yes.'

'You couldn't swear on it?'

There's a teasing smile in her voice. 'Fran, what's this about?'

I tell her the story in a garbled way, knowing I haven't quite got her full attention; unable to convey the strangeness of Ellie's post.

When I stop to draw breath, she says kindly, 'Could Ellie just have picked up the wrong pair before taking the photo? Kids have so many clothes. We were given bags of hand-me-downs by friends before we had Daisy. It's probably just a mix-up.'

I exhale. 'Do you really think so? It just seemed so odd.'

162

'Why don't you call her?' Caroline suggests. 'Ask her about it?'

Silent for a moment, I lay a hand across my forehead. I can't tell her, I realise, that I won't call Ellie because that's not something I've ever done since she moved. That she comes and goes as she pleases. That most of the time I don't know where she's living – let alone if she's back in the country. That we haven't had what you'd call a normal relationship in years.

And I can't say anything to Caroline, of all people, because it's important she thinks Ellie has been in France all this time. In case anything more should come out. In case Charles decides to share his suspicions with the police.

163

30

After Ellie joined me at Chesterfield, it was easier. When I walked around the school with her, people looked at us more; they smiled. Even teachers would regard us more indulgently, which I came to learn, later in life, is the way the world tends to look upon the beautiful. People – boys, mainly – would sidle up to me and ask innocent-seeming questions – how are you and what was that homework assignment – before moving on to what will you be doing this weekend and does your sister have a boyfriend.

The interest in her only grew stronger as Ellie got older. A couple of years after Ratings, when Ellie was in fifth form, Dickie developed a crush on her. He'd appear by her side after meals or hover outside her classroom at the end of the day, offering to carry her satchel, which she always refused. If Ellie seemed mildly annoyed by this, she tolerated him, answering his questions politely but shaking off his attention in the way a beloved pet shrugs off too much love – slipping out of the room at the earliest opportunity.

'Cradle-snatcher,' Juliet said to Dickie once, before English. 'She's only fifteen.'

But Dickie was oddly quiet. 'It's not like that,' he said, uncharacteristically reticent, refusing to be drawn.

Juliet toyed with the friendship bracelet Charles had given her. She was put out by the fact her most loyal admirer was distracted. She didn't seem to want Dickie for herself, but she didn't like his interest in someone else.

She and Charles had been together a long time by this point, and though he was always a gentleman in front of me, mindful of my feelings, Juliet had no such qualms, whispering loud details of their latest exploits within hearing distance – what Charles was like as a kisser, the secret places they frequented. Usually, I'd put my Walkman on and hum along (so loudly once that Juliet checked to see if I was all right – 'We thought you were having some kind of fit').

Ellie's mind, all this time, was on swimming. She still struggled with her school work – even with Mother and me coaching her in the evenings. There wasn't the same support for learning difficulties that there is now and it looked unlikely she'd pass her exams, but the school made allowances on account of her swimming talent, reducing the number of GCSEs she had to sit. She always won everything at interschool competitions but her focus that year was further afield, on the European Junior Swimming Championships.

Chesterfield's Victorian pool would probably be

considered a health and safety hazard these days, and has long since been razed to the ground – but Ellie loved it and would train while Mother, on her nights off, sat poolside on a damp bench darning or tacking nametapes into our clothes. Sometimes, when Mother was working, I went in her stead, trying to read as condensation dripped down from the vaulted roof, blotting the pages. It wasn't my natural milieu, but I was proud of Ellie: it was a privilege that she was allowed to use the pool on her own.

Dickie's pursual of Ellie sometimes brought him to the side of the pool ('Leching at her in her swimming costume,' remarked Juliet), where on a couple of occasions he sat a few feet along from me on the wooden bench, timing her with a stopwatch when she asked.

'She's like a fish, isn't she?' he said admiringly as she climbed out after a record-breaking length.

There was certainly something creature-like about the way Ellie sped through the water, but it was always an otter I thought of when she emerged like this, her hair slick against her shoulders, her eyes closed in bliss.

Dickie leapt to his feet to bring Ellie her towel. She buried her face in it, taking a moment to recover. 'Thanks,' she said. 'How did I do?'

He punched the air. 'Smashed it again.'

She rewarded him with a wide smile, stooped to dry her feet before pushing them into her flip-flops.

'Look at that,' he noticed. 'Your toes are webbed. So that's your secret.'

'It's not exactly a secret,' said Ellie, wrapping the towel around her.

'I mean to your success,' he teased, 'though if I told the other boys, we would have to knock a half mark off your perfect ten.'

Until then, it had never been confirmed but now I knew: Ellie had been the first girl in living memory to get a perfect score. The information was bittersweet. Only recently someone had let slip – a friend of Juliet's – that I hadn't even been given a mark. Like a test paper so bad the examiner didn't bother with it. Or, perhaps, as I told myself, it merely made me indecipherable. An enigma.

'I won't tell them, though,' Dickie promised Ellie. 'It can be our secret.'

'You can if you want,' said Ellie. 'I don't care.' And she walked off, her flip-flops slapping against the wet tiles.

'It's incredible, isn't it?' Dickie remarked to me. 'That she's so pretty and you're so . . .'

He didn't finish the sentence, but it was clear that whichever word came next wasn't going to be a good one. To this day, I'm not sure if he intended to be unkind – as a way of lashing out at Ellie's dismissal – or if it was just an accident: a thought of his I happened to overhear. Which would have been even worse. I hoped in that moment that he'd get his comeuppance for being so swayed by beauty. Perhaps now he has.

31

The problem with working in a public place is anyone can wander in. A couple of days after seeing Charles, I return from my lunch break in a happy daze only to slow down when I spot Fiona leaning over the counter, our Christmas-edition bag dangling from her arm. She seems to be having a cosy chat with Brenda.

I'm not sure whether or not my meeting with Charles is a secret. He never said, but I suspect it is. Hopefully Fiona's presence here is just a coincidence. On seeing me, her face lights up.

'Fran!' she says. 'I've been having a lovely chat with your colleague here.'

Brenda blinks a couple of times. 'Thank you,' she says quietly. She pauses to gather herself. 'It takes someone who's been there to understand.'

Fiona gives her a meaningful look and turns to me. 'I was going to suggest we grabbed a bite somewhere, but I hear you've just had your lunch break.'

I blink stupidly, unbreathing. Fiona and I have never 'grabbed a bite' anywhere. We've never spent any time at all one-on-one, so why is she pretending we're friends? I don't say this out loud, of course, and not just because of the kindness she showed me at the auction. She's someone with natural authority – the sort who was probably head girl at school. She has a slightly bossy riding teacher manner that maybe comes from a youth spent around horses. They've always made me nervous – you never know when they could spin around and kick you in the face.

'Perhaps we could have a word here?' She takes a few steps away from the tills, standing close to the two-for-one table. 'You see lots of Caroline, don't you?'

Air starts to flow around my lungs again. I exhale. It's OK: this isn't about Charles. 'From time to time,' I say, looking down at the sad, scuffed pattern of the shop-floor carpet.

'I was wondering, if she seems . . .' Fiona pauses, running a finger along one of the stickers on a book cover in front of her. 'Distant?'

She picks the edge of the sticker. I wish she wouldn't – we'll only have to smooth it back on.

'I'm worried she's drinking again,' she says quietly. 'In secret.'

I'm torn between my loyalty to Caroline and the importance I feel in having my opinion sought. I recognise this feeling – the cloying need to please. 'She seems OK,' I say in the end. 'I mean, she's grieving, so . . .'

'Yes, of course.' Fiona looks stricken for a moment. 'Of course, I realise that. I'm not saying . . . We're so worried about her. And there are times when she's seemed . . . so I just thought I'd mention it.'

My hand goes to my forearm where Caroline gripped it that night, leaving crescents imprinted on the flesh. I remember how uneasy I felt the next day; how I couldn't shake the sense there might be another side to her.

I hesitate. 'Well, there was one thing.' Even before I begin the story, I regret it.

Fiona leans forward.

'It's probably nothing, though.' I glance at the till. 'I should get back.'

'Please, Fran. Just say – whatever it is.'

I swallow, then say the words quickly, 'When I was staying, Caroline sleepwalked into my room. She said later it was something she usually did after drinking.'

'And she hadn't?'

'Not with me – that was the night of the auction.'

'Ugh,' Fiona says. 'I was so ill.'

'Did they ever find out what that was?'

'Food poisoning, I think. Ghastly – like being pregnant again.' She glances at Brenda. 'I had hyperemesis gravidarum, like Kate Middleton – I could barely leave the house.' She waves a hand to dismiss the subject. 'Anyway, was that all? She just walked in her sleep?'

'Well, there was more than that,' I say, bridling at her tone. 'She grabbed me.'

'Grabbed you?'

'She was a bit aggressive, that's all.'

'Poor you – it sounds quite upsetting.'

'It was.' I tidy a pile of books on the table in front of

170

me, patting them into place. 'But it doesn't mean she was drinking.'

'Hmm,' says Fiona slowly. 'Well, let's keep an eye on her, shall we? I'll give you my mobile number. Just in case.'

She asks Brenda for a scrap of paper and jots down her contact details. The pair of us watch her go, walking smartly in her high-heeled suede boots with no hint of a wobble.

'What a nice lady,' says Brenda. And she goes back to her work contentedly, as if Fiona's visit has made her day.

I keep gazing after Fiona, pondering all the omissions in our conversation. Neither of us mentioned Charles or that I've seen him recently – so it's quite possible that she doesn't even know. I need to speak to him.

32

'Have you told Fiona?' I ask Charles when I next see him in the National Gallery café.

We're in the corner, watching visitors line up at the canteen opposite. Our spot feels secluded, cut off from the hustle and bustle of visitors fetching trays and pushing them along a counter like at school.

'Told her what?' He pauses with his cup of coffee hovering close to his lips.

'That we've seen each other like this.'

He stops and puts the cup back on the table without drinking from it.

'Actually, no, I haven't got around to it yet.'

'But you will?' I check, although the idea disappoints me. If he does tell Fiona, then perhaps it's nothing after all. Perhaps it's all in my head.

'Do you think I should?'

I can't read his tone. His face is grave but is that a smile tugging at his lips? It gives me hope. I want to ask him: what is this? Is it what I think it is? But I have no experience, nothing to compare it with – aside from Gareth's clumsy approaches.

Occasionally, very occasionally, over the years, a customer has taken to me, like the man who bought the bullying books for his daughter. It's usually someone older, with whom I've struck up a lively conversation about a novel. As our chat concludes, he might say something about a pub nearby or a restaurant he likes – and it's not until later, after he's gone and I haven't responded in the right way, that Brenda might observe, 'Think you have a fan there.'

It's funny because I started reading so early – Mother made me a set of flashcards when I was three. She never held back from using longer words when she spoke to us and, as I got older, I started making a note of them. *Precarious. Phony. Ineffable.* But when it comes to people, I can't read them at all. I sometimes wonder if it's the way I feel – or don't feel – about sex: if it locks me out of a whole other world of meaning and motivation.

This much I know, though: if Charles doesn't tell Fiona, our meetings remain a secret between us. And secrets can link people like chains.

'I don't think you need to tell her,' I say with a coy smile. 'I mean, it's not as if we're doing anything wrong, are we?'

'Absolutely not,' he says solemnly. But there's still a gentle twinkle in the way he says it, which keeps me guessing.

'She came to see me in the shop the other day – she wanted to talk about Caroline.'

'Yeah?' He scratches his head absent-mindedly. 'She worries too much.'

It's a glimpse of their intimacy, like looking through a crack in a curtain into their house: Fiona restless in the kitchen, wiping at imaginary specks of dust, Charles with a newspaper, reading, thinking, minding his own business, but she can't just leave him alone, can she? I peeked on a scene like this on a night-time visit to Honeybourne. As usual, they had no idea I was there. Fiona pestering and pestering. Not quite dusting him down with the cloth but flitting around him like a mosquito. She keeps trying to start a conversation but even though I can't hear the words I can tell he doesn't want to be drawn in. He'll say something briefly then return to his paper. And she'll start again. *I would know,* I want to tell him, *when to leave you alone, let you read.* In the end, he gives up, pulling her by the wrist onto his lap and kissing her firmly to shut her up. I don't stay around for long to see what happens next. Only for a bit. It's the closest I've got to it – watching Charles. I'm not proud of that. Quite the opposite.

Of course, I can't tell him any of this. Any more than I can tell him I witnessed Dickie's death. I've left it too late now. There are secrets between us too.

'Did you speak to Juliet?' I ask.

Charles sighs. 'I mentioned it. Carefully. She says she went home earlier in the night – that she'd left South Kensington by the time it happened.'

She would, I want to say, annoyed that he didn't push it. Juliet has wriggled off the hook, as usual.

'And you believed her?' I persist, bolder than I'd normally be.

174

He gives me a sidelong glance. 'Why wouldn't I?'

He always sees the best in people. We are quiet for a moment, listening to the clinking of the canteen, the hiss of the cappuccino machine, the murmur of voices around us. I feel torn between irritation that Charles hasn't taken Juliet's proximity seriously and guilt about pushing the matter. I was there myself, after all, and it doesn't make *me* culpable. But then I'm not Juliet – I didn't have her twisted relationship with Dickie – or a history of hurting people. Not the way she did.

'I think about Dickie all the time,' Charles says quietly. 'I dream about him too. As if he's haunting me. Punishing me.'

'Punishing you?' My attention returns to the room. To him.

'For not pulling him back; for not saving him.'

'But Charles . . . you couldn't have – it happened so fast.'

The words slip out too quickly.

'Accidents do.' I take a scalding gulp of tea to slow myself down and check for his reaction. I seem to have got away with it. 'Are you going to say anything? To the police?'

He shakes his head. 'I don't think so. It wouldn't be fair to Caroline. Anyway, maybe the CCTV will confirm one way or another.'

Relieved, I take a bite of my brownie. I realise that perhaps I've brought up Juliet again to keep the focus off Ellie. But there's nothing to worry about, I tell myself. There's no way she was there that night. I swallow and change the subject. 'Do *you* think Caroline's drinking again?'

'I don't know.' He looks out at the room beyond us. 'It's complicated.'

He pauses. An elderly couple make for the table next to us. She is using a walker; he carries the tray for both of them, a large pot of tea and a scone.

'I mean grief always is,' Charles continues. 'But Dickie had problems. There were times when Caroline would call us in tears. He was such a complicated mix – he could be so cheerful, such fun. And then he had this dark side. We were at prep school together before Chesterfield, you know. We started on the same day. Friends all the way through. But if he fell out with someone – like he did with the housemaster's wife – then that could be very bad for them. She was always on at him – "Dickie, pull your socks up; late again; brush your hair." That sort of thing.'

'What happened?'

'Well, he took her cat. She really loved that animal. And he put it in the washing machine, set it off. She found it in there herself . . . I walked into the room at the time. It was terrible – the mess. Her shrieking. One of the worst things I've seen.'

I put my brownie back on the plate. I imagine the woman, alone in that boys' boarding house, surrounded by men. How the cat might have been her only friend. Her pleasure at tickling under his chin and waiting for him to purr. The way his paws would tread and catch in her woollen skirt but she wouldn't care about the snags because they were worth it, to know he was content.

'That's . . .' I can't think of a word strong enough. 'Wicked,' I say. But it sounds childish. A word from a fairy tale. 'Evil,' I add, but that's not much better.

'I know.' Charles's grey eyes find mine for a moment. 'She had her suspicions but I never let on when they asked me – "snitches get stitches" and all that – but it was a heavy secret to carry. She wasn't the same afterwards. I saw her looking at us boys as if we were something to be scared of.'

'I can see why.' I stare at my brownie glumly. I don't feel like eating now.

'When I asked him about it, he said it was as if he was watching a stranger. An out-of-body experience. Like what happened with your sister. He said sometimes he just wanted to see what he could get away with. Maybe . . .' he pauses; his gaze falls to my plate '. . . he hurt the wrong person. Maybe they decided to hurt him back.'

I'm quiet. My mind flickers to Ellie again. Could Charles mean her – or someone Dickie had damaged more recently? I can't bring myself to ask. I don't understand how he could ever forgive Dickie, but I don't want to ruin today by bringing all of that up. 'It's funny,' I say instead, 'I've been thinking about Ellie a lot at the moment.'

As if I don't always think about her a lot.

'When I was staying the night at Caroline's, I saw these drawings Dickie did. They made me think of that time at Chesterfield.' I can't say any more than that, but Charles will know what I mean. 'They were horrible, his drawings. These strange underwater creatures with webbed feet.' I shudder.

It comes back to me, how that night I lay with my heart hammering in my chest, and when I fell asleep my dreams were haunted by what I'd seen.

I shake my head. 'I can't help but think . . .' I pause. I've never said this aloud to anyone. 'I can't help but think that what happened at Chesterfield made Ellie the way she was as an adult – so restless, so . . .' I don't know how to put it. I think of *flibbertigibbet* – a word I loved as a child – but that's not right: Ellie was too much of a tomboy. *Flighty* is closer. 'I got Rose a present – a pair of dungarees,' I say instead, changing the subject.

Charles waits for me to go on. I suppose at this stage it's not a terribly interesting story.

'But then,' I continue, 'when Ellie posted about it online, to thank me, Rose wasn't wearing the pair I sent, but another one – in a different colour.'

'Maybe she picked up the wrong pair.' Charles shrugs. 'Children have so many clothes.'

I don't seem to be able to convince anyone that this matters. 'That's what Caroline said. I guess it's just care-lessness.' I give up, let it go.

Someone in the queue knocks a plate to the floor.

'Fran.' Charles takes my hand for a moment. 'Ellie loves you.'

I feel the warmth of his skin on my mine. The years don't matter. Just that Charles Fry is holding my hand.

'I remember how close you were at school,' he continues. 'And she still talks about you with such fondness.'

'I never see her.' I want to ask him how she's doing, what she says about me, but I can't move, in case I break the spell. 'I miss them so much. Her and Rose.' How can I miss Rose, whom I've never met? But I can. 'I wish I could make it right between us.'

'Maybe you can. Just give her space. Let her work things out in her own time.'

I look down at Charles's hand on mine and remember how the rift had started long before that awful day three years ago – the last time I saw her – how Ellie's pregnancy had made her secretive. Yes, it had started then – and, try as I might, I couldn't bridge the gap between us.

It seems selfish to say it but, for women like me, there can be a sadness to other women's pregnancies. They remind us of the division between the mothers and the un-mothers – the unknown world the women we love are about to enter. How we'll never really get them back.

When I get home, I examine my hands to see if they look different now that they have been held by Charles, as if there will be visible evidence. It is a strange thing when something you have wanted for so long starts to happen. The world blossoms into a different place. The sky stretches higher above me, the ground sings beneath my feet. Even colours seem more vivid, I note, as I admire the shade of red Rose is wearing in Ellie's latest post.

It's a photo of her peering into a shop window – another Rose reflected back at her in the fairy-lit glass. She's wearing red wellies too, and a tiny red bowler hat with a white scarf and tights. Mother was funny about red and white together – particularly when it came to flowers. It was a superstition that came from her own mum who, as a nurse, associated the colours with blood and bandages.

Ellie was never particularly interested in photography but her pictures of Rose are exquisite – she frames them like a professional. Perhaps she always just needed the right subject. In the way it took Charles to come along to inspire my journals at school. Perhaps we're all waiting for the right person to set us alight.

You don't need to be a mother yourself to see how good children are at doing that. Last time I went up to Whitby I shared a train table with a new mother and her baby. The woman was young and French, and perhaps that's why it sounded so lovely as she crooned and sang – pointing out the landscape flying past to her baby when he grew restless, or jiggling him on her knee. In other circumstances, I might have been tempted to remind her we were in the quiet carriage but I could tell that she wouldn't have cared, that there was nothing in her bubble of existence except this baby. And anyway he had softened me too, in the way babies do. They're clever like that.

It's appealing, that love, the singularity of it: how it might save you – or promise to save you – from everything else. I notice in the shop how Brenda's eyes are drawn to certain sights – a mother tying up a child's shoe or picking up a toy from the floor and placing it companionably next to her baby. There's a purity to this kind of love: the way it pushes everything else out.

Perhaps that's what I find in my passion for Charles. I return to my collection now, adding the latest items: a postcard I picked up in the National Gallery shop to remind me of this day and an empty sachet of sugar, from Charles's coffee. There's a smattering of granules left and I empty them into my palm, touch them with my tongue, where they melt like snowflakes.

33

I can't stop looking at Caroline's beer. She arrived at the café in Waterloo before me and ordered first and now I'm behaving as if I've never seen a pint before. It's my fault. The café I suggested has morphed into a late-night drinking spot. I dropped in with Mother years ago and enjoyed a custard tart and a cup of tea, but now, after dark, it's different. The lights have been dimmed, candles lit in jars on the small round tables, cocktail menus laid out. The pale features of Caroline's face are shadowed in candlelight.

'It's nice to come for an adult night out,' she says, looking around us at the speakeasy style of the place – old gramophones and bric-a-brac, fairy lights and bare brick walls.

I wanted her to like the place, to admire it in the way she is, but the drink in front of her is so distracting that the thought of it has inflated like a balloon, pushing out everything else in my mind. Fiona was right, after all,

181

and Caroline's not even trying to hide it. But perhaps she trusts me in a way she doesn't trust Fiona.

The words on the menu blur in front of me, as I imagine the things we can't talk about stacking up on the table between us. Fiona. Charles. Dickie. Her drinking. I wish we could sweep the secrets away. I wish we could start again.

'How was your day?' she asks.

'It was fine, quite busy at this time of year. How about you?'

'Lovely.' There's a flush to her cheeks, probably the alcohol. 'It was my day off and we went swimming and then to Baby Boogie in the afternoon.'

I imagine her driving around Ealing with Daisy in the back of the car. My eyes keep returning to the glass on the table, a ring of condensation gathering at its base. I know I shouldn't be looking but it keeps drawing my gaze back.

'We need to keep busy at this time of year,' Caroline is saying, as if everything is just the same. 'With Christmas coming up, it's going to be difficult.'

'I always find it hard too,' I agree. 'On my own.'

It's true. I struggle at Christmas. It's the one day – as Charles Dickens demonstrated so well – that we can't escape ourselves. Where the reality of my life is held up to me like a mirror – no Mother, no Ellie, no Rose. There's so much I can forgo – so much I have forgone. Stockings and crackers and shared jokes and quarrelling over the meal preparations. Mother's bread sauce recipe, which I inherited, handwritten on a yellowing scrap of paper, but which never tastes the same now she's gone. I would give up every single Christmas accessory – all of it, I barter silently, if I could have them back.

'We'll be on our own too,' Caroline says, turning the glass in her hand.

Anger tingles in my arms, my belly. The fact that Caroline says, '*We'll* be on our own,' says it all. People like Caroline – with children and friends and full lives and Baby Boogie, they think they know what it's like.

But I've seen the photos on Facebook – her and Dickie in roomfuls of people with crooked cracker hats and ironic Christmas jumpers playing party games. Charades or the one with the cereal box on the floor that gets shorter and shorter (Fiona always wins). Dickie posted videos of them a couple of Christmases ago and I gorged on them while I sat on my own, making my way through a family-sized tub of Quality Street. If you stripped one person from those photographs, even the most important one, you're still left with a roomful of people.

'You have Daisy,' I point out.

'Yes, you're right,' she says. 'I need to be grateful for what I have. That's the sort of thing I learned with AA.' Then, ironically, she takes a gulp of beer. 'Do you want to come over? Spend the day with us?'

'Me?' I almost have to stop myself glancing over my shoulder to check she doesn't mean someone else.

'Yes.' She laughs. 'Why not? Better to be glum together.'

'But what about all your other people?'

She shakes her head. 'I don't have other people. I'm an only child and my parents are gone now. Dickie's parents are being kind, and I know they'd like to see

183

Daisy, but they're so far away in Scotland – I can't face the journey on my own with a baby.'

An image slips into my head of Caroline, Daisy and me around the Christmas tree. Daisy tearing open her parcel from me, settling herself on my lap to read one of the books I've given her, tipping her head back to look at me in the way she does. Then her face merges into Rose's face and I blink the image away. I still haven't entirely forgiven Ellie for messing up Rose's present, in spite of her apologetic messages – both on Facebook and in email – for photographing Rose in the wrong dungarees.

I'm sorry, sis. Life is so chaotic with a little one. She doesn't quite say, 'as a mother', but the implication is there.

'Are you sure?' I ask Caroline. It strikes me as an astonishing invitation. 'You don't want to be with Dickie's parents?'

'That big old house.' She shivers dramatically. 'I'd much rather be in my own home, eating the food I want to. And being away from alcohol.'

I glance again at her beer.

'Oh, Fran.' She puts a hand to the glass. 'This is non-alcoholic.'

'Oh.' I begin to breathe again.

'I wouldn't do it,' she says. 'Not with Daisy. I promise.'

'Of course,' I say apologetically. I feel like a fool. 'I'm not saying . . . I was just worried. That's all.'

She gives me a sad smile.

'How long have you been sober?' I ask.

'About fifteen years,' she says. 'Since my early twenties. It started at university – I'm talking about the really committed drinking. The kind where you come around from blackouts not knowing where you are or who you're with. I don't know why it started exactly but everyone at Newcastle seemed to have so much confidence and I had none, and the only way I felt I could cope with it was by getting out-of-my-mind drunk. Then I could do anything.'

I nod. 'It's difficult,' I agree vaguely, thinking of my Open University degree and how things ended.

'You know Dickie was at Newcastle too?' she says. 'We met once or twice at parties but I'm glad we didn't get together then. We were both such a pair of wreckheads. Of course, plenty of people are like that at uni so you blend in at the time, but you know you have a problem when you can't stop living like that in the years afterwards. You think everyone else is doing it too and then one day you wake up in your mid-twenties and you realise that all your friends have proper jobs and proper lives, and you're sleeping in the garden, still drunk from the night before, and you didn't even notice things changing.'

No one's ever spoken to me in this way – so open, so confessional. Ellie would share bits and pieces about her life outside the flat, but she always held so much back. I like Caroline confiding in me – it makes me feel special. Trustworthy. Perhaps, despite the secrets, it's not too late for us to become real friends.

'When I saw Dickie at that first meeting – a mutual friend had suggested he come to my group – he was so pale and shaken,' Caroline continues. 'I recognised him from university – a cheeky-chappie type with so much front you couldn't see the person behind it. I knew he was keen on me early on and I was quite strict with him at first.' She smiles. 'But I think he liked that.'

Those days when he was pursuing Ellie showed a different side of Dickie, too, something softer, gentler – I saw glimpses of the person I imagine Caroline fell in love with: someone doggedly loyal and anxious to please. Like the way he would time Ellie's lengths. Perhaps something would have happened between them if the boys hadn't lost that game.

'Public schoolboys like a firm hand.' I smile, but an unsettling memory closely pursues that thought. 'Life could be quite tough at Chesterfield,' I say, picking my words carefully. 'I can imagine it did its own damage. It made monsters of all of us in one way or another.'

Caroline nods. 'I know Dickie was haunted by it in some ways – the things he did back then. There was some dreadful story about a cat he alluded too, and I know he never forgave himself for what happened with your sister.'

I never forgave him either. I want to tell her that the dreadful thing he did to the cat was before Chesterfield, but I can't let on that I've spoken to Charles. I glance at the couple at the next table, the way their hands are knitted together.

'But when I spoke to Ellie, she seemed completely unperturbed by it,' Caroline says. 'It was as if she could barely remember.'

'She said that?' I ask, keeping my face impassive.

'That's how she put it.'

I remember Ellie's description of the colours: blue moving through yellow and then black and finally white

186

– the yellow the most painful, so that afterwards she would flinch at the colour. In the weeks after it happened, she would lie in bed, limp-haired, staring at the wall, and I have often thought how, if you were mapping out her life, the highs and lows of it, that would be the point where she changed from someone irrepressible, hopeful, to someone else. So do I think it's likely Ellie has forgotten? Well, she might have lost details – trauma mashes up your memory, but I know in my bones that, wherever she is, Ellie would never forget.

The thing is, I realise, as I scratch at a drop of wax on the table, it's clear, for whatever reason, she wants Caroline to *think* she has.

Close behind that thought, another follows: perhaps Caroline wants me to believe Ellie doesn't remember. She knows we don't speak much these days. But why would she do that? To diminish the event? To protect Dickie? Or, by association, to protect herself?

The memory of Dickie's aquatic sketches nudges at me. I find I want to see them again. Perhaps there's something I missed before – some kind of clue to his state of mind – so when Caroline, drained by the conversation, suggests I come and stay, I take her up on her offer.

'It's the nights,' she says. 'They're the hardest part. I promise I won't sleepwalk again,' she teases, touching my arm as we leave the café.

I make a mental note to lock the door of the spare room this time, if I can.

34

When we get back to Caroline's house, Daisy is in the arms of the same blonde babysitter as before. She is wailing, inconsolable, even when Caroline guiltily takes over, sweeping her from the arms of the other woman.

'Fran, please could you order Maja an Uber,' she asks, passing over her mobile with one hand, while she smooths Daisy's hair with the other.

'Of course,' I say, knowing it's not the time to point out I've never done that and I'm not sure how.

Finding the app isn't too much of a problem. I open it and select 'My trips' from the sidebar menu, where I can see a couple of journeys from here to an address in Acton.

'Is that your address on Eastfields Road?' I ask.

Maja nods from where she's standing by the sink, drinking a glass of water. Her cheeks look flushed and I'd guess she's had quite a night of it with Daisy, that she's keen to be going.

I'm about to order her car when something catches my eye. And once I've seen it, there's no way of going back, though I wish I could.

It's another late-night journey from Caroline's address, taken quite a while ago, but this one's to South Kensington in October. I know the date well. It's imprinted on my memory. The night Dickie died. I stare at it for a couple of seconds and consider taking a screengrab. Then I remember that I'm still using Caroline's phone.

My mouth feels as dry as sawdust. I try to swallow, to concentrate on putting my fingers to work in ordering the car. Luckily, Daisy's wailing blocks out any conversation, so I don't have to say anything for a while beyond telling Maja her car is on its way.

I take myself to the loo and sit on the seat for ages, hearing Daisy's cry echo through the house. Questions race through my mind. Snippets of conversation with Charles and Fiona about Dickie's drinking – and Caroline's fear of him – are stirred like sediment.

Maybe she was frightened of him, says a voice in my head that sounds like Ellie's. *Maybe she had had enough.*

Fortunately, Caroline doesn't seem to notice any change in me when I return from the loo to a quieter house. By that stage, I've splashed cold water on my face and pulled myself together. Daisy has settled down, too.

On the sofa, hot drinks in hand, Caroline says: 'I meant what I said about Christmas. I want to do something different. With no association with the past.'

I take a sip of hot chocolate. 'I don't know if he said, but Dickie and I weren't exactly friends at school.'

My new knowledge has liberated me. I feel I could say

189

anything now. Anything except: *What were you doing that night, Caroline? Why were you there?*

She glances at the fire. 'He was mean to you – he told me that. But I think you might have been surprised by how much he'd changed.'

I gulp my drink again. It's too hot, but it gets me out of having to say anything.

'My colleagues at Haven – they loved him,' she continues. 'A lot of people who end up working for charities have some personal connection to that cause. He would come and talk to people, really listen to their stories.'

She's working so hard, like she always has, to make him seem kind. Sympathetic to the plight of women. Sensitive. That's what you might do, isn't it? If you needed to persuade people you had a happy marriage.

'I just thought I should tell you,' I say. 'Before Christmas – I thought I should mention it. It's not right to pretend.'

'If I ask you something, will you give me an honest answer?'

I nod. In my experience, people asking that question never truly want what they say, but normal niceties matter less to me in this moment.

She tucks her pyjamaed legs under her. 'What did you make of Dickie?'

I swallow, choosing my words carefully. 'We didn't always see eye to eye,' I say. 'But when Dickie cared about someone, he really cared.'

I don't add: *until he didn't.*

'That's why I like you, Fran – you tell it how it is,' says Caroline, looking pleased.

190

I aim for a modest smile and return my gaze to the fire. Caroline might have things to hide but she's not the only one. As I sit in her living room, sipping hot chocolate, I try not to think about how I watched Dickie fall to his death all those weeks ago and never said a thing.

35

In the spare room I lock the door behind me, as planned. I lie in bed listening to Caroline wander from her room to the bathroom – a tap running, a squeak or two from Daisy and then her mother's murmur. I wonder what Dickie would make of me, Freaky Fran, here with his wife and daughter.

When the house is quiet, I get out of bed as quietly as I can, creep to the desk and open the drawer where Dickie's sketchbook was, but, to my disappointment, it's nowhere to be seen. Caroline must have moved it.

After everything that's happened tonight, I'm worried I'm not going to sleep. I want to ask Caroline about her trip to South Kensington, but I need to decide how. It's not something to do late at night when I'm alone in her house. Caroline doesn't seem dangerous, but I check my bedroom door is locked again before I get into bed. It's all become so messy, so unsettling.

I long for someone to talk everything through with.

For someone non-judgemental. For Ellie. She's the one who knows the best and worst things about me, in the way siblings do. I'm the same with her. It's the closest I've ever got to seeing the world through the eyes of another person, to feeling their pain.

The day everything changed between her and Dickie, we'd gone along to watch the boys in a rugby match. It hadn't even been Ellie's idea; it'd been mine. Charles and I were in upper sixth by then. I knew there wouldn't be many more opportunities to watch him play and I wanted to take advantage of every chance I had. You could tell how pleased Dickie was to see Ellie there, though, raising a happy hand in greeting when he saw her – about as bold as writing a signed love letter at Chesterfield.

They shouldn't have lost: with Charles, Dickie and Tom all in the First XV by then it should have been a shoo-in, so the mood was sour afterwards. Wellington were the school to beat and they gloated afterwards, riling the boys up. Someone – I think it was Tom Bates – muttered something about how it was unlucky to have girls at a match. His father was in the navy, with its own superstitions about women, which was probably where he got the stupid idea from, and before too long the rest of the boys joined him in blaming Dickie for being distracted.

Dickie was the scrum half – it was his job to get the ball from the scrum and spin it out to the backs who'd run with it. He wasn't a leader like Charles, the team captain, or big like Tom, the number eight, who headed the scrums, but Dickie usually excelled at scrabbling for the ball in this terrier-like way. It was true that perhaps his mind wasn't on the game that day, but he didn't deserve what happened later.

It was a social dance that Saturday and, though the boys' preparation wasn't as lengthy, or as obvious, as the girls' – for whom things might start early in the afternoon with soaking and shaving, plucking and primping; I was a little hazy on the details because I tended simply to wash my face with Mother's oatmeal scrub and run a comb through my hair – you could tell Dickie had made a particular effort that night with gel in his curtained locks and buckets of aftershave. That was how we found him, standing with his hands in his pockets next to the upright piano in the party room waiting for Ellie, the same bright smile on his face from earlier.

There was a strange atmosphere that evening – too meek and calm, as if someone had planned something. Which, of course, they had.

Ellie and Dickie had been goofing around most of the night, but when Des'ree's 'Kissing You' came on, they started to dance together in the centre of the room, with their hands on each other's shoulders. It began as them fooling around, but you could tell how happy Dickie was from the way he looked at Ellie and I thought to myself, as I watched them, that if they became girlfriend and boyfriend, Charles might realise that we belonged together too. He and Juliet were nowhere to be seen at this stage, though I'd spotted them earlier in the corner of the room, watching Dickie and Ellie, Charles's arms slung around her shoulders in a bored manner as if he'd really rather be doing something else.

It was while Dickie and Ellie were dancing that a silent

194

signal was exchanged between the boys and they pounced, surrounding the pair of them on the floor and separating them.

'What's going on?' I asked a boy in Ellie's year – less intimidating than one of my peers.

'They're debagging Dickie for losing them the match.'

He didn't join in but he folded his arms, as if waiting for a show to begin. It was Tom Bates who grabbed Ellie and pulled her out of the way, while the rest of them were on Dickie like hyenas, removing his shoes, then pulling at his trousers.

'Stop it, guys,' he shouted at first, trying to keep it light-hearted, but his cries became increasingly anguished – you could hear the crack in his voice, the desperation – with Ellie there and all of us girls – and of course they'd chosen a moment when there were no adults in the room to prevent it from happening.

Group mania took over, gaining momentum like a boulder rolling downhill. I looked around frantically for Charles, for Juliet, for someone with the power to stop it, but there wasn't anybody. Just a squirming scrum with Dickie buried at the bottom of it all. They had his trousers off by this stage and Will Lovell was going for his boxers. Will was a slight guy, like Dickie, not solid like Charles or Tom – perhaps he knew, that if it hadn't been Dickie, it could have been him. Perhaps he was pleased that someone so popular was getting his comeuppance. Either way, he made the most of his moment, glancing around him like a magician – after all, the act would have lost its power if no one had been there to see it.

There was a whoop at the unveiling from the boys, giggles from a couple of the girls and then it was done.

I turned away – I had no interest in witnessing Dickie's humiliation – and made my way over to Ellie who had launched a knee into Tom's privates and pulled free. She ran to Dickie.

'Are you OK?'

He was sprawled on the floor clutching his trousers to his groin, snot and tears smeared over his cheeks.

'Just fuck off, will you? Leave me alone.'

Ellie blinked a couple of times in shock. Dickie had never spoken to her like that before. She went over to Will, who was brandishing the boxers like a flag, and pulled them sharply out of his hand. She returned them to Dickie, sitting up by this stage, and dropped them at his feet, and then she did as he requested and left him alone.

We heard later from Meilin, who'd missed this sorry scene, that a rumour had been started – by whom we didn't know – that the whole thing had been Ellie's idea, that she lured Dickie with a dance in order to humiliate him in front of everyone. Vengeance, perhaps, for the way he'd bullied me years before. It was just a stupid story, but enough people believed it. Ellie's looks won her enemies, as well as admirers. She tried to tell Dickie, on numerous occasions, that she'd had nothing to do with it, but he never spoke to her again.

It was an event that taught me two important things.

The first was that Chesterfield could be as brutal for the boys as it could for us girls; it was a place where you couldn't trust anyone, where tender alliances and secret desires were seedlings that could be wrenched away from you if you weren't careful, if you didn't guard them with everything you had.

The second was that someone out there didn't want Ellie and Dickie to be friends.

And look where that led.

36

The next day begins with an unexpected message from Charles.

I don't s'pose you can meet me again at the National Gallery for lunch?

I lie in Caroline's spare bed looking at the text for a long time, thrilled that he has used the apostrophe correctly. After drafting a few replies in Notes, I go for something breezy but positive.

I can, as it happens, Mr Fry. 1pm?

As soon as I send it, I begin to regret it. Mr Fry? Is that peculiar? Should I have made more of the occasion? Less? I jump out of bed quickly and wash my face at the sink, taking a moment to examine it to see if it passes muster. Round and pink, as always, it both does and doesn't look different from any other day. I flatter myself there's a glow to my cheeks, a knowing twinkle in my eyes.

'Something is happening,' I tell myself in the mirror.

'Your life is changing. You've been waiting for this for a very long time. So don't mess it up.'

Over breakfast I feel anxious around Caroline. I sit perched at her breakfast counter, while she tries to feed Daisy mashed banana, wondering how I can bring up what I saw on her Uber account. I run through different ways of broaching the subject in my head, but all of them sound abrupt and strange. And I don't know how she might react. *It's broad daylight in Ealing,* I tell myself. *Nothing's going to happen. What are you expecting? That she might threaten you with that baby spoon?*

Still, I delay the moment, asking instead, 'You know Dickie's sketches – the ones he did before he died. Can I see them?'

It's a bit of a long shot – and I'm not even sure she'll remember telling me about them, but I want to know where the sketches have gone.

Caroline stops what she's doing for a moment, wipes a smear of banana from her forehead. 'I think they're in your room. The spare room, I mean.'

She looks pale today. I heard Daisy cry a couple of times in the night and Caroline's stumbling footsteps from her room to the nursery.

'Dickie did them when we came back from Oman in October.' She picks up a cloth and mops down Daisy's face and hands. 'I thought it was because he'd been diving – but they're dark. Not just pretty pictures of fish.'

'Can I see them?' I ask again.

'Sure.' She drops the cloth at the side of the sink. 'They're in the top drawer of the desk.'

Daft though it is, I perform the charade of going

upstairs to look for the sketchbook when I know it's no longer where it was.

Returning empty-handed to the kitchen, I say, as casually as I can, 'I couldn't find them.'

'Oh, how strange,' says Caroline, heaving Daisy out of the highchair. 'Maybe I moved them.' She smiles. 'I'm so sorry – I've got to get Daisy to nursery this morning. But you know your way to the tube, don't you?'

'Yes, of course.' I feel like I've just been dismissed. Perhaps she's keen to get me out of the house. Is it possible she's guessed what I saw on her phone?

'What are you up to with your day off?'

'I'm not sure,' I say, my hand reaching for my mobile in the pocket of my cardigan, to caress Charles's text. 'A spot of Christmas shopping perhaps.'

After all these years, you might think the effect of him would tarnish in the way silver does, but that's not the case. His smile when he spots me makes my heart twist. I smile back – I can't help it – my face aches from the joy of it. He kisses me in greeting on both cheeks and he smells so good – so fresh and clean – like new beginnings.

'I thought we could show each other our favourite paintings,' he says. 'Me first. It'll give you time to think.'

He takes me to the Rokeby Venus and I blush at her pearly backside lounging in front of us so flagrantly. I do what I often do when I get nervous and regurgitate all the facts I know about her – how her name comes from Rokeby Park, a grand house in County Durham where she used to hang on the wall; how Velázquez, in painting her, didn't want to give her face, reflected in the mirror, the distinctive features of any one woman, so she remains blurry, leaving the viewer to fill in the gaps; and how, because she was supposed to be the most beautiful character in the world, she became a target and was attacked by the suffragette Mary Richardson.

Charles laughs indulgently and says, 'Always the straight-A student.'

I flunked my A-levels in the end. I don't tell him that. We'd left Chesterfield by then.

When it's my turn, I panic and I take him to the Arnolfini Portrait – not because I like it; I wouldn't say that was the word – but because it's one of those paintings that stays with you, like the Mona Lisa. No one can pin it down.

A couple looks out – a man in black who resembles Vladimir Putin and a woman in a rich green dress with her hand on her protruded belly. There's a small dog at their feet and a circular mirror between them, in which you can catch a glimpse of the artist, Jan van Eyck.

'I don't think I know it,' Charles says on our way there.

'You do,' I tell him. 'You'll recognise it.'

When we get there, he does.

'She's pregnant, isn't she?' he asks.

'Actually, they're less sure these days. They think it may just be her dress, the way she's standing.'

'She looks pregnant to me,' he says stubbornly.

I concede the point to him. I suppose, with two children, he would know more about that than me. It's hardly my specialist subject. When Ellie first told me about Rose, I'd had no idea.

'I don't want you to freak out and go all . . . but I

201

have something to tell you,' she'd said on her way out to work.

Looking back, I'm sure she timed it that way, so that the conversation wouldn't go on for too long.

'Go all what?' I asked, irritated.

'I'm pregnant.'

'Oh, Ellie.' I got to my feet. 'How? Who?'

'Well, I don't think I need to explain the process to you.' She laughed. 'But it's someone I know from work. A customer.' She was working in a cocktail bar at the time. 'But he's married, so he won't be part of all this. You can't mention it to anyone. It's kind of a secret.'

'A secret baby.' I was shocked, but excited. I couldn't stop looking at my sister's belly.

'I guess she won't be a secret when she comes out.'

'She?'

'I don't know that yet.' She smiled. 'But I have a hunch.'

She looked so pretty and carefree that day, leaning against the counter. You would never guess that she was cooking a baby. Rose. As big as a raspberry.

'What will you call her?'

'Christ, Fran.' She rolled her eyes.

'Please,' I asked. 'Call her Rose. After Mother.'

In response, she came over to where I was sitting and pressed a kiss on my head. 'Don't freak out,' she called over her shoulder as she left the flat for her shift. 'You promised.'

I remember thinking I had done no such thing.

Charles and I stop in the café again afterwards, sitting peaceably together, looking out at the room. A melancholic mood takes over me after all my thoughts of Ellie. Charles, of course, can sense it. He moves his hand to the small of my back and strokes me there, almost imperceptibly. A private place that no one can see. It's a tiny circular movement, no bigger than a two-pence piece. It's nothing much – just the small motion of a digit through two layers of clothes, but for a few minutes it's as if the whole of me resides there.

If you were passing by, you wouldn't look at us twice. You wouldn't know that everything has changed between us or that I've been waiting thirty-seven years for this. That my waiting has finally paid off. That lives can alter course in a few moments in the National Gallery café in this way. To anyone hurrying on their way, we'd just look like a pair of old friends catching up over a cup of tea.

37

After so much happiness, it catches me unawares. These sorts of things always do. I wake up thinking I'm going to have a normal day – busy, no doubt; it's the run-up to Christmas after all – but not a day that will stay with me, stirring up dark feelings like silt at the bottom of a riverbed. If I had known what was to come, I wouldn't have gone into work at all.

We have to be very organised in December, with a certain number of us on the tills at all times. A great deal of thought goes into organising our shifts, our breaks and so on. It's a military operation. I like it, though. The busyness, the sense of purpose. I'm on the late shift, so Caroline and I have planned to meet at three when I have my lunch break. It's a Friday, her day off, but when she arrives, she's come alone, without Daisy.

Caught at the till with a customer, I wave at her when I spot her waiting by the Crime table and I'm so pre-occupied that I don't really notice that she doesn't wave back, that she keeps standing there with her arms by her sides, watching me the way she did a couple of months ago in the street before I knew her.

'That's my friend,' I tell Ingrid. 'I'm off on my break now.'

I'm not ashamed to say that I do it with a flush of pride; to show off to Ingrid that I have a friend, someone waiting for me, which is perhaps why I greet Caroline a touch loudly, my voice jollier, brassier than it might ordinarily be.

'I won't be a moment – I'll just get my coat.'

She shakes her head. 'We're not going for coffee.'

And I can't believe it's taken me so long to work out that there's something terribly wrong. Up close, she smells sweet like fermented fruit, something that's softened and melted in the bowl. After Fiona's warning, I've been looking closely for signs that Caroline has been drinking, never knowing how obvious it would be. Not that she's slurring and stumbling but there's a heaviness to her now – a dark energy. Her face is sheet white; her eyes look black.

'When were you going to tell me?'

There's a slight tremor in her voice she's working hard to hide and that makes it worse: that what I've done is so terrible she has to make an effort to control herself around me. The intensity of her emotion leaks out at the edge of her words.

'Tell you what?' I ask, but I know what she means.

She shakes her head. 'I trusted you,' she whispers. 'I thought you were someone I could rely on.'

'You can,' I say. 'Let me explain.'

205

'You watched my husband die in front of you. You have let me go on about that night for *weeks* and you never said.'

Blood rushes to my face. A couple of customers glance up from their Christmas shopping. At the till, Ingrid gives Liam a nudge. I try to work out if Caroline's fury is simply because I was there or because she thinks there's a chance she might have been spotted. But I can't think straight in these conditions. I just can't tell.

'I thought you would find it weird,' I mutter.

'It *is* weird,' she hisses. 'I don't know which is weirder – your being there, or your not saying anything.'

'I was only there for Charles,' I blurt out. 'It had nothing to do with Dickie.'

I've said the words without stopping to think. Now they're out there I feel exposed – there's no taking them back.

Caroline folds her arms. 'That, in itself, is strange. If no one's told you that by now, you ought to know.'

I want to remind her how she stood in front of me, her head tilted to one side, saying, *I understand addiction*, but what I want more – more than anything – is to move this discussion outside of the bookshop, to somewhere I won't be able to feel the prickle of everyone's gaze on my back.

'Can we go outside?' I ask.

She nods sharply. 'Fine.' She slings her handbag over her shoulder, sending a pile of books flying from the apex of Gareth's carefully constructed pyramid. 'Fuck it,' she says loudly and marches out.

I'm not keen on drunk Caroline.

206

We huddle in the street glaring at each other. Caroline's arms are folded again; her breath comes out in angry little puffs.

'Everyone said you were weird,' she says. 'But I didn't listen – I thought I'd give you a chance.'

Everyone. I try not to dwell on this. 'Who told you I was there that night?'

She shakes her head. 'That doesn't matter.'

'Was it Meilin?' I persist.

I think of Daisy's Christmas presents already neatly wrapped. I won't get the chance to give them to her now.

'She promised,' I say. 'She *promised* she wouldn't.'

'Why were you there?'

'I wanted to see Charles.' It sounds pathetic when I say it out loud. 'I just wanted to watch him, from a distance. I wasn't doing any harm.'

How must that sound to someone like Caroline? Someone who has known a happy marriage, motherhood, challenging work, family life. That sometimes I would just go to where Charles was and hang around from a distance. And – what? Not much more than that. Imagine scenarios in which I could bump into him and strike up a conversation. A conversation in which he was finally wowed by me; he finally got it. That I could offer him something Fiona never could: a meeting of minds.

It hadn't happened like that, though. It hadn't panned out. Charles never shared much on social media so I had to follow Dickie's leads of what the pair of them were up to. Which is what I was doing that night when they met at Charles's club on Cromwell Road. It was so easy to pop round after work, have a drink in the public bar that night and wait for them to emerge from the private club upstairs. Easy too to remain invisible: women like me – big-boned, of a certain age – often do. Dickie and Charles wouldn't have been looking out for me. But I wasn't the only one there that night, was I? I know that much. I know that Caroline was in South Kensington too.

'You were there as well,' I say quietly. It's easier to say it now our friendship is over. I have less to risk. And what's the worst she can do to me right now on a busy street? 'I saw your Uber history. You made a journey to South Kensington that night.'

The colour drains from her cheeks. 'That was nothing,' she says. 'It's not the same.'

'Why *were* you there?' I persist.

'I was so worried about Dickie drinking.' She begins to cry. 'I had a bad feeling. A premonition. I scooped Daisy up and got into an Uber and then, when we arrived at the club, she started to wail, and I thought, "What am I doing? Spying on my husband?" So I got a black cab back home again, because my phone had run out of battery. Stupid. Just a stupid waste of money – and I wasn't even *there* when he died. I could have been and I wasn't. I walked through the door at home, plugged my phone in and saw I had a couple of missed calls from Charles. Then it rang again. That was him telling me about Dickie.'

Her face is red and blotchy. People slow down as they walk past us, trying to eavesdrop on the drama.

'Caroline, I don't know what to say.' I feel bad for pushing it, for getting it so wrong.

She seems calmer now she's wept. She wipes away her tears with the back of her hand. 'You could start by explaining why you never told me.'

'I didn't know how to,' I say. 'And then after I'd missed my opportunity the first couple of times – at the memorial, when we went for tea – it got harder.'

I didn't try that hard, though.

'You were only there for Charles,' she says disbelievingly. 'Yes.'

'Just watching him?'

'Everyone does it,' I say. 'Not quite like that, but to an extent. You came to see me at the shop once – I spotted you across the road. And we all watch each other on social media, don't we? It's just what we do. It's not so bad, is it?'

'Now you're back in his life, aren't you?' She ignores my plea. 'Dickie's death has been a good thing for you.'

There are things I haven't told her – Charles in the National Gallery, his hand on my back. The joy I have experienced in the last few weeks – the heart-thrilling joy. Our cups of tea, our chats. Our time together. Now I think of it with guilt, dark and sticky as treacle. Dickie's death *has* been a good thing for me. I'm less alone than I have been in a long time.

'How did Fiona get sick at the auction?' Caroline continues in a determined manner, as if she has a list of accusations to get through. 'Jules said that was weird – the timing of it. And then Charles made that bid on you . . .'

The idea that I could have 'poisoned' Fiona is laughable. But then Juliet knows my dark side better than anyone.

'What did she tell you?' I ask. 'What did she say?'

'Just what happened,' Caroline says. 'How she got those scars.'

'Did she explain what led up to it? What *she* did? What she stole?'

Caroline looks at me.

'And I'd *never* do anything to harm Fiona. As if I could have . . .'

'As if I could have . . .' Caroline repeats, sarcastically.

I know I've offered up the wrong answer again. That there will be nothing I can say to convince her that it's just a matter of being in the wrong place at the wrong time. That it's something I'm good at. If *good* is the word. That bad things have a habit of happening around me and I don't seem to be able to stop them.

'I didn't have anything to do with it,' I say. 'Her or Dickie. I was a bystander.'

She looks at me for what feels like a very long time. 'The fact that you even have to say that . . .'

'Listen,' I say, desperate, 'what do you want to know? Anything. You can ask me anything about Dickie. There might be something . . . something that could help.'

'I've already asked Charles.'

'But I had a different view. I saw . . .'

'What did you see?' Her voice becomes fierce. 'You saw my husband die. I would have given anything – anything – to be there instead of you.'

She fishes in her pocket for a pack of cigarettes and lights one now, glaring at me, daring me to say something. I am quiet for a long time, breathing in her second-hand smoke uncomplainingly.

'I don't know if it was an accident, that's all,' I say in the end. 'There was a group of women on the platform. Some of them were in fancy dress – wearing wigs and glasses. Their faces were covered. And they were really close to him.'

'What are you suggesting?'

'I'm . . .'

'Just say it.'

'I had a hunch he saw someone he knew,' I say. 'A feeling – from the expression on his face.'

I've finally said it. The secret I've been holding on to for so long.

Caroline rolls her eyes. 'He probably just saw *you*.'

What an anti-climax, after all this time worrying. I shake my head. 'No, it wasn't that. It was someone right behind him. Look,' I continue more urgently, 'someone could have pushed him in that crush and it would've been hard to tell.'

'But did you *see* anyone do it?'

'No, not that exactly.'

'Then what use is this – or you?' she snaps.

Nothing I say is helping.

'You watched him die.' She looks at me steadily, holding the cigarette still burning in her hand. 'Someone you knew – not a stranger – and you didn't lift a finger to help him. You didn't speak to the police, or leave a witness statement. You just vanished.'

She's right: I could have gone to Charles and held him. I could have waited with him. I could have said what I'd seen.

These might have been things I would have done for

a stranger, but I didn't do them for Dickie. And I want to explain to Caroline the reason I didn't; I want to tell her the full extent of what Dickie and Tom did to my sister.

But instead I ask, 'What could I have done?'

'I guess we'll never know,' she says, dropping her cigarette on the pavement and folding her arms again.

She doesn't say goodbye, just turns, with her arms still folded, as if she's holding herself together, and walks away. It's only a matter of moments before she's swallowed up by a crowd of shoppers and I can't see her any more.

38

By the time I call Meilin, I'm crying so hard my voice is thick with snot.

'Did you tell her?' I ask.

She has no idea what I'm talking about and I have to repeat the question three or four times before she understands.

I half-shout, at last, 'Why did you tell Caroline I was there when Dickie died?'

'I didn't,' Meilin says. Her voice echoes, as if she's standing in a corridor. 'Why would I? *How* would I? I don't know her.'

'You met her at the memorial. And there's Facebook – did you message her on that?'

'I'm not really on it – I don't have the time – and why would I?' she asks again.

'You said I should go to the police – share any information I have.' The passion of my sobs has subsided now, replaced with a cold clarity.

'Yes, I thought you should, but that doesn't mean I would take matters into my own hands. It's not the sort of thing I'd do.'

'You were the only person who knew,' I insist. 'The only one. Who else could it be?'

'I wouldn't do that. And if you can't see that . . .'

'Things were going well.' A wave of self-pity washes through me. I don't tell her about my Christmas with Caroline and Daisy – what it would have meant. 'They were finally going well.'

'Fran.' Her manner is so conciliatory, so grown up, as if she is soothing a child. It nudges my recalcitrance into fury.

'You've always been jealous,' I say. 'You couldn't bear it – Charles picking me out all those years ago. You couldn't bear me to be happy.'

Even as I say the words, I'm unconvinced by them – Meilin knows nothing of my friendship with Caroline, or my Christmas plans. And she's shown no interest in Charles since school, when most girls had a soft spot for him. But my rage blinds me to all of this: I have a hammer in my hands and I want to smash something.

'I think you need help,' she says quietly. 'You need to talk to someone professional about your problems, rather than taking it out on your friend.'

She doesn't say *your only friend*, and I am grateful for that. But she hangs up nonetheless.

When I return to the shop, Gareth is no more sympathetic, calling me into his office.

'We can't have that kind of scene going on in front of the customers,' he tells me.

I nod, focusing on a strange box of tat in the corner – a bunch of plastic flowers, an old piece of paisley fabric, a bald doll with a vacant gaze.

'Are you all right?' he adds, more gently. 'I know things have been difficult between us, but I want you to be OK, you know.'

He was kind, Gareth. In that moment I missed that about him: his constancy, how every time we went on a date he had a plan for the next one, how he'd always get the pudding menu in the restaurant because he knew I had a sweet tooth. And then I think of Charles, how his thumb touched the small of my back as if he were unlocking me, how I checked that spot in the mirror later to see if he'd left a mark in some way and my heart thumped so boldly as if it wanted to jump right out of my chest.

For the rest of the day, everyone gives me a wide berth, exchanging looks behind my back but not addressing me directly. I focus on tasks that keep me away from people, putting stock on the shelves, finding returns. At one stage, Brenda tries to ask me about Caroline but I snap at her so nastily she flinches, and I'm immediately ashamed. Shame layering on shame.

On the way home, I buy a cake, a huge dark chocolate gateau, freshly made and sticky with icing. It reminds me of a similar cake Juliet was given by one of her godparents at school.

'Don't go eating it all by yourself,' Juliet's mother instructed her when she dropped it off. 'You're looking a bit porky as it is, darling.'

The cubicles in our dormitories didn't offer us any privacy at all. The partition between each bedroom was only paper-thin and didn't stretch to the ceiling. You could always hear everything, unless people whispered.

Juliet had never looked porky in her life, but her mother, who was ramrod thin herself, didn't strike me as someone who would have a balanced view on such things. The cake was too big for Juliet's tuckbox, so she slid it under her bed in the crisp white cardboard box it came in.

'I don't really want it – I have to keep my figure trim,' she said after her mother left, laying a hand on her washboard stomach. 'You can have it.' She waved at me and a couple of others who'd gathered outside her cubicle in the hyena way people did when something interesting was going on.

She was true to her word and we were allowed a piece of her cake whenever we fancied it, but, each time, we had to go through the humiliation of asking. She'd cut you a huge slice – too big, really, certainly the sort of slice that would have daunted her – and then say: 'You can eat it in here.' And she'd gesture imperiously at the chair at her desk and watch closely as you ate, licking her lips occasionally as if she was gaining a vicarious pleasure from it.

I think of this as I hurry back home, the cake in its posh box in my arms. I know there is an element of punishment as well as consolation in what I'm about to do and, if I dwell on that for too long, I won't be able to see it through.

At home, I open the cake box on the kitchen counter and cut my first slice. A large one of the sort Miss

Trunchbull cut Bruce Bogtrotter in *Matilda*. Still standing, I take a first mouthful. It hits the spot – the dark chocolate, sugar and cream are like a comforting hug. I chew and swallow. Pushing away the thoughts of the afternoon: Caroline's demeanour, pale and haggard; the way she said, *You watched him die*; the hurt in Meilin's voice; the censure in Gareth's. I cut myself a second piece and continue – even though the initial pleasure is already beginning to curdle.

The project of the cake is a distraction from my thoughts: Ellie caring so little about what I'd given her that she'd dressed Rose in the wrong thing; Rose on her tricycle so far away, never knowing how much I longed to see her; Caroline's face.

I eat and eat and eat. The chocolate smears my fingers and my face as I push slice after slice into my mouth. The cake settles like cement in my belly, but still I eat. I do well. I'm proud of my progress, in fact; I get almost two-thirds of the way through the cake when my stomach starts to churn and I begin to hiccup in a sickening sort of way. I don't like to admit defeat so close to the end so I try to push one more mouthful down but this proves to be the last straw and I know, with a dizzying rush, that I'm about to be sick.

I make it to the bathroom in time. It's an unseemly position to be in, kneeling on the floor like this – vomiting this expensive treat back up. I haven't binged like this for years, not since my school days when some unkindness would drive me to bed with a packet of biscuits, where I'd eat them as swiftly and silently as I could. The idea is to forget – not so much *death* by chocolate as oblivion, I tell myself as a joke. But I don't feel like laughing.

The emptiness afterwards brings peace. A clarity. I lower the lavatory seat and rest my head against its cool surface.

It's only then that the thought settles, fluttering down like a feather. Meilin wasn't the only person I'd told I was there the night Dickie died.

Ellie knew, too.

39

When I wake my eyes are puffy and my throat feels scratched and sore. Worst of all is the creeping shame – how differently Caroline looked at me yesterday, as if she were regarding a stranger. You'd never know I was someone she had passed her baby to or invited over for Christmas. No need to check if that is still on the cards, or whether I'll ever cuddle Daisy again. Self-pitying tears fill my eyes but I brush them away. I can't start the day weeping.

My feet are cold and I call out for Branwell. He jumps onto the bed and pads towards me sullenly as if he's doing me an enormous favour. I look at the ceiling tiles for a long time. I'd hoped, as I fell asleep last night, that I might dream of Charles. But, in the end, it was Ellie who appeared. Ellie before she left, her face contorted with rage.

I have to approach things carefully with her. She spooks so easily – and I don't want to lose the little contact I

219

have. But it is a difficult question to ask lightly: Did you tell Caroline I was there when Dickie died? And why would you?

I test it out a few ways – delete and start again, but however I put it, it still sounds like an accusation.

When I finally send it, the answer comes back more speedily than usual: No, of course not, sis. I don't really know her – and I wouldn't tell your secret.

The word secret makes me blanch. It sounds so deceptive, but how else would I describe how I've behaved? I get out of bed and press my feverish forehead against the glass of my bedroom window, trying to decide what to do about Charles. I've been too much of a coward to get in touch but I have to face the fact there's a good chance Caroline will have told him.

I picture Fiona sitting next to Caroline on the sofa, her arm around her, saying, 'I knew never to trust her.' Or maybe, worse: something pitying. Something charitable. While Charles listens to them from his armchair, keeping his counsel, not agreeing or disagreeing but perhaps making the private decision not to see me again. The idea leaves me bereft, makes me want to claw at the window in misery. I know what it is to feel betrayed and I can't bear that I've done that to Charles. I have to reach him first, to explain things in my own way – the folly of my old lonely habits before I was sure of his love.

Mother used to say: *Your sin will find you out* – to teach us not to lie – but I'm not even certain of the worst of my sins: was it being there in the first place? Was it keeping it a secret? Or was it finding happiness with the people Dickie left behind?

If I go to the police, perhaps that will assuage my guilt. After all, I'm the one with all of the information – the only one who is still convinced Dickie was pushed that night. If I could help the coroner get to the bottom of things, if I could make amends, then perhaps Caroline might forgive me. And I might be able to prove, once and for all, that Ellie had nothing to do with it. If only to myself.

But first I need to see Charles. I have to talk it through with him. This could save me, solve all of my problems. We could go to the police together, side by side. United in our determination. Now I've made the decision, I act quickly, throwing on an old tweed suit I picked up from a charity shop, which I think makes me look respectable, credible, and dashing for the door. It's a Saturday, our busiest day, but I text the shop with an excuse about feeling poorly. They won't believe it after the scene yesterday, but I deserve one fake sick day in seventeen years of loyal service. I switch my phone off and hurry to Paddington, hoping to make the 10.50 train, which I do. I spend the journey looking out of the window at the bleached winter sky, longing for a miracle.

When I reach Honeybourne, the house is quiet. I knock on the door a couple of times and then make my way around the side, peering into windows, keeping my ears open for any noise. We were so close, Charles and I, in the National Gallery. I can't have Caroline destroy everything I've waited for for so long. I need him now more than I've ever needed him before. Standing alone and cold outside his empty house, my earlier mood of resolution plunges into one of despair.

On the shore of the lake, I stop to look out over the water. It's generous to call it a lake – it's a large pond, really, stretching around the back of the house. I decide to head for my favourite bench, where I sit and watch Honeybourne on my secret visits. I started my trips after Ellie went. She wouldn't have allowed it as long as she'd been around – she would have been furious. But I've always been careful not to be caught here. I come at dawn or at night-time when I know they'll be inside. There's no sinister intent – I just watch the house as it sleeps and learn details about Charles's life, preparing for when he'll want me to take Fiona's place.

Sometimes the twins see me. They're big enough now to be able to climb up onto one of the beds and peek out of the window. I've glimpsed them once or twice – their small faces pressed up against the glass. I wonder if they ever mention me to their parents. If they do, perhaps Fiona and Charles think I'm no more than an imaginary friend. The lady in the garden. Something they'll grow out of.

Today my usual bench is dripping and untempting. I fold up my scarf and sit on it, watching the shadows the bare branches cast across the water. The dark thoughts of yesterday return. What is the point of any of it? Who do I have left? Caroline, Meilin, Gareth: I have let everyone down. I tell myself I'm a good person, but am I really? Creeping around. Always there uninvited. Weighed down by secrets.

Even with Charles. Did he really want me? And if he did, where is he now when I need him most? Maybe it's already too late to explain myself. Maybe he's made up his mind. Maybe it would be better for everyone if I wasn't here any more, I think as I watch the wind flutter over the surface of the water.

'*Willows whiten, aspens quiver / Little breezes dusk and shiver*,' I say aloud to a couple of cold-looking mallards. Mrs Fyson made us learn *The Lady of Shalott* at school and called on us at random to recite a verse. I never had the sort of recall that Mother did – you could set her off on Shakespeare or Emily Dickinson and she'd be away – but I found *The Lady of Shalott* easy to remember because of the rhyming scheme. I've never understood exactly what drove the heroine to the water, but I feel it now. I understand. She wanted Lancelot to look at her. She just wanted to be seen. And if she couldn't be seen, she wanted to be obliterated. He was all she had left.

There's no boat here, so I can't take to the water that way, like she did in the poem. No matter. I kick off my shoes and take a step into the lake. It's so cold it burns. But what is there to lose? Almost all of it has gone now. Mother, Ellie, Caroline, Daisy. Maybe Charles. Maybe I never even had him in the first place.

I don't want to have thoughts like this any more. I don't want to feel any of it. Any of the pain, any of the longing – I've had enough.

As I make my way deeper in, the bite of the water almost stops my heart in my chest but, still, I push on. I'm committed to this course of action now: wherever it leads, it can't be worse than where I've come from. The humiliation, the loneliness. The loss. I'm braver than I think. I can tolerate the pain, after all.

The ducks shoot past me, looking alarmed. By the time I'm up to my shoulders, my stockinged feet start to get tangled in the weeds. I try to swim, but it's hard in these conditions. The water's thick as treacle and the tweed I'm wearing becomes as heavy as a constrictor clamped around my limbs. The small island in the centre of the lake, with its weeping willow, seems to stretch further away as I head towards it. There's a spot there I've noticed before, where it never ices over, where the water must be warmer. I don't know why I think of that now.

I kick down but I'm out of my depth. The tweed clutches me more tightly. My arms are as slow and heavy as oars. I turn on my back to look at the angry sky. There is only one hope: that he'll find me here. Like the first day we met, he'll say, 'Fran can share with me.' But this time, he'll mean his house. His everything.

Not so bad, I think, to die here. Where he is. I kick out again but there's no solid bed beneath me – and the island's still out of reach. My limbs aren't doing what I tell them to do and I experience a moment of genuine fear.

'Fran?' I hear Fiona's voice cutting across the water. 'What in God's name . . .?'

Not her. I don't want her. I open my eyes. Four figures on the edge of the water – Charles, Fiona and the twins. The adults in the middle with a child either side. A neat, symmetrical unit in Barbours and wellies. Completing the picture, their large chocolate Labrador woofs happily and trots in to join me.

'Fuck, Charles.' Fiona actually sounds frightened. 'I think she's drowning.'

40

His arms around me, warm and strong. Just like I always imagined.

'Come on, old girl. Steady as she goes.'

I giggle, leaning into him as he swims me in. 'The good ship Francesca,' I want to say, but my teeth are chattering so badly I struggle to formulate the words.

'Jesus, you gave us a shock,' Charles says as we stagger out. 'What were you doing?'

I swallow. Though the water had a numbing quality, now I'm out of it I begin to shake violently. I notice Fiona and the children have slipped back into the warmth of the house, taking the dog with them.

'I feel a bit strange,' I say.

'You're all right.' Charles puts his arms around me. 'You just need to warm up slowly. Let's get you inside and out of these wet things.'

It's like something from a dream. If all I needed to do

was jump in the lake to get his attention, I would have done it a long time ago.

Inside, Fiona is at the Aga, stirring soup in a saucepan.

'We need towels,' says Charles and he disappears, leaving Fiona and me alone.

She hands me a cup of tea. 'You'll need this to warm up.' She pauses and adds sharply, 'Is this about your fight with Caroline?'

'How did you know about that?' Self-consciousness creeps over me, as I stand dripping in her kitchen.

'I spoke to her earlier.'

My hands burn with the heat of the mug. I put it down on the table. 'How did she find out? Who told her?'

I can't leave it alone – I need to know.

'She asked me not to say. But look, Fran, it's better that it's out in the open. The truth is always the best option.'

She reminds me of Ellie when she says that.

Fiona looks out of the kitchen window at the lake. 'Why are you here?'

My gaze falls to the slate floor, where a small pool is forming around me. I consider sharing my plan to go to the police, but I'd rather talk it through with Charles first. As far as Fiona knows, I'm just Ellie's sister. An acquaintance from school. As far as she's aware, I haven't been here for years. She doesn't know the half of it.

'I wanted to speak to Charles,' I say quietly. 'I thought he might be able to help me patch things up with Caroline.'

'And why did you get in the water?' she persists. 'You could have died if we hadn't come home. If we hadn't found you.' She shakes her head in disbelief.

I return my gaze to my feet, unable to put it into words. 'I can't explain.'

'Fran, I realise we don't know each other very well,' she says, returning to the soup. 'But I think you might need some help, some kind of support. Doing something like that at this time of year . . .' She leaves the words hanging. 'Look, anyway, I have the number of a good therapist. Someone I went to see when we were trying for the twins.' She leaves the saucepan for a moment and goes to her handbag, fishes out a business card, which she passes to me. 'I'll talk to Caroline and explain about today – it might help for her to know how upset you were.'

'Thank you,' I say meekly.

'In the meantime,' she says, 'I've got to go out with the kids in a bit, but I'll ask Charles to run you a bath. You need to warm up – slowly, though. Have some soup first.'

Charles appears then with towels and a dressing gown and in the downstairs cloakroom I dry off and wrap up in the robe. He takes my wet clothes from me, to hang in front of the Aga, and offers me a bowl of soup at the table. Fiona sits with me, nursing a cup of tea, while Charles tends to the children.

'Don't worry about Caroline.' She pats my hand. 'She'll get over it eventually.'

'I feel terrible about it – I should have said earlier.'

'This too shall pass.' She smiles. 'A helpful mantra when you're delivering babies.'

'I'm sure you were very good at it.'

I mean it as I say it. I've always seen her as my rival

but I see now how she's the kind of person who could handle anything you throw at her. The kind of person it would be good to have on your side.

As I wallow in the bath, I hear the children's voices, the sound of the television, then light footsteps pattering down the staircase, a car door slamming, the burr of an engine. I get out reluctantly, tying the bathrobe tight around me.

The house is quieter now. Someone's turned the television off. The kids have left the building, gone to their grandparents, perhaps. Fiona's family live nearby on the stud farm where she grew up, learning a few of her practical skills, no doubt. Her toughness.

I realise I'm not sure where my clothes are, where Charles is. I stand on the landing for a moment, listening. My heart thuds in my chest.

'Fran.' Charles's voice comes from the bedroom.

I pop my head around the door, suddenly conscious of the fact I'm only wearing a bathrobe. So is he, fresh out of the shower. I don't know how to hold myself or what to say.

'Fiona and the kids have gone out.' He smiles. 'In case you were wondering.'

His voice is different: gentler and inviting. When he is around Fiona, he speaks with a crisp efficiency like her own. But that shell has fallen away now.

'Our bathrobes match,' I say, because I'm stuck for words and it's true.

We're in his and hers versions, white and fluffy. The lights are dim in the bedroom; someone's lit candles too, drawn the curtains. The carpet is thick under my bare feet. I realise that I've never actually been alone in a room with Charles – not really. At Chesterfield, at the auction, even at the National Gallery, we were alone in a crowd. Now the moment is here I don't know how to act. In books and films, people instinctively understand how to behave in these situations. They act smoothly, moving confidently towards the inevitable clinch. But I don't feel smooth and confident. I'm shivering still from my swim. Unable to shake off the cold. Unless it's excitement. Or fear.

'Where's Fiona?' I ask, although I've guessed the answer.

'She's at her parents'.'

I realise I want her to come back. That I don't know how to handle this new situation.

Charles stands, just looking at me. Then he opens his arms for a hug and I go to him, resting my face on his warm chest. I'm still shaking.

'You saw Dickie die,' he says quietly, sadly.

'I'm so sorry I never said.' I murmur the words into his chest, grateful he can't witness the hot shame on my face.

It's worse, somehow, than it was with Caroline, because Charles was there himself. It was his face I saw afterwards. A spectator in the way I have been at other times in his life. Intimate moments I shouldn't have witnessed. And I slipped away when I could have stayed. That would have been the noble thing to do. The right thing. But then I would have been exposed for what I was. Someone who creeps around, watching from a distance, looking through windows, longing to be let in.

I begin to cry. 'There is so much I'm ashamed of.'

'Me too,' says Charles. He pulls away from me and sinks into the bed, holding his head in his hands. 'I wish I had saved Dickie.'

I perch next to him. 'There's nothing you could have done.'

'Are you sure?' he asks urgently. 'You were there. Do you really think so?'

'Yes, I'm sure of it.' I hesitate, steeling myself to continue. 'Charles,' I say at last. 'I've been thinking. About what you said before. I don't know if it *was* an accident. I believe Dickie was pushed.'

He looks up at me.

'I couldn't tell you before, because you didn't know I was there. But Dickie saw someone he knew just before he fell. I think that person could have pushed him.'

'Caroline said you'd told her something like that,' he says doubtfully.

I can tell by the tone of his voice that Caroline still doesn't believe me.

'I didn't see who it was.' I look into those slate-grey eyes I have loved for so long. 'But I thought maybe I should go to the police – share the information I have. Something doesn't add up.'

There are still things I can't mention. I know if I say anything about Caroline's Uber trip, she won't forgive me, so I keep quiet about that. And of course I won't breathe a word about the woman who looked like Ellie. But I need to do this: I need to find out what happened that night. It will prove my love to Charles, my friendship to Caroline. *As long as she didn't do it herself,* adds a quiet voice in my head.

'Will you come with me?' I ask. 'To the police. I'd really like you to.'

Charles takes my hand. I look down at my nails, clean and white after the long soak. 'If you need me there, I'll come with you,' he says kindly. 'But could we wait until after Christmas – for Caroline's sake? It's a hard time, as you know. And she's just fallen off the wagon. Let's do it when things have settled and she's got her drinking under control.'

I nod. 'Of course.'

He exhales and flops back on the bed, sinking into the duck-down duvet. I stay upright for a moment, looking ahead, but he pats the spot next to him and I lie back into the crook of his arm, though in a less relaxed manner than him. We keep still, listening to the sounds of the house: the gurgle of the radiators, the caw of a crow outside. I look up and see us reflected in a mirror above the bed. It occurs to me why Charles and Fiona must have hung it there and the realisation makes me blush from the roots of my hair.

'Fran,' he says quietly, 'why were you in the lake?'

'I just wanted to . . .' I glance away from the reflection. 'I don't know,' I say. 'I can't explain it.'

'Did you want my attention?' he says quietly. 'For me to rescue you?'

We catch each other's eyes in the mirror and I nod. I can feel a trickle of sweat in the hollow of my throat.

'You like me, don't you?' He doesn't wait for an answer. 'You've always liked me.'

231

I stay as still as a doll. Now we're here, lying in bed, I don't know what to say next. With Gareth I had been able to explain and he had understood. He had patted my hand and said we could still be companions, that the other stuff wasn't so important to him either, but with Charles I can't find the words. I hear Dickie's laughter then, ringing in my ears. *Freaky Fran, you finally have your chance and you're going to blow it.*

'Charles,' I say in the end. 'I've never . . . you know. I don't know if I'm like everybody else . . .'

He takes my hand in response and gives it a squeeze. There's another silence. I hear a car in the distance and I wonder how long we have – if this will be our only opportunity to lie like this.

'Do you remember that time you caught me and Juliet together?' Charles pulls me closer, murmurs in my ear. 'Perhaps you just like to watch.'

I don't respond. My face burns with shame.

'We knew you were there but I think Juliet enjoyed it, having an audience.' His breathing is thinner; I feel the thump-thump of his heart through the robe.

He means in the sports hall at Chesterfield, how I followed him there one evening, not sure exactly what I wanted. Juliet was one of the athletics prefects, so it was her job to check the students had left the sports complex at the end of the night. I'd hung around, waiting for ages in the girls' changing room, just sitting there in the dark.

When I'd heard heavy breathing, a moan from the boys' changing room next door, I'd crept towards the sound. I can't remember what I told myself. Perhaps that someone was in trouble, that they might need help. Or maybe it was simple curiosity. Nosiness. I don't know, but the door was ajar. They'd left it like that. Juliet supine, facing the ceiling, her eyes closed, her school skirt thrown up. The back of Charles's head, bobbing up and down. Her eyes opened, just for a second, and she saw me. The brief shimmer of pleasure I'd experienced shattered like fireworks.

I ran back down the corridor, out of the sports hall, to the boarding house, where I got into bed with all my clothes on and feigned a migraine.

'Some people just enjoy watching.' There are whisky fumes on his breath. 'Maybe you're like that, Fran? A voyeur.'

He's a different Charles then, his face hot and close, his hand heavy on my bathrobe. I don't like it; I don't understand. I want to pull away, so I can admire him again from a distance. This is too cramped. Too strange. And there's another thought – something I try to push away as hard as I can. Juliet isn't the only woman I've seen him kiss like that. If it had just been her, it wouldn't be so bad.

I curl away from him – only a fraction but he senses it, takes his hand off me.

There's a long silence between us.

'Is this real to you?' he asks in the mirror. 'Or is it just an old schoolgirl crush?'

I glare at him. What a ridiculous, childlike word. Meaningless, reductive. The way I feel about him has always been so much bigger than that. Anger wells up so quickly I find I want to hurl something at him for misinterpreting everything. For mistaking my love for sordid desire.

'A crush?' I want to say. 'Are you insane?'

But almost as quickly as it started my rage U-turns into grief. I sit up. My shoulders tremble, and I swallow hard, but it's too late. The emotion of the day spills out in furious tears. Maybe he's right, I realise. Maybe it's all just an idea. Maybe the most important thing in my life isn't real.

'Fran.' He leans forward to touch me, but I rear away, abandoning myself to paroxysms of grief.

When I finally manage to speak between the sobs, I don't want to talk about my feelings for Charles any more. It's not even him I'm thinking about; it's not his name on my lips.

'Ellie,' I cry. 'God, I miss Ellie.'

41

When we were children, Ellie and I would leave a glass of sherry and a mince pie by the fireplace for Father Christmas, a carrot for Rudolph. We'd wake early in the room we shared in the cottage in Yorkshire, condensation dripping from the windows, and creep downstairs, where our stockings would hang by the fireplace. There'd be a smattering of icing sugar – snow as we thought it then – with the print of a big boot, the carrot gnawed to its stubby end, the mince pie reduced to crumbs, the sherry vanished. Sometimes I think of Mother crunching her way through the raw carrot, which would have given her the hiccups, eating the mince pie and downing the sherry. Her reward for wrapping and filling our stockings on her own at the dead of night. But where did she find a boot big enough for the Santa print? It was far too large for her. And where did she keep it the rest of the year?

You don't appreciate love like that until it's gone.

But I'm an adult now and, despite what *A Christmas*

Carol and *It's A Wonderful Life* would have us believe, I know there are no ghosts or angels. No second chances. No way of calling our loved ones back. No way to unsay the terrible things we've said.

And yet I try my best to cast my own spell, think of everything I can do to tempt Ellie back. I fill the fridge with her favourite food – brandy butter, salmon, Brussels sprouts – she was weird like that. A stack of books waits for Rose under the tree, a beautiful vintage-style swimming costume for Ellie. She should face her fears and start swimming again; we should move on from the past.

Before I go to sleep, I even consider leaving the door on the latch for them, as if they could slip back in the night. It's a silly thought, really. Ellie has a key, after all.

Do you remember that footprint Mother used to leave in icing sugar? I wrote in a Facebook message to her last week after that dreadful day at Honeybourne. I've been thinking about that a lot. About her. I would love you to come back for Christmas. You're both always welcome here. Always.

I haven't been in touch with Caroline, but I noticed on Facebook that she's changed her mind – she'll be spending Christmas with Charles and Fiona, not on her own, after all. I try not to think about how they will all be waking up together, cosy and warm in that golden house, unwrapping presents under the enormous tree in the hallway or by the fire in the living room.

The last Christmas I spent with Ellie, three years ago, we exchanged presents after lunch, both slumped, full and woozy, on the sofa. After I'd given her hers, she passed me an envelope. Things were better between us by then. I'd

236

had time to get used to the idea of her pregnancy and she'd told me a little about Rose's father, Roberto, even shown me his Facebook profile – he looked like a poor man's George Clooney. Handsome, older, married.

I was a little underwhelmed by the envelope. I had worked so hard, on a tight budget, on her presents. I always found it difficult because she wasn't much of a reader but in addition to lots of spoiling treats – cashmere socks, Babygros and a few books for my future niece – I'd managed to nab one of the scans Ellie had shown me on her phone, by emailing it to myself, and had it framed professionally.

Ellie was never much of a crier when we were children – I was always the one who wept, frequently and easily at the injustices of the world, but even when the worst things happened, Ellie would remain dry-eyed and as silent as a stone. That day, though, her hormones must have been wild, because she started weeping afresh at every new present she opened, 'Oh, Fran,' she'd say, opening a beautiful edition of *The Velveteen Rabbit*. 'You shouldn't have.'

'I can't wait to read it to her,' I said.

But that only made her cry even harder.

When she opened the final present – the scan – she was so emotional she could barely look at it. She pushed it back into her box of presents, wiped her eyes and handed me the envelope.

It was a letter from Nationwide about our mortgage.

I could feel Ellie's gaze on my face as I read it. As soon as I finished, I began to read it again. It wasn't a complicated letter but I couldn't believe what it was saying: Ellie had paid off our mortgage all on her own, without my knowing.

'What do you think?' she asked.

'I just don't understand,' I said. 'How you did it so quickly.'

In truth, what I didn't understand was how someone who had given up her job had managed this. She looked at me so eagerly that I tried to mask how worried I felt. Where had all this money come from?

I knew I was naïve about the world Ellie inhabited – cocktail bars and nightclubs; men who splashed out on pretty girls – knew, too, how angry I would make her if I framed my worries in the wrong way.

'Aren't you pleased?'

'Yes, of course,' I said quickly. 'It's just such a lot of money.'

I held off asking where it came from.

'Roberto helped,' she said carelessly, as if it was nothing. 'He's the father of my child, after all.'

'He's not going to live here, is he?'

Ellie laughed sharply. 'No, don't worry about that. He just wants us to be secure.'

She began to tidy up our wrapping paper then, scrunching it into tight little balls and throwing it into the recycling box. I was left with the feeling that our presents had shaken things up between us like flakes in a snowglobe, rendering us indecipherable to each other. Unreadable.

42

I wake early on Christmas Day with the children next door thundering up and down the corridor, exultant. The day yawns before me. 'Happy Christmas,' I say to Branwell and he scowls and begins licking himself furiously.

The first thing I do is drag my laptop to bed and check my email. There's nothing from Ellie. Nothing from anyone except a few emails from companies like Pen Heaven and Marks and Spencer, wishing me a very happy Christmas. I watch one of the Christmas ads a couple of times but it's a story about sisters wearing matching festive jumpers and it makes me feel unspeakably maudlin.

I drag myself out of bed for a long hot bath. I scrub every inch of my skin until it's pink and glowing. And, almost out of habit, I think of Charles and wonder what he'll be doing now. Will he still be in his pyjamas or has he changed into his cords and old jumper with patches at the elbows? Later, Fiona will nag at him to put on something smarter, but for now she'll let him be comfortable.

I ruined everything by crying on him the way I did the other day. It changed the atmosphere as swiftly as turning on the lights would have done – or Fiona arriving home. We'd sat upright on the bed until my sobs subsided, with Charles patting my knee from time to time. He found me tissues and a glass of water, but you could tell, more than anything, he just wanted me to go. I'd thrown away my golden opportunity. Then why, on the train back to London, was my overriding feeling one of relief?

It's not much consolation against today's sadness as I imagine them all together. The children will be in matching tartan pyjamas, one of the adults in a Santa hat. Perhaps Caroline is nursing a coffee, thinking of Dickie; Fiona gives her shoulder a squeeze and returns to scrambling eggs. Caroline should be with *me*, I think, with a sudden flare of anger. I understand what it is to be sad at this time of year; I wouldn't have tried to chivvy her up with crackers and party games. We could have watched *Brief Encounter*, wallowing in what we'd lost.

When I get out of the bath, it's only nine-thirty. It's going to be a long day.

'Were you trying to kill yourself?' the therapist had asked about my dip in the lake.

I'd kept my promise to Fiona and gone to a trial session with the woman she recommended. Out of good will, after Fiona's kindness, but at that price I wasn't sure there would be many more. I liked the therapist, though. She was around Mother's age, sensibly dressed in woollen tights, a corduroy skirt and the sort of flat, stout boots you could climb a mountain in.

'No, it was more of a poetic thing,' I said. And I tried to explain about *The Lady of Shalott*.

'Were you trying to get someone's attention?' she asked.

I shook my head. I thought of Charles, of course, but I didn't want to talk about him. Not to someone who knew Fiona.

'Do you ever think of suicide?' she persisted.

'Yes,' I replied bleakly. 'I *think* of it. I think of a lot of things I wouldn't do.'

I told her a story I'd heard once about a woman who jumped off the Monument to end it all, but whose crinoline skirts slowed her fall like a parachute so she landed alive on top of a carriage. 'I imagine she thanked the gods and rethought her decision,' I said. 'And then, of course, she fell off the carriage and was trampled by horse's hooves.'

'What do you take from this?' she asked gently.

You wouldn't say she was someone who could just appreciate a story for the sake of a story.

'Don't jump off the Monument?' I suggested. 'Or any building marking a tragedy. It's in very bad taste – do you know some people say more died jumping or falling off the Monument than in the Great Fire of London?'

'Or that it's worth staying alive because you never know what's going to happen next.'

'Or that,' I conceded.

Still, later, I find myself staring at the black water of the Serpentine. I don't have to push myself too hard to wonder at the woman's state of mind before she jumped. This time, Charles wouldn't be here to pull me back in. You

241

must have something to live for, I always say at the shop, and I have always had Charles, but on a day like today when everyone you love is so far away, when the sky is so white and heavy it almost touches the ground and the water is dark and magnetic, you do wonder. Maybe when I've gone to the police, I'll feel better. Perhaps Caroline will forgive me, perhaps this black cloud of despair will shift.

When I get back, the dealer is sitting out in the communal garden with one of his buddies, a small toothless man wearing a Father Christmas hat. The dealer's dog, jaunty in a tinsel collar, runs over to sniff my feet.

'Happy Christmas, Franny!' says the dealer.

'Happy Christmas to you,' I reply, glad I've been able to say the words, in person, to someone today.

'Want one of these?' He waves a spliff at me.

I look at it – I've only smoked once or twice before, and never marijuana. Tobacco tends to make me cough – I've never really seen the point of it, but today, well, I *do* see the point – or, at least, I see the point of doing something different.

'Why not?' I say. 'What do I owe you?'

'Nah.' He looks affronted. 'I wouldn't charge today. Anyway'—he grins—'it so happens I've come into some money.'

In the flat, as I smoke, Branwell adopts the body language of a judgemental prefect. He essentially folds his arms in a goody-goody manner and gives me a look as if to say, 'Let's see how this pans out.'

As it happens, it pans out rather well. I realise I'm not the first person to discover this, but Christmas is vastly improved by being mildly out of it. Perhaps everything is better when you're stoned. I can't believe I've missed out on this pleasure for so long. I chuckle my way through *Christmas in Connecticut* – and then turn my attention to the food. Ah, the food! I heat up my turkey-for-one and gobble it down, and then I eat Ellie's salmon because she hasn't answered any of my messages, so why not? Then I start on a few of the treats I got for Rose, like pigs-in-blankets – I bet they don't have those in France.

The only thing I don't bother with is the Christmas pudding because I can't face the palaver of lighting it on my own. It does make you realise, doing it like this, how much of Christmas is performance. I can suit myself. It's liberating.

I sit spooning Ellie's brandy butter straight from the pot, thinking, *Take that, SIS. I'm having a wonderful time without you. Wonderful!*

I consider catching the Queen's speech but decide against it and switch over to watch *HMS Pinafore* instead and, before long, find myself leaping around the room singing along with Little Buttercup.

Look at me, I taunt Ellie in my head. *I couldn't do this with you here. I'm actually having a lovely time.*

The neighbour on my right bangs loudly on the wall and then my phone rings. *Ellie,* I think. *Charles. Ellie. Ellie. Ellie.*

I dive for the phone while desperately trying to mute *Pinafore* at the same time.

'Fran?'

It's Meilin, I realise, my chest sharp with disappointment.

'Have you seen?'

'Seen what?'

'The news?'

'No, I was having a bit of a jolly to *Pinafore*.'

'You'd better turn over now.' Her voice is quiet and serious.

My stomach drops. 'Is it Ellie?'

The picture on the television comes into focus. It's a picture of Tom Bates under the headline 'Brit found dead'.

'It's Tom,' says Meilin. 'He drowned.'

I sink into my armchair. What I can feel pulsing through my veins – though I mustn't say it – is relief.

It's not Ellie. Just Tom Bates. Horrible Tom Bates. Whose face made me feel so sick that I scratched it out of my team photo.

'How dreadful,' I say at last. 'His poor family.'

'It's awful, isn't it?' says Meilin.

'Yes, awful,' I parrot, trying to work out what they're saying on the news. There's a reporter on a bridge, a river stretching behind her.

'It's just . . .' She hesitates. 'They're not sure if it was an accident . . .'

She's holding something back. It's irritating – that and not being able to make out what the anchor is saying. My head is still foggy. I'm trying to play catch-up. The bridge on the television is as pretty as a postcard. The reporter points at padlocks latched to the railings behind her. They're scrawled with love notes – *Carol* ♥ *Colin*; *N & J 4Ever* – those sorts of things.

I realise where I've seen padlocks like that before – on Ellie's Facebook page when she first got to Paris. That's what Meilin is not saying. Why she sounds so strange. Tom has died in France. Where Ellie is.

The screen has changed again now; the camera is panning over the river. 'Drowned in the Seine,' a new headline reads.

I remember then, with appalling clarity, Dickie's face as he glanced over his shoulder before he fell. As if he'd spotted someone he'd once loved. Someone he'd hurt.

'First Dickie and now him,' I say. My voice sounds strange and formal. I barely recognise it. 'What a terrible coincidence.'

43

Like Dickie, Tom had been drinking. He was last seen alive in the small hours of Christmas Eve in a bar in the Marais, a trendy district by the river, the news reports inform me. He left alone and staggered back to his hotel in a bad state, but never made it. Yesterday a family on a festive stroll spotted his body floating in the water.

Tom and Dickie both fell to their deaths. I wonder if Tom's fall took him by surprise. A hand to the chest propelling him into the icy river. I wonder how long it took; if he died with his eyes open. Perhaps he was forced to look at himself and what he'd done.

I need to speak to Ellie. It's the only thing that will calm my racing heart. No matter what happened between us, I need my sister to reassure me she's still in Tignes. That she's nowhere near Paris. That she and Rose are safe. I don't have her number but I look up her apartment block on the internet and find a phone number for the concierge team there. I dial it immediately. A harried-sounding woman picks up, and my GCSE French abandons me.

'Ellie Knight?' I say desperately. 'Can I speak to her?'

I don't catch what she says in reply and, after repeating it several times, she hangs up.

I message Ellie instead. Have you seen the news about Tom Bates? I need to talk to you immediately, Ellie. Please.

I am begging now. It's too clear in my mind, too easy to imagine: Ellie in the corner of a bar, having dyed her hair, perhaps, or wearing a wig, or maybe just doing the kind of thing I used to when I followed Charles – a hat pulled down low, a scarf around her face. Maybe she didn't have to make much of an effort to disguise herself because Tom wasn't looking for women our age.

Did she watch as Tom poured beer after beer down his thick throat? See the way he approached those young girls with a teasing touch, a clammy hand? Did she pick up something sharp then just to see what it felt like?

After messaging her, I stare at the screen for a long time, my fists clenched, panic a fluttering bird in my chest.

I call Charles and then try Caroline. Neither picks up. I glance at the clock – it's just past four – they'll be sitting down for Christmas lunch. I imagine them in the dining room with wine-red walls or, less formally, in the conservatory overlooking the lake. Cracker hats and candlelight. I think of something catching fire – a paper hat, a lock of Fiona's hair – how it could all go up in flames. Their safe cosy haven. I wish them ill, I realise. It frightens me when my mind turns this way.

Next, I try Meilin. I don't know what else to do. I

need to speak to someone. I can't be left with these thoughts alone. She's a little breathless when she answers.

'I'm scared,' I say. 'Sorry, I didn't know who to tell. It's too much.'

'It's OK,' she says. 'It will be OK.'

The words remind me of Mother, sitting by my bed stroking my hair when I'd got myself in a state.

'I'm sorry I blamed you for telling Caroline.' My words spill out quickly, nervously. 'If you say you didn't, I believe you.'

'I didn't,' she assures me. 'Like I said before.'

'I've got a lot of things wrong.'

'Well,' Meilin sighs, 'to err is human.'

'Ellie could be the one who told Caroline,' I say. 'I thought of that later. She knew I was there.'

Meilin pauses for a long time. 'Are you sure she wasn't there herself?'

'Of course not,' I snap. 'What are you saying?'

But I know what she's saying. There it is again: the flash of white-blonde curls I saw on the platform. She could have been there; it could have been her.

'It's a strange coincidence – both of them dying like that, so close together; you said it yourself.' Meilin sounds weary.

For a long time, I stare into my lap. For all her steeliness and athleticism, Ellie is a tender person: gentle, empathetic. The idea of her pushing people to their deaths is fantastical. Ridiculous. But, and this is the only thought that catches me in its grip, Dickie Graham and Tom Bates weren't just people.

'Would it be possible,' I begin, 'I mean I know it's a

248

big ask, but could I come to yours? I don't want to be alone.'

She pauses. 'You can't, I'm sorry.' Her voice is warm but firm. 'I have someone here.'

'Oh.'

Her colleague, of course. Even Meilin has someone to spend Christmas with.

'Let's talk tomorrow,' she says.

'Please don't say anything to anyone about Ellie. Not yet.'

'I wouldn't,' she says reproachfully. 'But, Fran, you really should get hold of her.'

After she's hung up, I decide I need some fresh air to clear my head. A walk around the block. I fetch my coat and open the door and the rush of air disturbs a light dusting of white powder just outside, where the mat would be if I had one: icing sugar with a footprint in the centre.

44

This time, though, the sight doesn't make me feel loved. It makes me feel uneasy. It makes me feel frightened. I tiptoe to the staircase as if I might disturb the air somehow. There's only one person who knows about the Father Christmas footprint.

'Ellie,' I call down the empty steps. 'Was that you?'

But when I hear the words echo down the stairs, I feel vulnerable and foolish, as if she – if indeed it is her – is taunting me. I return to the safety of the flat and stand in the hallway for a few moments, unsure what to do with myself. Then, almost without thinking, I find myself climbing upstairs to Ellie's room and doing something I've never done before: I get into her bed and pull the covers up to my chin. I stare at the pattern of the dark sky through her Velux window and concentrate very hard on sending a message to Ellie: *Stop hiding, come home.*

I realise I've never had a firm grip on where she is – that I've never quite been able to keep up with her, ever since we were children. She was always a faster runner, a stronger swimmer, better at hiding.

I close my eyes and think.

Perhaps Tom drank until the others in the bar began to shift away from him – the women, with imperceptible movements, nudging away from his touch, the men rolling their eyes.

Perhaps it was then he felt he'd outstayed his welcome, that he decided to go back to his hotel. And Ellie, hiding in the corner of the bar, followed him out into the night.

Perhaps it didn't take much as he staggered across the bridge, unwitting, unknowing. Two hands to his chest. A sharp push. Him squirming in the water, her staring down at him, unsmiling. A reversal of the last time.

Perhaps, I think, lying in her bed, shivering with cold, even though I'm under the duvet, if I'd known what she was going to do – that that was her plan all along – I would have done it with her.

Ellie only told me once. It was almost a year after we left Chesterfield. I was miserable. We both were. I'd been finishing my A-levels in a sixth-form college, where the set texts were different and no one talked to me. Withdrawing into myself, I didn't speak, unless I had to, for the rest of the year.

Ellie didn't say much, either. She had begun speaking again in our last days at Chesterfield after weeks of silence, but she kept her words to a minimum. She'd started dancing – something Mother was pleased about – taking classes in the evening, working in a coffee shop during the day. Though Mother home-schooled her for a while, she failed her GCSEs and didn't want to take her studies any further.

Our mother never got over what happened to Ellie at school. I caught her looking at my sister in a different way in the years afterwards: watchful, attentive. In her last night with us, when I woke in my chair beside her bed to hear her ragged breath in the darkness, Mother gripped my hand. I wanted to get Ellie – I'd promised I'd wake her if there was any change – but before I did, Mother said in a weak voice, 'You must look after your sister.' I said to her I did, that I always would, but Mother wouldn't let go of my hand. 'You must promise,' she said. 'She's not as strong as she seems.' It was only after I'd reassured her a couple of times that she let me stand up and fetch Ellie.

She never stopped worrying it might happen again. After Chesterfield, she made us attend a self-defence course taught by a short, bald man with a background in martial arts and a curiously calm demeanour for a person who spent most of his working day fighting. Ever since that class, I've looked at the world differently: keeping my eye out for items that could be used as weapons. A glass; a lamp; on one occasion, on the night bus home, when the driver was acting strangely and I was the sole passenger, one of those hammers strapped to the wall for breaking through the window. A tiny, bright orange thing, which looked like it could do some damage. If it came to it.

'Do you know why women are so easy to overpower?' he asked us once.

'Because we're not as fucking strong,' Ellie said.

252

He overlooked her expletive with a benign smile. 'Well, there is that,' he said, 'but, also, when you fight, you don't fight to kill.'

One white winter morning, Ellie had climbed into bed with me and started talking. She must have guessed I was full of questions I'd never ask. That all I'd known was that Charles had carried her from the swimming pool, dripping wet, wrapped in a towel, to the staffroom in the boarding house.

Mother and Mrs Morgan closed the door, while Dickie hovered outside for a while. When I asked him what had happened he told me to fuck off with such vehemence I knew to leave it alone.

I sat outside the staffroom pretending to read a book. After an hour or so, Mother came out and told me to go to bed. Her face was puffy from crying.

'I don't know what Dickie had planned,' Ellie said to me in bed that day. 'I don't imagine it was purely innocent fun. Maybe he was going to sneak up on me while I was swimming or showering.'

He'd never forgiven her for what had happened after the rugby match – and she'd given up trying to persuade him it had been nothing to do with her. Anyway, somewhere along the line, Dickie had mentioned his idea for revenge to Tom, perhaps forgetting, or unaware of, Tom's role in Dickie's debagging. The boys were always quicker to overlook each other's crimes than those of the girls.

I think of Ellie swimming her lengths, goggles on, the sounds of the world beyond the pool muffled by her movement in the water, her immersion in her task. I've heard it said that that single-mindedness is a masculine trait, that women are better at multitasking, juggling, spreading their focus – but when I recall the way Ellie trained, I'm not so sure.

Suddenly, a shadow fell across the water and she knew she wasn't alone. She found her footing in the shallow end and saw Dickie and Tom were by the side of the pool, fully clothed. She scowled at them and said, 'What are you doing?'

Dickie made a quip like, 'We've come to rub you down.' Something stupid like that. But while she was talking to Dickie, she kept an eye on Tom. He was so quiet you could never tell what he was thinking.

At first, when Tom stooped to unlace his shoes, Dickie started making jeering noises, 'Ohh, look out, Tom's coming to join you.' That sort of thing.

Ellie didn't like it. She should have just hauled herself out then, but she wasn't thinking straight. She turned back and began to swim into the deep end. All the time, Dickie was dancing around on the side, 'like a prick', Ellie said, while Tom stripped methodically. He already had his swimming trunks on underneath.

Ellie was a fast swimmer – and because of her training she had a pretty good idea of how long it would take her to get to the steps in the deep end and, from there, out of the pool.

'I almost made it,' she said, the time she told me, her voice catching on the words. 'But Tom headed me off by running along the side and jumping in.'

She felt his hand on her foot, like he was catching her in a game of tag. Dickie was still yelping and jeering at the side of the pool. Ellie darted away from Tom the first

254

time, but the second time, just as she was in reaching distance of the steps, he got a firmer grip.

We'd all sometimes play-fight in the swimming pool, but this wasn't that, said Ellie. Tom held her down until she thought her lungs were going to explode. Dickie's noises changed from jeering, to bartering, to fear. She lost her goggles, the chlorine stung her eyes; at first there was the blue of the swimming pool, and then there was the yellow of the burning, and then it went black and she lost all sense of orientation, which way she was facing, whereabouts in the pool she was, even whether she was conscious or not. When the world went white, she felt certain she was going to die. And when you think you're going to die, she said, you'll do anything you can to survive. So she stopped fighting, and Tom let her breathe again, and he did what he wanted.

45

It doesn't take long for the world to start joining the dots. By Boxing Day, someone has spotted that Dickie and Tom were in the same year at Chesterfield. It begins as a sentence or so at the end of a story online, but, as the day progresses, the excitement begins to blossom and spread: one publication unearths an old team photograph – the same one as I have, though in this one Dickie's and Tom's faces are still intact, their eyes bright at the sight of Juliet's red bra behind the cameraman. Another paper mentions a 'Chesterfield curse'; a third links 'TV personality Jules Bentley' to the boys.

The first thing I do, after a terrible night's sleep, is switch on my laptop and check for messages from Ellie.

There's nothing – no email, nothing on Facebook, no change. But on my phone I have five missed calls. Three are from Charles and a couple are from a number I don't recognise. There's an answerphone message from Charles and one from Juliet.

'Fran, it's Jules. I got your number from Charles. I can't believe it about Tom. I need to talk to you. Will you call me?'

She sounds frightened, but I can't deal with Juliet now. I delete it and call Charles instead.

'Fran,' he says in a low, urgent voice. 'I got your message; I saw the news.'

'The papers know,' I say. 'That Dickie and Tom were at school together.'

'I'm afraid it's all going to come out,' he says.

'No.' I stop pacing and sink into the sofa. The thought makes me sick: that Ellie's private anguish might be shared with the world.

'We can't stop it,' he says. 'It's already happening.'

For a ridiculous moment, his words remind me of a disaster movie. I imagine snow gathered in clouds at the top of a mountain the moment before an avalanche begins.

'Fran,' he says. 'Where's Ellie? It's been such a long time since we saw her.'

'Tignes,' I say. 'Last time I heard. Not Paris.'

I think of the icing sugar on my doorstep last night; I don't know if it'll complicate things, but it might show Ellie was here.

'OK,' he says. 'If you're sure.'

A voice in my head says over and over: *I don't know, I don't know, I don't know.* It's so loud I'm surprised Charles can't hear it.

'It's not as if she would . . .' I whisper.

'Yes, I know,' he says. 'It just helps. That she's in a different place. That she wasn't in Paris.'

He's being polite, careful with my feelings. Neither of

us points out that it wouldn't have been a difficult journey for her to make. A child's scream breaks the silence between us. I wonder if it's Daisy.

'Fran,' he whispers. 'Are you still planning to go to the police?'

I swallow. There's a small tear in the arm of the sofa and I begin to pull at the stuffing. It comes out in easy clumps and I wonder why I haven't done this before. How simple it is to tear it apart in this way. 'No,' I say quietly. 'Let's wait. Like you said.'

I can't say it to Charles, but I'm sure he can guess: if Ellie is involved, there is no way I'm speaking to anyone official. Not voluntarily.

'I'm just worried,' he says apologetically. 'Caroline is too. We all are.'

'Is she still with you?'

'Yup.'

'Is she OK?'

He's quiet for a moment. 'She's shocked.'

I can imagine what Caroline is thinking: if it looks like Ellie could have killed Tom – if that's something they've all been discussing – then there's a chance she could have killed Dickie too. One violent death could be an accident. But not two.

I know that must be what's going through her mind, because it's spinning around mine like a record and I don't know how to stop it.

46

The story is everywhere the next day. Tom's and Dickie's faces, side by side like mugshots, peer from the front pages of the papers. I pick up one from the newsstand at Sloane Square and skim-read the piece, shivering. Like the other stories I've read, the article links Dickie and Tom to Chesterfield – the same year, both in the First XV – and summarises how they died in unexplained accidents within weeks of each other. The piece focuses on the prestige of Chesterfield; how much the fees cost – they always mention that; before referring, more tentatively, to a historic sexual assault case at the school. I stop for a moment. I can't read on.

'Are you going to buy that?' asks the man at the stand.

The world continues to move as usual. Resentful commuters on their way to work grip their coffee cups, faces sallow and hungover or determinedly cheery, still wearing Christmas jumpers, twinkling earrings, the odd

Santa hat. I think I can smell chlorine. It's filling my nostrils, burning my sinuses.

I ignore him for a few moments more. My eyes return to the story and I see, with relief, they're unable to name the victim in the sexual assault. She's protected by anonymity. At least for now. The detail in the story is shocking, though. Only someone well acquainted with Chesterfield could have shared that kind of information – the terrible bruising on Ellie's arms, her silence after the attack. Who's been talking to the papers?

'Actually,' I say in the end, 'can I buy them all?'

It starts to drizzle as I walk up the Kings Road. The pile of newspapers becomes soggy and heavy with rain. I don't know what I'm going to do with them. When I get to work, I'm still carrying them as I walk into the staffroom.

'Fran.' Gareth looks up from making a coffee. 'What's all this?'

The sudden heat of the room and the weight in my arms become too much for me. The floor leaps up and hits me in the face. As I fall, the papers don't scatter in the way they might if they were dry but drop in sticky clumps around me.

Gareth picks one up and looks at the front page.

The tears, when they start, are hot and unstoppable. I don't even bother to climb to my feet but remain weeping on the floor. Gareth comes to sit next to me. 'This is your old school, isn't it?' he asks.

I nod.

'Was it you?' he asks. 'The girl in the pool?'

'No,' I say quietly.

260

'Ellie.' It's not a question.

Gareth and Ellie met once or twice when we were together. Despite how different they were, they always liked each other.

'What a terrible thing to happen,' he says. 'No wonder she ran away from everything.' He gives my hand a squeeze. 'Where is she now?'

I blink the tears away. 'France,' I say. 'They're implying she did it. But she would never . . .' I can't finish the sentence.

Gareth returns to the paper and reads a bit more. 'I don't think they are at the moment,' he says thoughtfully. 'It's true they're making links between the stories but they don't have much. Just two disparate incidents in different parts of the world and a historic case they can't say much about. It could be nothing but a weird coincidence.'

My fingers uncurl. I feel calmer than I have in the forty-eight hours since I heard the news. 'Are you sure?'

'There's no proof. You can't go round calling people murderers without proof.'

The solidity of his body is a comfort against mine.

'It's just that people from school reckon it looks bad for Ellie.'

Gareth gets to his feet. 'Think about it logically: unless there's anything linking her to either crime scene – it's just a story. An idea, really,' he says. 'It'll die down. It's Christmas – they're looking for things to fill the pages.' He gathers up the pile of papers. 'I'm going to take these out to recycling and then let's have a cup of tea.'

I pick myself up off the floor, put the kettle on and wash my face. When I come back, Gareth has made our drinks and we sit on the tired old sofa in the staffroom, staring at the noticeboard opposite.

'It was really awful what they did to your sister,' Gareth says, after a couple of minutes.

'Yes.'

'Your school sounds like poison.'

'It wasn't all bad.' I think of Mrs Fyson, Meilin, Charles. 'There were good things, wonderful opportunities. People who were really on my side.'

I remember Charles, then, cradling Ellie's dripping body as he carried her into the staffroom, his face sheet white, how he could barely look at Dickie. Things might have been strange between us recently, but I'm so grateful for his kindness, his constancy.

Gareth gets to his feet, drains the last of his tea. 'Are you sure you'll be all right to work today?'

'Yes. I can't be on my own at the moment.'

'Let's find you a job where you won't have to talk to anyone,' he says.

First, I sticker up a pile of books for the sales table, then Gareth hands me a list of returns to find from the shelves. I get on with my tasks as calmly as I can. I'm interrupted from time to time by the odd customer, but, on the whole, it's a quiet day. The work soothes me. I come round to thinking the situation is not so bad, after all. Perhaps all I need is to speak to Ellie. Just to hear my sister's voice, for her to reassure me. I'll try to call her again tonight.

Mid-thought, a tap on my shoulder makes me turn round.

'Are you Francesca Knight?'

262

The woman in front of me is very slim and sleekly fashionable – dark wool dress, nail varnish the colour of dried blood.

'Yes.'

'I'm from *The National*,' she says. 'I'd like to speak to you about your sister, Ellie. About what happened to her at school.'

I hug the book to my chest.

'As I'm sure you know, there's lots of interest in the current climate, about this kind of toxicity in famous institutions. Sexual assault at university, in parliament, our schools.'

'How did you know it was her?' I say in a small voice. 'Isn't it against the law? To identify her?'

'We wouldn't have to,' she says smoothly. I notice she's ignored my first question. 'There are different ways of doing things: for example, she could speak off the record. Lots of women did to the *New York Times* about Weinstein.'

I shake my head. It doesn't feel real. I remember the kinds of comments I've seen online. Some of the things old pupils have already said on Facebook. It wouldn't take any time to identify her.

'Why would she relive the worst experience of her life?'

'I know it's a lot to think about,' she says. 'But she might find it frees her to tell her story.' She lowers her voice. 'I know what it's like – this sort of attack. I've been through something similar. These men need to be brought to account.'

'I don't know.' I think of all those damp newspapers Gareth dumped earlier, of what further exposure might do to Ellie. To Caroline. 'I'm pretty sure she won't want to talk.'

'But will you ask her for me?'

'I don't know,' I say again.

'Think about it,' she says. 'Talk it through with her.'

She passes me her card and, just as I'm taking it in my sweaty hand, Gareth appears by my side.

'What's going on here?'

'I was just asking Francesca about her sister.'

'Please don't pester my staff on the shop floor.'

The journalist looks contrite. 'Well, you've got my details. Pass them on to Ellie, if she wants a sympathetic ear. She lives in France now, doesn't she?'

'That's right,' I say. 'Well, she moves around, but she was in London on Christmas Day.'

I blush as the words come out. Gareth glances at me.

'Oh.' She slows down. 'I hadn't realised. She was with you?'

'Not all day.' My cheeks flush again. 'But she popped by.'

'Interesting,' she says, before making her way out of the shop with Gareth following a few steps behind to ensure she's gone.

'Is that true?' Gareth checks when he returns to me. 'That Ellie was in London?'

Glancing down at the stack of books on the counter, I manage to avoid his gaze. 'I didn't see her,' I say quietly. 'But she left a present for me on the day.'

I don't mention that the present was a footprint in a smattering of icing sugar. That I'm not sure if it was a greeting – or a warning.

47

It's a relief when it's time to leave work. To have a break from Gareth's eyes on my face – worried and, on occasion, suspicious. As if he's trying to work me out. The wind is bitter and I pull up the collar of my coat and wrap my scarf around me tightly. The door of a neighbouring restaurant swings open and the smell of Italian food sweeps out. I've never gone in – the food is overpriced and it's not a place for dining alone. It's cosy, with small tables, soft lighting: the kind of place you go with someone you're intimate with, where they could lay a hand on the small of your back and no one would know any better.

As I pass, I catch a glimpse of the journalist who came into the shop earlier. Kat is the name on her card. Her face is sympathetic as she listens to the person opposite her. Someone elegant, with long dark hair, whose earrings – a pair of tiny jewelled skulls – catch the light as she speaks, whose long, thin fingers tap on the table. Whose right wrist is striped by old scars. I take a couple of steps closer to check, though I already know.

It's Juliet.

I walk away, with my chin tucked into my chest. Thoughts occur to me thick and fast. The insider details in the story about Ellie – they must have come from Juliet. But *why*? I ask myself as I pace to the tube – what did she stand to gain from talking? I step off the pavement without looking and a sharp car horn makes me step back in fright. Shivering, I hold myself together, clutching my bag so tightly the strain of it hurts my arms.

Juliet never had any compunction about sharing other people's secrets, I remind myself. They were currency to her. I don't know why I'm still shocked by her after all these years, but I am. Her final act of cruelty was something I could barely think about. Something I kept wrapped up tightly, pushed away into a dark corner.

I didn't pick up the signs in my last English class at Chesterfield. Everybody was very quiet when Mrs Fyson came in. Unnaturally quiet. Expectant, you could say. As it was the last lesson of the Easter term, Mrs Fyson had said we could bring any book we chose to read out a favourite passage.

'Who wants to go next?' she asked.

Juliet's hand shot up. It was most unlike her.

'Juliet, what would you like to read?' asked Mrs Fyson.

'It's a creative piece,' she said.

'OK,' said Mrs Fyson, sounding confused.

On the one hand, she seemed pleased that Juliet had

written something of her own. On the other, quite rightly as it turned out, you could tell she had her doubts about the endeavour.

Charles, who had been slumped over his desk, raised his head and glanced over at Juliet, who was sitting, as always, by the window. I was in my usual place in front of her. I don't know why none of us had moved over the years, as we progressed from GCSEs to A-levels. It was just the pattern of things. The same group of people, the same seats.

'Today he left his jumper behind in English,' Juliet began. 'It gave me a little thrill. I loitered behind at the end of the lesson and picked it up on the pretence of returning it to him. I don't think he remembered where he left it. Another item for my Charles collection.'

Those were *my* words. From my journal. Where had she got it? The panic was heavy, pulling me down into my seat, the heat of it staining my face like ink.

I stared down at my desk as if it could tell me what to do.

Leave, Fran, I thought. *Get up. Go.*

Mrs Fyson frowned. 'What is this?'

'I suppose you'd call it a love letter,' Juliet replied innocently. She didn't pause for long. 'I wore it in bed that night after Lights Out,' she continued. 'It still smelled of him. I wrapped my arms around myself and pretended it was Charles Fry holding me.'

The class started to titter. Perhaps because of my burning complexion, a couple of people began to glance from Juliet to me.

Charles hissed: 'For fuck's sake. Stop.'

'Yes, Juliet,' Mrs Fyson agreed, forgetting to upbraid him for his language. 'That's quite enough of that.'

Juliet got to her feet, raising her voice. 'I have no experience of physical passions, but in his strong arms I would be as Jane Eyre to his Mr Rochester. I would melt like ice at his manly touch.'

I knew what was coming next, knew, too, that I had to stop it. Without thinking, I was on my feet, launching myself at my precious journal. In the intervening scuffle, Juliet somehow managed to carry on, shrieking: 'I, Francesca Knight, would sacrifice my virginity for such a love.' She held the book away from me. 'But it must be a meeting of spirits as well as bodies.'

She was taller than me, so she had the advantage, stretching the book high above her head so she could continue with this definitive performance – a way of keeping Charles's eyes on her, as usual. At a time when he'd started to pull away.

It's true that in that moment, when the red mist took over, I didn't care what happened to either of us. I saw nothing but my journal, my determination to get it back, to keep my secrets safe. But I didn't make her do it. It was still an accident.

I leapt for the book and she whipped it away from me without looking at what she was doing. There was a terrible sound as she punched her hand, holding my journal, through the window next to her. Shattering the glass. Slashing her wrist. There was a moment of quiet before the classroom erupted. As if we were all waiting for some silent instruction on what to do next.

Juliet looked down at the blood pulsating from her

wrist and made an unholy noise; Mrs Fyson scrabble
the drawers of her desk, crying out for a first aid kit,
looked to Charles in panic, but Charles had frozen in
horror.

Meilin was the first to reach Juliet, grabbing a wad of
tissues from Mrs Fyson's desk and pressing it hard against
the wound to staunch the flow. 'Fran,' she said. 'Find
help.'

I ran out of the classroom, without looking back. Blood
still spattered on my shirt.

48

Dark thoughts pursue me all the way back to my front door, where Branwell is waiting. In the corridor there's a familiar scent: I can't place it but it's as if someone has been waiting here, has only just left. I let Branwell in and begin to run a hot bath. I don't seem to be able to stop shivering. While it's running, I try the number for Ellie's apartment block again, listening to the phone ring and ring. I try to picture where it might be: in the concierge's office perhaps – on a desk littered with paper, next to a brimming ashtray. Or ringing in an empty corridor – I imagine Madame, an older woman in court shoes, coming to pick it up, to fetch my sister. But nobody does.

In the tub, I lean back and close my eyes. I don't want to think about Juliet but my mind is tugged back to that dreadful night when I was waiting for Ellie outside the staffroom. After Mother told me to go to bed, I couldn't help myself, I went to Juliet's room. When she answered the door, her eyes were pink as a mouse's. Guilt, I thought. The boys shouldn't have had access to the sports hall; they shouldn't have been able to get through to the pool. Ellie knew the key code as a special privilege, because of her training, but the only other student who would have known it was our athletics prefect. The person I'd caught messing around in the changing rooms with Charles. Putting on the kind of show she hoped someone would see.

There was a strange atmosphere in the boarding house that night. Girls whispered as they got ready for bed, between brushing their teeth, washing their faces, but there was no giggling, no music. Or is that my memory playing tricks on me? Is that just how it felt?

In the staffroom, there was a conversation about whether Ellie should see a doctor, if the police should be called. My mother won the first battle, but lost the second. No police, said Mrs Morgan. Their friendship was never the same after that.

The boys were suspended, but they were allowed to sit their A-levels the following term. By then, the three of us were long gone. We wanted a fresh start and stayed at first with Mother's aunt in London, before finding the flat on the estate.

That day, when I went to Juliet's room, it occurred to me that, for the first time in my life, I didn't feel scared of her.

'How did the boys get into the swimming pool?' I asked.

'Fuck off, Fran,' she said, slamming the door in my face. 'You don't know anything about it.'

271

She was quick, but I was quicker. I put my foot in the door. 'What did Dickie do to Ellie?'

'Please go away,' Juliet said. She started to snivel again. I just watched her.

I didn't understand what had happened to Ellie, but I knew from the way Mother had sent me away that it was something unusually bad, with the power to make grown-ups cry.

'You don't understand,' said Juliet. 'The pressure that comes with . . .' She shook her head and managed to push me away, slamming the door.

She never said what the pressure came with, so I was left to guess what she meant: her beauty? Going out with Charles? I wasn't sure, but it was the first glimpse I had of another Juliet. One with an inner life of her own. Regrets, perhaps.

In the weeks between the assault and the end of term, Charles and Ellie grew closer. He started to visit her in Mother's room. He was the only one she'd see, apart from Mother and me. I think that's when their friendship began to take root, and Juliet didn't like it. By our final English lesson, a few weeks later, she'd recovered sufficiently to exact her revenge.

Lying back in the bath, I dip my head under water, comforted by the heat of it. My mind flickers back to Juliet standing next to Tom on the night of the auction. The pair of them watching as our taxi pulled away. Was that an alliance between them as I had thought, or something else?

And was Juliet talking to the journalist purely out of

malice? Even for her, I found that hard to get my head around. I thought of her fingertips tapping nervously on the table. The voicemail I'd never answered.

After Dickie and Tom, was Juliet frightened she might be next?

Beneath the water, the world sounds different – the whir of the washing machine, the footsteps of the children next door. I hear knocking but I can't tell where it's coming from in the building or how long it has been going on for.

It stops for a moment and I imagine a neighbour answering the door, throwing their arms around a loved one – a relative, an old friend. It's a bittersweet thought. Then the knocking starts again. I sit up in the bath and listen more closely. It's coming from my door.

Ellie, I think. *Is it possible?*

I leap out of the bath and dry myself hastily, throwing on the clothes heaped on the bathroom floor. What shall I say? How should I greet her?

'Hello?' I call through the door. 'Ellie?'

'It's not Ellie,' says a crisp voice from the other side. 'It's Kat. The journalist. We met earlier today at the shop.'

Kicking myself for not being more cautious, I open the door carefully, keeping the chain on. 'How did you find out where I live?' I say. 'Was it Juliet?'

'It's my job to find things out,' she says with a sly smile. 'Would it be possible for me to come in? I'd really like to talk to you some more.'

I don't make any move to take the chain off.

'I think it's in your interest to speak to me.' She is less deferential in private, I notice. Away from the arena of the shop floor. She pauses, as if weighing up whether to say more. 'Juliet has told me a lot – including some pretty strange things about you,' she continues quietly through the gap in the door. 'About your temper, for example. And the fact you were there, on the scene, when Dickie Graham died.'

She says those last words lightly but the impact of them is like being punched in the chest.

I have always known it might come to this, since the night it happened when I paced the streets on my way home, rehearsing my explanation. I have always known someone might come to my door and ask: *Why were you there?*

It felt inevitable, but I didn't imagine it like this. I thought it might be a pair of policemen with buzzing walkie-talkies and handcuffs – not a slight journalist carrying a reporter's notebook. The pen is mightier than the sword, though. I should know that.

'You'd better come in,' I say, and lead her through to the front room.

I don't want her standing on the doorstep, where the neighbours might be able to hear.

The flat has a neglected air – sticky crumbs on the counter, a sofa covered with Branwell's hair. It's not how I'd want her to see the place. From nerves more than anything I grab a cloth and make a last-ditch attempt to wipe the surfaces down, but she seems most interested in the globe in the corner, my *1,000 Places* book next to it and the framed photograph of Ellie and Mother in Whitby.

'The night Dickie died,' I begin, trying to call to mind

the speech I'd rehearsed all those weeks ago, but the words evaporate like smoke. I turn to her with a cloth in my hand. 'It was a coincidence,' I say inanely. 'Merely a coincidence.'

'It's a strange coincidence to be there when someone you hate is killed,' she says softly. 'I've heard how you felt about Dickie.' She is quiet for a moment. 'I don't blame you – I know what that feels like.'

I stare at her, wondering what else she knows about Dickie's death. The women on the platform, Dickie's glance over his shoulder: does she have any idea?

'None of this looks good for you and your sister,' she says in an oily voice. 'But I'm on your side, believe me. I want to help – and the best thing would be for you to talk to me. Both of you. You mentioned she was with you for Christmas, for example. I'd like to hear more about that.' She glances down at her notepad. 'You should make that information public, don't you think?'

Folding my arms, I glance over at the globe – the piece of Blu Tack that follows Ellie around the world. Two things occur to me. The first is that I need to make this woman go away. I need her out of my flat, so I have space to work out what to do.

The second is that, above everything else, I must get hold of my sister and find out what she knows.

Or what she did.

'Look,' she says, pushing harder, misinterpreting my silence, 'either way, I'm going to do this story. About the abuse at Chesterfield. With or without your help. But I think it would be much better if you and your sister were part of it.'

'I'll speak to Ellie,' I hear myself saying, 'and we'll talk to you together. You're right – we need to tell this story.'

What we really need is to clear our names. She knows it and I know it, but if this is what it takes to make it all go away . . .

'You promise?' she says. 'You still have my card?'

I nod. 'I'll get in touch with her immediately.'

49

As soon as she's gone, I call the number for Ellie's apartment again and listen to the phone ring and ring. My heart leaps when someone picks up – the same woman as before, I think – but once again my schoolgirl French abandons me and I'm forced to bellow, 'Can I speak to Ellie Knight?'

'*Qui?*'

'Ellie Knight,' I shout again. '*Une fille anglaise.*'

She says something too quickly for me to grasp and hangs up.

Just as I'm intending to try again, there's another knock at the door. I curse under my breath. Surely the journalist can't be back so soon.

'Fran, it's me,' says a female voice. 'Caroline.'

I open the door and there she is with Daisy in her arms and enough luggage at her feet to give the impression she might be attempting to move in permanently.

'Hi,' she says quietly. 'I think we should talk.'

I'm so grateful to see a friendly face I want to fling my arms around her, but there's something about her bearing that warns me off. She's still unsure about me, still making up her mind. She looks sober, though, and I can't smell alcohol on her in the way I could before. There's no trace of the dark, heavy energy she had when she was drunk – just the sense of someone who is fatigued. Wary.

'Take a seat,' I say over my shoulder. 'I'll make some tea.'

'It's OK,' she says quietly. 'I wanted to talk first.'

She doesn't sit, but props Daisy up on the back of an armchair in the front room, facing her rather than me as she speaks.

'I'm so sorry about what happened to your sister at Chesterfield,' she begins. 'I had no idea.'

I stand with the kettle in my hand.

'When she replied to my email about it,' Caroline continues, 'she made it sound so much more insignificant – like a prank.'

'It was worse than that.' I turn to switch the kettle on.

'Yes.' She pauses. 'I always got the impression from Dickie that it was.'

'He didn't really do anything – it was Tom – Dickie just watched.'

'But to watch and not do anything to stop it,' Caroline says. 'That's as bad in a way, isn't it?'

Looking down at my feet in Mother's slippers, I consider her question, remembering cases in the news – ubiquitous at the moment – in which people did terrible things while everyone else just watched.

And was I any better? I hadn't stopped Dickie and Juliet's bullying at Chesterfield. Or reported my suspicions about how Dickie died. Bad things happened around me all the time and I did nothing to stop them.

'I know you're probably wondering if I think Ellie did it,' Caroline continues, 'if she killed Dickie and then Tom. Or, if it wasn't her, was she behind it somehow?'

I keep quiet, letting her speak.

'But I can't bring myself to believe she did. I spend my days looking out for victims, believing them. And the way Dickie spoke – he always felt so bad about Ellie – it never seemed like he saw her as a threat.'

My breathing changes, slows.

'Charles dropped the gravy when he heard the news,' she says. 'We were clearing the table after lunch and he switched the television on in the kitchen. That's how we found out. Fiona and I were in the dining room with the children and we heard the crash.'

I can picture Charles standing like that, cold gravy congealing on the floor while he stared at the screen.

'I didn't know who Tom was until then.'

It strikes me that she's very keen to make this clear.

'He was at the auction,' I say. 'Sitting on the table next to yours.'

Tom's face as Charles made his bid. The rest of the room smiling, clapping with encouragement, but not Tom. Why was he there after all those years if he and Dickie hadn't stayed in touch? If Caroline had no idea who he was?

'I don't remember,' she says. 'There were so many people that night. Anyway, they told me he was the other

279

boy. That hurt Ellie. When I heard what they did, I threw up in their downstairs loo – I just couldn't believe it; that Dickie could be involved with something like that.'

'Tom was worse.'

Caroline sighs. 'Did Ellie talk about it much?'

'Only once,' I say. 'She didn't like to.'

'That's understandable.'

Daisy kicks her feet against the back of the armchair and her mother moves her to the floor, where she rubs her toy giraffe on the sticky linoleum and then pops it in her mouth.

'There's a woman from *The National* who wants to interview Ellie and me,' I say. 'She knows I was there when Dickie died.' I glance at the floor in shame. 'Juliet has been talking to the press.'

'Why would she do that?'

'I think she's scared.'

'Why?'

'I don't know,' I say. 'That she might be next? Maybe she thinks if she talks it'll protect her somehow. I always suspected that she might have had something to do with it. That she let the boys in.'

Juliet was never quite the same after what happened to Ellie. Nor was her relationship with Charles. They didn't break up immediately but he started to avoid her in those last weeks and she seemed to wander the corridors like a ghost. I'd hear her husky voice asking: 'Have you seen Charles?' like a refrain. People would dart into their rooms at the sight of her coming. And Charles hid from her like the rest of them, concealed behind doors as she swung them open looking for him.

'Poor Juliet,' Mrs Morgan used to sigh. 'Misery loves company, but company does not reciprocate.'

Mother was silent in response. We were all miserable by then – Mother, Ellie and I. Ellie lay in bed for weeks, stopped washing, stopped speaking, except to Charles, when he popped by to see her. Perhaps because he was the one who rescued her, he became the only person she'd confide in. The only person she trusted.

'We need to talk to Ellie.' Caroline's voice brings me back.

'I agree.' I get to my feet, knowing what we have to do. 'Do you speak French?'

'Yes, not badly.'

'Could you call this number?'

My hands are shaking as I pass the scrap of paper. Caroline dials it from her mobile and then there's what feels like an eternal wait as the call tries to connect and fails.

She hangs up and shrugs.

'Let's try again,' I say. 'Try from the landline.'

Caroline picks up the receiver, dials the number and waits again. The sound of the ring echoes down the line and I imagine the noise of it filling an anonymous corridor. A voice at the other end.

Caroline speaks. '*S'il vous plaît, je peux parler à Ellie Knight?*'

She is quiet as the murmur of Madame's voice fills the receiver. I imagine her explaining that Ellie is out for now and that we should call back later. Or maybe she's saying – I dare to hope – that she will just put us through.

My heart beats a little faster.

Ellie and Rose in their apartment. Rose tucked up in bed, her hair tumbled across the pillow. Her chest rising and falling.

'*Attendez une minute s'il vous plaît.*' Caroline places a hand over the receiver. 'Ellie is short for Eleanor, isn't it?'

'Yes,' I say, trying to read her face. 'Why?'

'*Y a-t-il une Eleanor? Eleanor Knight?*' she asks. '*Y a-t-il une jeune femme britannique avec un bébé?*'

She pauses again and then there's another murmur.

'*C'est étrange,*' Caroline is saying. '*Merci.*'

'That was quite weird.' She puts the phone down carefully as if it's something fragile. 'She said there wasn't an Ellie there. Or an Eleanor.'

'That *is* weird. I suppose it's possible she could be using another name?'

Caroline shakes her head. 'That's the thing – she said there wasn't a woman with a child living there. Whatever Ellie told you, it's not true.'

50

Sometimes fear feels like hunger. A strange fluttery feeling you can't place. An emptiness or a need for reassurance. I tear into a packet of digestives. Caroline shakes her head when I offer her one, but Daisy's more interested and sucks on a piece while I tell Caroline about Christmas Day.

'Ellie left me something.'

'A present?'

'No – it sounds silly – a footprint in icing sugar. It was a family thing – something our mother used to do.'

Caroline's face softens. 'Where?'

'Just outside my door.'

'But you didn't see her?'

'No.' I glance down at my hands. 'I haven't seen her for three years. Since 2014.'

'Can you be sure it was her?'

'It's just . . . It's not something anyone else in the world knew about.'

283

'What happened?' Caroline asks. 'Why did you fall out?'

I look over at the globe in the corner of the room. I'd come back from work early. It was a bright, wintry day. The sun low through the window in the front room overlooking Great Western Road. Light pooling on the sofa. Ellie pulled away from him when she saw me and pushed down her dress. I caught a glimpse of her belly as swollen as a loaf. It seemed sacrilegious, that she would do that with my niece so big inside her. Disgusting. My rage was unlike anything I'd ever known.

'We fought over a man,' I say simply.

Daisy tries to stand, clinging to her mother's fingers as she does. If Caroline guesses who the man is, she doesn't say. She keeps her focus on her child.

'And you haven't seen her since?'

'No, I know she's been back in London from time to time – she leaves me things: flowers, that footprint in the icing sugar. But I've never seen her, never met Rose. That's my punishment.'

'That's terrible.' Daisy falls flat on her bottom and begins to cry. Caroline scoops her up and kisses her cheek. 'I'm so sorry.'

'Sometimes I think I deserved it,' I say quietly beneath Daisy's wails. 'Because of what I said.'

Ellie hit me. I deserved that too. A sharp blow to the side of my head that left my ear ringing. I liked the pain. It was better than the suffocating weight of my fury.

I'd said the thing I knew would hurt her most. I hadn't rehearsed it – it had been instinct – sisterly instinct. I'd always known.

She was weary when we came to this point, weary of the argument, of her pregnancy. Weary of all the words.

'He's a *friend*,' she said for what seemed like the millionth time. 'Charles and Fiona both are. You know that.'

She still hadn't said much; hadn't confirmed or denied what I'd seen. She wouldn't be drawn. She evaded my questions, turned away then, dismissive.

'I can't help it if I get that sort of attention,' she added, exasperated.

Sometimes dismissiveness can be the hardest thing to bear. Sometimes it can be worse than open hostility. Or was she just trying to get away from me before the argument became poisonous? I wanted her full attention. I needed something that would get it. As if I had something sharp hidden in my hand, I had always known what could do the most damage.

'Maybe you ask for it.'

Was I talking about Charles? What he did? Well, yes, but there was the other thing behind it, too. The thing, years before, she had crawled into my bed to talk about. The thing she never asked for.

I knew it was terrible to say it, but I said it anyway. And then she hit me.

There was a moment or two of ringing pain, of almost enjoyable self-pity – but the buzz didn't last long. By the time it had worn off, Ellie was in her room, throwing things into an overnight bag. I hovered outside as she packed, called her name in a weak voice – a voice that wasn't really expecting an answer – and then I left her alone.

If I had my time again, I wouldn't have loitered at the doorway. I would have gone in and shouted over the abyss between us, I would have apologised, I would have hugged her. She would have forgiven me. She never would have left.

'She packed in such a rush,' I say to Caroline now, glancing upstairs. 'And then she was gone. I still keep her room for her. Just in case she comes back.'

Caroline strokes Daisy's cheek. 'Can I see it?'

I look at her, trying to work out what she wants. She says she doesn't believe Ellie is behind Dickie's death, but is that really true? Perhaps, whatever she thinks, she suspects Ellie is the key to finding out what happened to her husband. If so, her goal is the same as mine: I need to find Ellie too – and Caroline might be able to help me. So far, she's been a useful ally.

'It's pretty empty,' I say, but I lead the way upstairs.

She follows me with Daisy on her hip. I switch the light on in Ellie's room and am struck by how bare it looks. Caroline gazes around her, taking in the poster on the wall, the duvet cover on the bed.

'Have you searched through her stuff?' Caroline asks.

'How do you mean?'

'For any indication of where she might be?'

'No.' I shake my head. 'Not really.'

There have been times when I've felt restless or curious, or I've just missed Ellie and Rose so badly I haven't known what to do with myself, and I've come to her room with the vague intention of looking for something. I've opened her cupboard and stared at the clothes she left behind – a couple of pairs of old jeans, a few woolly

286

jumpers, her old dance shoes and leotards – as if they held an answer.

Ellie wasn't a hoarder, nor a reader like Mother and me, and there's not much in the way of paperwork or books. Only a dance textbook or two, one on photography and a couple of travel guides stacked up on a shelf above the desk.

I pull the drawers out of the desk, one by one, in part to satisfy Caroline. The first contains a bunch of old receipts, a packet of AA batteries, a small torch. In the second, a deeper drawer, there are some old bank statements, tax forms and other papers. Ellie was terrible at staying on top of her admin. As I pull the drawer out to have a closer look, something at the back of the desk, wedged between drawers, plops onto the dusty carpet. I pick it up.

'What's that?' says Caroline, her voice sharp, curious.

I can tell that she already knows, that she's already spotted it, but I say it anyway. 'It's Ellie's passport.'

I open it up and look at the photograph of her pulling a serious face for the camera. The expiry date is July 2015, the year after she left. She must have lost it and applied for another one. Unless she never left the country.

51

In the passport photograph, Ellie's hair looks like a living thing, just as it always did. I touch the picture with my thumb, remembering how her curls used to feel when she was a child, as light and fragile as moth wings.

'Can I have a look?' Caroline asks.

I hesitate. I feel as if I haven't had long enough with it: that there's something it can communicate to me, something I might be missing. After a moment or two of flicking through the pages, remembering certain trips Ellie took – the one to Thailand in 2012, India the following year – I hand it over.

'Could Ellie have got another one before she went away?'

'Yes, she could have,' I say. 'But it's the kind of thing she would have mentioned. It's such a hassle getting a new passport and, because of her dyslexia, she hated forms – she usually asked me to help her with stuff like that.'

We're silent for a moment, perhaps both mulling over the other options. Could Ellie have travelled without a passport – on a boat, perhaps, or a private jet? Even on a fake one? But those options seem too fantastical. Something from a spy story.

'There are so many pictures,' I think aloud. 'On Facebook and Instagram. So many landmarks – the Eiffel Tower, the Taj Mahal.'

'Let's think.' Caroline sits on the bed, still staring at the passport in her hands. 'What do we know? That she's not at the address she gave you in France; that she didn't travel on this passport, though she might have got another.' She pauses to consider. 'You haven't seen her since the night you quarrelled – but how about other people? Has anyone else stayed in touch?'

Fiona standing on the doorstep at Honeybourne all those weeks ago when I delivered the fruit basket. What had she said then? Something about Ellie being in the country.

'I think perhaps Fiona sees her – Fiona and Charles – when she's back.'

'Well, let's give her a ring and find out when that last was.'

The three of us return downstairs. Caroline asks if she can prepare a snack for Daisy and I leave her in the kitchen, stepping into the hallway with my phone. It would be much more natural for me to call Charles but I remind myself of Fiona's recent kindness, and she's the one who mentioned Ellie being back, after all.

'Hello Fiona, it's Fran,' I say, when she picks up.

'Fran.' Her voice is warm. 'How are you doing?'

'Well, it's been difficult really.'

'I'm sure it has,' she says. 'I bet you've heard from the police and all sorts.'

In the background, their dog is barking at something. There's the squeal of children's voices. I can picture Fiona, her bare feet against the slate of their kitchen floor, the phone sandwiched to her ear while she efficiently sees to another task.

'Not the police,' I say. I don't add, *Not yet*. 'But there's been a journalist investigating – she's desperate to talk to Ellie – so I was wondering . . .' I pause. I hate that it has come to this. That I am begging Fiona to tell me where my sister is. 'I was wondering,' I begin again, 'when you last saw her?'

'Just a second, Fran,' says Fiona.

I hear her voice lowered as she says something to one of the children.

'Now,' she says, returning to the phone, 'when I last saw who?'

'Ellie,' I say patiently.

'Oh gosh,' says Fiona, 'we haven't seen Ellie in years.'

52

I take a deep breath and hold the phone away from my ear. Next door, in the kitchen, Caroline coos as she feeds Daisy. It seems odd to me that everything is continuing as normal. I have the sensation I'm falling. Tumbling down a steep hill, rather, trying to clutch anything that will save me.

The closer I think I'm getting, the further away my sister seems to be.

I try to remember exactly what Fiona had said about Ellie. She slipped it into conversation so casually but then perhaps she wouldn't have known how it'd affect me to hear my sister's name mentioned in such a throwaway fashion when we were estranged.

'But you said . . .' The words sound childish. Impudent. 'You said you'd seen her.'

'I'm sorry to have given you that impression,' Fiona says. 'But we don't. We're in touch by email occasionally, and on Facebook, but we never actually see her.'

'Has Charles . . . ?'

'No, neither of us,' Fiona says smoothly. 'What's going on?'

I hesitate, pulling at the corner of my cardigan, unsure of how to continue.

'We found her passport,' I say in the end. 'We don't know what to make of it.'

'We?'

'Caroline and I. She's here, with Daisy.'

'How peculiar. I suppose Ellie must have got another one.'

'Yes, you would think,' I say uncertainly.

'She must have done,' says Fiona. 'How else would she have travelled abroad?'

She sounds so confident that I'm reassured for a moment. That's Fiona's way. In spite of myself, I think again that she must be a comforting person to have on your side. So logical; so certain of herself.

'Ask her when you next speak to her.'

'Well, she's not really replying to anything at the moment.'

'She's probably just trying to get her head straight after everything that's happened. Give her a day or two.'

'It's strange that you haven't seen her.' I pull at a thread on my cardigan. 'I really thought you had.'

'No.' Fiona's voice is cooler. 'I can only apologise for giving you the wrong impression.' She sighs and says more kindly: 'Sometimes we just convince ourselves of things because we want to believe them.'

After she hangs up, I think of how wrong she is – how I would never want to believe that Ellie preferred her company to mine. I imagine Fiona going to find Charles, wherever he is in the house – by the fire in the living room or maybe upstairs in their bedroom – and relaying the conversation.

I'm left feeling disorientated. I half-wish Caroline weren't here so I could gather my thoughts on my own. In the front room, she and Daisy are sitting on the sofa eating Marmite rice cakes. Caroline looks up eagerly when I return.

'What did she say?' she asks.

'She hasn't seen her.' I perch on the armchair. 'Not for ages.'

'Oh,' says Caroline. 'I thought you said she had.'

'No, I got it wrong.' I look down at my hands. 'She's only been in touch through email and Facebook.'

Caroline is quiet, watching Daisy as she sucks on a rice cake. 'Is there a reason she'd be avoiding everyone? Did she have anything to fear?'

'To fear?'

'I don't know – is Rose's father possessive?'

'Not as far as I know.' I try to recall the few conversations that Ellie and I had had about Roberto. 'He was older than Ellie and married, but I think he was always happy to admire her and Rose from a distance.'

It occurs to me that perhaps Roberto is a watcher, like me. *Voyeur*, Charles said, but I don't like that word and its connotations.

'He always showered them with money,' I add. 'That made me worry. That he wanted something in return.'

Everyone wants something in return. I can't bring myself to tell Caroline that I owe this stranger my home;

that he paid off our mortgage. It's too much. Too humiliating.

'Does he live in the UK?' Caroline asks, reaching over to take the disintegrating rice cake from Daisy.

'Yes, as far as I know.' I fetch her a piece of kitchen roll. 'I've never met him – only seen him on Facebook.'

'Can you show me?'

On my laptop, I show Caroline Roberto's profile. He doesn't post often but his account gives an impression of the life he leads – yachts, skiing, family photographs. Four daughters with the same Mediterranean looks as him and a wife who could have been mistaken for one of them. I don't know how Rose would have fitted in – the odd one out, pale and mousy-haired, at the end of the litter – but he doesn't seem to have any interest in seeing her.

Yet there's no escaping it – it's his money Ellie and Rose are living off. His money, too, that has kept me in my home. Not blood money, exactly, but certainly guilt money.

'That must be hard for Ellie,' says Caroline, looking at the family photograph.

'I don't know,' I say. 'She never seemed bothered – she wasn't really jealous in that way.'

'It might be worth getting in touch with him,' she suggests. 'To ask when he last saw her. If you're sure he's not any kind of threat.'

It's funny, I think, but don't say: Ellie didn't seem to be scared of Roberto, but the only time she seemed spooked, back then, was when she'd seen Dickie.

She came in one November afternoon, shutting the front door carefully. I heard her as I sat on the loo, where

I'd been fretting about our latest money worries. I didn't know then that Ellie had plans to pay off our mortgage. I found her, as I came out, sitting on the staircase like someone who barely had the strength to climb it. She was so big by that stage. I could hardly believe that someone so slight had the strength to carry that enormous belly around.

'Are you OK?'

The lights were switched off in the hall, so I couldn't see her properly, but she was holding her head in her hands.

'Yeah,' she said quietly. 'Just had a shock.' She moved along the step so I could sit next to her. 'I saw Dickie Graham,' she said. 'Ran into him on Wimpole Street.'

'Oh.' I couldn't think of anything better to say. 'What were you doing in that part of town?'

She waved a hand. 'Doctor's appointment. I had a scan.'

'That's fancy,' I teased, trying to hide my stung feelings. I'd have loved to have gone with her to one of her scans, to hold her hand as we heard the baby's heartbeat, but no matter how many hints I dropped she never asked me. 'Did Dickie recognise you?'

She nodded. 'And he looked at my belly; he could see.'

Over the years, I'd thought about that night in the swimming pool so much that sometimes I felt the burn of chlorine in my own sinuses, the tightness in my lungs. I'd imagined it so many times that there were days when it almost felt as if it had happened to me, but perhaps that's just what love is like. We can't separate the other's pain from our own.

'Did Dickie say anything?' I asked.

She shook her head. 'Just my name.'

'What did you do?'

'I ran away like a coward.'

'You're the bravest person I know.' I took her hand in mine. It felt icy and limp. 'And you're safe now. He can't do anything to hurt you.'

'I shouldn't have gone out.' She pulled away from me. 'Roberto keeps saying I should take it easy.'

'He can't confine you,' I said.

She laughed nastily then. 'For the money he's paying he can do what he wants.'

'That reminds me,' I said guiltily. 'We're behind with a couple of our bills.'

'How much do you need?' she asked. 'You only have to say.' She struggled to her feet. 'Please don't hide them from me – I can help now. Or Roberto can.'

It was a short spell of intimacy during the tricky period of her pregnancy. Nothing much – just the briefest of interludes. That night, as I dozed, she crawled into my bed. I felt the nudge of her belly next to me, tight like a drum.

'I wish I hadn't seen him,' she said. 'I wish he didn't know.'

Usually Ellie was so pragmatic, so down-to-earth, but she seemed particularly spooked that night – as if seeing Dickie had been some kind of curse for her and her baby.

Maybe it was.

53

After Caroline and Daisy leave, I do as she suggests and write Roberto a message. The first to the father of my niece in all these years.

> Dear Roberto, We've never met but you might know that I'm Ellie's sister. I'm trying to get hold of her with some urgency. Are you in touch? When did you last see her?

As I pause to decide what to write next, my mind races to Dickie and Tom. The impact of the train against Dickie's body, Tom's floating in the water. Horror-film images, too lurid to seem true. I can't bring Roberto into all of that. It's important to keep it simple. Finally, I add:

> I haven't seen Ellie in some time. It would mean a lot if you could help me find her.

All in all, it sounds plaintive and overly formal. I send it anyway and spend a long time on Ellie's Facebook page, looking at her last post – the picture of Rose reflected in the shop window. Yasmina, a girl with bright red hair I've noticed commenting on Ellie's posts before, has written, Can't wait for you to come back, baby girl. We need to hit those margaritas again.

Come back from where?

I look at Yasmina's profile photograph. She's lounging on cushions in a rooftop bar, a mauve sky behind her, though I can't tell if it's dawn or dusk; hot air balloons rise from the ground like bubbles. It's not a view I recognise, nor one that gives any clue of where Ellie might be. Yasmina's account is private but I ask to Friend her. It's something I would have been shy about once, but I don't care about that any more.

At work the next day, the mood is cheerful. It's still just three days after Christmas, though it feels like weeks have passed. With most people at home with their families, we're busy only in bursts, with clusters of shoppers on post-prandial walks or, in lonelier cases, looking for company, lingering at the till and stringing out their small talk with us. At ten to one, Gareth and Brenda exchange a look and he announces, with forced jollity, 'You two should take your lunch break together. Treat yourselves to a drink.'

'Are you up for that, Fran?' asks Brenda promptly. 'The Phoenix does a lovely mulled wine.'

I have to say, their little performance is quite touching. It's clear they've discussed me. *Poor Fran and her problems. We must look after her.*

Sure enough, a couple of sips into her mulled wine, Brenda asks, 'How are things? Gareth said they'd been difficult.'

She doesn't say any more – whether Gareth had mentioned any specifics about the newspaper report. Some days, all I want to do is talk about Ellie, but things have developed so strangely now, I don't know where to begin.

'I had some upsetting news,' I say vaguely.

'It can be a difficult time of year.'

I recall, for a moment, my Christmas Day, staring down at the Serpentine, leaping around to Gilbert and Sullivan on my own, as high as a kite, the phone call from Meilin, the footprint on my doorstep.

'Yes,' I agree.

'For me it can,' Brenda says. 'Without children.'

It's a relief that she's distracted from the subject of Ellie. I make a sympathetic noise and remember my precious time alone with Daisy in the café. What it had been like to be mistaken for a mother. Just for a few minutes.

'It was better this year,' she continues. 'Because we finally made a decision to give up on IVF, to explore a different route – adoption or surrogacy, we're not sure which yet.'

'How long have you been trying?' I ask.

'For years,' she says bleakly. 'For years and years.'

I'm briefly ashamed that I never really asked about it. All those doctor's appointments. Her move from the children's department. Unexplained tears. I was so busy wanting something of my own that other people's desires slid past me.

'It's a terrible thing,' she says. 'Nothing took. Thousands of pounds it cost us – for each cycle. It wiped out almost all of our savings, and my parents' savings too. But each time the drugs arrived, it felt so exciting. Like Christmas. That this time it might work. So many drugs – I can't tell you. Boxes of the stuff. Boxes of needles. It was so extreme. I was obsessed – as soon as one round failed, I would want to get going with the next. But none of it worked.'

As she takes a large gulp of mulled wine, I wait for her to continue.

'I don't mind telling you,' Brenda says. 'Because I think you might have an inkling of what it's like: to get to our age and be childless.'

With Daisy, there'd been a flash of happiness so strong and sudden it had taken me by surprise – a glimpse of a place on the other side of the mirror. But as for a wish – to have children, to be a mother – that has never been mine or, at least, not at any cost. Perhaps I couldn't allow myself to want that. Perhaps I sensed where that kind of overwhelming desire might lead for a person like me. What I feel is different – not a longing for children of my own necessarily but for *Rose*: to read her stories or give her advice or stroke her head as she falls asleep. It's family I want more than anything. Intimacy.

'You discover a hatred you didn't know you had,' Brenda says quietly. 'You notice things – mothers passing you in the street with five kids in tow, snapping at them, not appreciating them. It's primal. You just can't understand why they have something that you want so badly.'

To want something someone else has. I know what that feels like.

'Your friend understood,' says Brenda. 'There are so many of us these days. It's the curse of our generation.'

It's funny, Caroline never mentioned any difficulties conceiving, but maybe it was something that came up in conversation between them. When Brenda goes to the bar again, I check my phone. There are three missed calls from Caroline and a couple from the journalist. I drain the last of my mulled wine.

Caroline is breathless as she answers the phone. 'Are you at work today?'

'Yes,' I say. 'Just on my lunch.'

'Can you come to mine tonight?'

'I don't know – I want to see if Roberto has messaged me back.'

'You can check that here,' she says impatiently. 'There's something I need to talk to you about. Something I've discovered.'

'What?'

'I can't tell you over the phone – I have to show you.'

'OK,' I agree. 'I'll come around later.'

After I've spoken to Caroline, I listen to Kat's message. 'I wondered if you'd had any luck getting hold of your sister?' she asks. 'It would be really great if you could let me know.'

The words are polite, but her brusque tone gives her away. I can tell she's onto me, that she suspects I'm hiding from her. Perhaps it's a good thing I'm away from home tonight, in case she turns up again. I don't want other people snooping any more into Ellie's affairs until I've had the chance to find out first.

I return, distracted, to Brenda, but the message on the phone leaves me spooked.

On the drizzly walk to the tube after work, I glance over my shoulder more than once. Kat is clearly not going to give up on the story easily. Spotting a woman in a hooded coat several metres behind me, I pick up the pace, just to be sure.

Caroline already has her laptop on the counter in the kitchen with Ellie's Facebook page up on the screen.

'I'm sorry to sound so cloak and dagger,' she says. 'But it's really been bothering me. I've been looking at your sister's photos on Facebook, going through them, one by one, and I found something extraordinary.'

She's speaking quickly, tripping over herself.

'Have you heard of a reverse image search?'

'No.'

'There's a TV show – *Catfish* – I binge-watched it while I was pregnant . . . They're always doing reverse image searches on that.'

I wish she'd give me the chance to take my coat off, to sit down. Her words are coming at me too fast; I can't process them.

'Can you slow down?'

'Fran,' Caroline says gently. 'This is important. You need to see it for yourself.' She grabs me by the arm and pulls me towards her laptop. 'I don't want to shock you, but, look, see this image of Rose . . .'

She clicks on the photograph taken before Christmas – Rose looking through the shop window, in her red coat and white tights. She saves it onto her desktop.

'Now watch,' she continues.

302

Caroline opens up Google Images and drops the photo of Rose from her desktop into the search bar.

'You have to follow the link through,' she says as the photo appears on the screen, 'and it will show you where else the image can be found.' She checks to see I'm paying attention and clicks on Rose, then clicks again. 'Here's the same photo,' she says.

I take a step closer. The image is for sale in a photo library. It's titled 'Little girl window shopping', with a price next to it – twenty pounds or three credits. Beneath the photo of Rose, there's a longer description and a list of words, starting with child, children, shopping, Christmas and going on to include happy, beautiful, cute.

'I don't understand.'

'Look at this one,' says Caroline.

She finds another photo of Rose – the one of her on the tricycle – and goes through the same process. It turns up for sale on a different photo library.

'I don't understand,' I say again. 'Why has she been selling photos of Rose?'

Ellie's photographs of her daughter are so beautiful, well lit, professional-looking. But still, I think, it's not like Ellie to sell something she loved. It's simply not the kind of thing she would do.

'Maybe that's not the question,' says Caroline quietly. 'You could ask: why has someone been buying library photographs and passing them off as Rose?'

I frown. 'Why would Ellie do that?'

Caroline is silent for a long time. She's miles ahead of

me, I realise. I'm stumbling after her in the dark, frantically trying to catch up.

A memory, unbidden. It's as if Caroline has disturbed something in my subconscious, shaking it like a hedge to see what might fly out. The thing is this: Ellie never called me sis. Not in real life. Not until she went away.

I curl my fingers around the kitchen counter to steady myself. 'Are you saying it's not Ellie at all?'

54

The fridge in Caroline's kitchen hums, an enormous Swan in eggshell blue. There's the faint buzz of the overhead lights, the tick of the clock. I try to focus on these sounds to distract myself from the panic rising in me.

What is happening? Where is my sister?

I'm not sure if I say these words out loud or not, but suddenly Caroline is beside me with a hand on my back, saying, 'It's OK. Take a few deep breaths.'

She fills up a glass at the tap and I drink in swift gulps.

'We'll deal with this methodically,' she says, pulling up a stool for me next to her at the breakfast counter. 'We'll go through every photograph on her Facebook page. I've made a start – some of the photos of Ellie seem to be genuine.' She pauses. 'It's the pictures of Rose that come from photo libraries.'

I hold my palms flat against the solid granite surface. 'We still don't know where they are.' I take another couple of deep breaths. 'Is this something we need the police for? To track her down?'

'Maybe,' Caroline says. 'I don't know – we'll need to show them more than a strange Facebook account.'

'But no one's seen her – she's run away from everyone.'

'Let's check what Roberto has to say.' Caroline pushes her laptop across the counter towards me.

Heart pounding, I log onto Facebook and see Roberto has replied. I read his message silently to myself and then out loud to Caroline.

Thank you for your message. I haven't seen your sister since she moved away with my daughter three years ago. I send them money from time to time but I'm sad to say that's our only contact. I'm sorry not to be more help.

'Fuck,' says Caroline. She gets to her feet.

'But he's sending them money,' I say. 'That counts for something.'

'Good point,' she says. 'Ask him where he sends it. I'll get Dickie's laptop out and carry on checking the photos.' She glances over her shoulder as she leaves the room. 'It would be an idea to message her other friends, too – the ones who say they've seen her recently.'

It feels as if my brain has vacated my body, so I follow Caroline's orders. She's good at this. Her line of work must help – she knows just what to do. I reply to Roberto and get in touch with everyone who mentions seeing Ellie recently. Yasmina, the red-headed girl who says she's missing their margaritas; a tall chap with steel-rimmed glasses and a bow tie; a mum friend of hers, who poses with a toddler on her hip in front of the Eiffel Tower.

I ask them all, in as undramatic fashion as I can manage, When did you last see my sister?

Next to me, Caroline returns with another laptop and begins to unravel Ellie's Facebook account. 'Look at this,' she says at a photo of avocado on toast swiped from another Instagram account. Minutes later, she tuts disapprovingly at a stolen image of the Astronomical Clock in Prague, which matches the one on another account, right down to the couple posing with a bunch of balloons below it.

It's a magpie's nest, built from pilfered things.

I stare at the photograph of Rose on the tricycle that had caused me such consternation. It's not even Rose. A thought rises like a bubble in my head, rapidly followed by another one. Whoever posted the photographs was clever enough to find plenty of the back of a child's head, or her profile, or a half-hidden reflection. That's why the photos of Rose's face were so few and far between, so we wouldn't be able to tell it was always a different child. I don't even know what Rose looks like.

A message pops up from Yasmina. A pulse thrums at my throat as I read it.

I haven't been in touch with Ellie for a couple of weeks. The last I heard she was on her way to Paris.

I close my eyes and see Tom in the water, shouting, perhaps – calling for help. Ellie standing over him, looking down from the bridge above, her hair wild. Doing nothing to help him. Her face impassive, unknowable.

'We'll get to the bottom of this,' says Caroline soothingly.

'You keep saying that.' My voice sounds high, unfamiliar. 'But it keeps getting worse. Worse and worse. If Ellie is in Paris, that can only mean one thing . . .'

Another message pops up from Ellie's tall friend. He thinks Ellie is in Paris too, but he's more specific – he mentions the Marais, the district Tom was last seen in.

The fear takes hold of me, spreading through my limbs like pins and needles.

'I could fly out there,' I say. 'Fly out and find her.'

'Hang on,' says Caroline. 'Let's think this through.'

She leans on the counter, resting her head in her hands. Then she clicks on the profile image of Yasmina – the one of her on the rooftop with the hot air balloons. 'Let's try something.'

Moments later, we're staring at the Instagram account of someone called Roksana Kowalska, with the same red hair and sharp features as Yasmina. And eleven thousand followers.

'As I thought,' says Caroline a touch smugly.

I'm lagging behind again. 'Why does she have all of Yasmina's photos?'

Caroline gives me a pitying look. 'I don't think Yasmina's real.'

She goes through the same process with Ellie's other friends. The results are the same – every single one of them has a double: another person on the internet with identical photographs, except more of them – more friends, more chance, Caroline says, of being the real version.

'They're all fake accounts.'

We stand, staring at each other. A thought nags at me.

Something incomplete like the last crossword clue that wakes you in the night, the answer on your tongue.

Then I realise what we have to do. I know it – but I don't want to.

Caroline looks up at me, as if she's had the same thought.

'Roberto,' I say. 'Is he real?'

My mouth is dry as paper as she clicks through to Roberto's profile, choosing the photograph of him with his daughters lined up next to him like ducklings. All with the same dark, handsome features.

But, of course, Roberto isn't Roberto at all. His name is Michel Billeaud-Chaussat. He has properties in Paris and Saint-Tropez, a yacht and four daughters.

He also has more than eight hundred friends on Facebook. Not one of them is Ellie.

55

A fat fly lands on the laptop and pauses to clean its legs.

'I don't understand,' I say, still staring at Michel's profile.

'This is quite worrying,' says Caroline.

'You think so?' I snap.

'We need to work through this logically. When did you last see Ellie?'

My nails dig into my palms. I don't want to think about that day. The low winter sun coming through the front room of our flat, blinding me as I walked in. Two figures on the sofa, folded over each other. The light in Charles's hair as he did to Ellie what he'd done to Juliet all those years ago. Physical love of the kind I'd never known. That, even when offered to me, I'd pushed away.

'I hate remembering that time.'

'But Fran, we have to.' Caroline taps the counter

310

impatiently. 'Perhaps, because of your fight with Ellie, you weren't thinking clearly – perhaps there was something you missed.'

I glare at her. How dare she? How dare she pull apart everything I've loved all these years?

'You didn't know her at all,' I say. 'She's mine. *My* sister. I don't know why you've taken over like this.'

Caroline stiffens. 'Why do you think?'

I know the answer, but I don't say it.

'Because I want to find out if she hurt my husband,' she says at last. 'If she pushed him.'

We glare at each other. The kitchen clock ticking through the seconds of silence between us. I remember the first time I saw Caroline, before I knew it was her – the way she tracked me down, watching me like a ghost in the rain. I've been foolish to think we were friends. She's always had her own agenda. I look at her pale, freckled face. I wanted a friend so badly I didn't stop to ask myself why she sought me out.

I try to keep my voice calm. 'She wouldn't,' I say at last. 'You don't know her, but she wouldn't.'

'I don't know what to think.' Caroline begins to pace. 'It's possible Ellie could have been in the crowd on the platform. That she could have pushed him. There's a chance. But not if . . .'

She stops, raises her hands to her face, thinks better of completing what she was going to say.

'What?'

'It doesn't matter.' She takes her hands away again, revealing a different expression. More subdued.

'Just say it,' I urge.

311

'It doesn't matter,' she repeats. 'I was only thinking out loud.'

A twisting pain in my gut. I know what she was going to say; what she's trying to shield me from.

'You must have thought of it – you must at least have *considered* the possibility,' she says more gently. 'That she might not be here any more.'

It's worse that she's still being so careful. That she won't say the words. I shake my head. 'You can't say that . . .'

'Why is someone faking her account?' she asks in the same tender voice. 'And all the others?'

'I can't believe you'd say that.' My voice is raised. Almost shouting. 'She could be here in London. You know she could.'

'She could be,' says Caroline. But her gaze doesn't meet mine.

'I'm leaving,' I say. 'I'm going home.'

'Let me get you an Uber.' She reaches for her phone.

'You've done enough.' It's a cliché, but it makes me feel better to say it.

'Please, Fran,' she says. 'Don't go like this. Whoever hurt Dickie might have hurt Ellie too. I think we should take care.'

I ignore her, kicking her garden gate on the way out so hard that the pain ricochets up my shins. It's raining heavily. On my walk to the tube, I find I'm talking to myself loudly, saying *no, no, no*. I can't even tell if I'm crying or not. None of it makes me feel any better. There's nothing I can do to stop the dread.

Most of the shops are shut now. I buy a family-sized bar of Dairy Milk from a late-night newsagent but it's not enough. When the sobbing subsides, I realise I'm desperate to speak to someone. To spill out my worries, be comforted, reassured. Almost out of habit, Charles appears in my head. The memory returns to me of him in the bedroom. The whisky fumes. The heat of his breath. I don't want *that* Charles – I want the old one. From my childhood. Either way, without Caroline, he's all I've got.

I fish out my phone. The call goes straight through to his answerphone.

'Charles.' My voice cracks on his name. 'I'm so scared. I have no idea where Ellie is – it looks like her Facebook account is a fake. And her friends too. I just . . .' I don't know what to say next. 'Please could you call me as soon as you get this.'

At home, remembering Caroline's warning, I hook the chain across and drag the chair from my desk to lean it against the door. For good measure, I pile books up on the chair. At the back of the kitchen cupboard I find a dusty bottle of sherry and pour myself half a pint of the stuff, knocking it back with an ancient sleeping tablet. I can't look at anything in my flat – the globe in the corner, the parcel of books waiting for Rose under the tree, Ellie's passport on the coffee table. I've been surrounded by lies.

56

I wake to the sound of a knock at the front door, something falling to the floor. Footsteps. My heart's racing but the sleeping tablet is slowing my reactions like fog and by the time I put my eye to the peephole, there's no one out there. A door slams in the flat below. I run to my bedroom window. Nothing.

In the loo, the fresh smell of marijuana drifts up from the cistern. I sit there, thinking. There is someone who is uniquely placed to know when I'm in the flat or not, whether I'm asleep or not, to nip upstairs and make a delivery. But he's got it wrong today.

I grab a coat and throw it on over my nightdress. It's too late to mess around.

When the dealer comes to the door, his clothes and hair are wet, as if he's been waiting in the rain. His dog is damp, too, cowering at his feet.

'Was it you?' I ask. 'Who delivered the flowers? Let yourself into my flat?'

His eyes are red and bloodshot; his hand is shaking as he lifts a joint to his lips. I think he's going to deny it for a moment, send me away, but he says quietly. 'I know it's not right.'

I stare at him.

'Ever since the trick on Christmas Day, I've been feeling bad about it. I don't know – it's nearly 2018. A new year. I thought I should make a clean start, come and talk to you about it.'

'What trick?'

'The print in the icing sugar.' He shifts uneasily.

The footprint. The thing that only Ellie knew about. *Think, Fran. Think.* I mentioned it in a Facebook message, didn't I? A reminder between sisters of a secret world – something shared between the pair of us. Something to make her long to come back to me. But someone else's eyes scanned that message – not Ellie's. Just as someone else has been reading all of my private musings to her for God knows how long.

My legs feel unsteady, as if they no longer want to do their job of holding me up, but I can't break down here. I need to be strong for Ellie. I have to get to the bottom of this.

I swallow hard. 'Who asked you to do it?'

'I don't know her name, but she has a posh voice.'

'Posh.'

'Yeah, like yours.'

That could be Juliet, I think. Or Fiona. Or Caroline.

That could be anyone I went to school with. The dread surges up then, because there is no one I can trust and the only person in the world I could is missing and I have no idea where she is.

315

'What did she look like?'

'I don't really know,' he says.

'Why not?'

'I only met her once,' he says. 'When she gave me the key. She was wearing big sunglasses and a hat. I don't think I'd recognise her if I saw her again.'

All these years we've exchanged friendly greetings. A nod in the entrance hall, a wave in the communal garden. You wouldn't call us friends, but the idea that he has been inside my home, laid flowers on my bed, makes me feel cold.

'Why did you do it?'

He sighs, glances at the flat behind him. 'It was just money. That's all it takes for most people to do most things.'

'I want my key back.' My voice is icy.

'You're not going to the police, are you? I couldn't . . . with my record.'

'Give me my key.'

He reaches into his pocket and hands it over.

All those faces on the internet, each one a double. It seems to me there are two versions of everyone. And he's no different. How could I be so easily fooled?

'You thought you could pull the wool over my eyes.' Even as I say it, it sounds like a daft expression. The kind of thing Mother might have said.

'Just a minute.' He disappears, leaving me standing at the door. 'You might want these.' He returns, a couple of moments later, with an envelope addressed to Ellie.

I tear it open, but it's just a marketing mail-out from a dance company.

'There's not so much post for her now,' he says sheepishly. 'But there used to be more – I wait for the post at the door, take out anything for Ellie and leave it in a brown envelope in my pigeonhole for someone to pick up. That's where the woman would leave instructions for me, too.'

'What name do you leave it under?'

'R Deal.'

R Deal. Roberto Deal.

Our deal.

Occasionally a piece of post would arrive for Ellie, but so rarely I'd always imagined she'd had it all redirected.

'You won't go to the police, will you, love?'

I feel so cold, so sick, that I can barely stand up.

'You've done a terrible thing,' I say. 'You've helped cover up a person disappearing.' I swallow back bile. I can't bring myself to say it. 'Or worse. Something much worse.'

57

My head spins as I climb back up to my flat. If Caroline is right about us getting what we deserve, then perhaps I'm being punished – taunted and followed by someone whose features I can't quite make out, just as I once followed Charles and hung back on the periphery. I call her, once the door of the flat is closed firmly behind me, but she doesn't pick up.

Adrenaline is pumping through my veins now. The metallic taste from the Zolpidem tablet lingers in my mouth, but I'm not going to bed. I'm determined to find answers. I march up to Ellie's room and go straight to the desk, pulling the drawers out and emptying them on the bed. Bank statements, receipts, old photographs and letters flutter out. I'm going to go through every single one. I look at every receipt, the date on it, the amount, what Ellie bought. The photographs she'd held on to – or left behind, depending on how you wanted to look at it. There weren't many. One or two of Mother and me, a handful from her years as a barfly, dark photographs, badly lit, crammed with pale, red-eyed faces I didn't recognise.

At nine o'clock, I send a text to Gareth saying I'm not well, I won't be in today, and then I switch my phone off and continue my search: opening the drawers under the bed and going through everything there, working my way through her clothes, looking in every pocket, every rolled sock to find out what my sister might have been hiding. Eventually, exhaustion overwhelms me and I crawl into Ellie's bed and close my eyes.

When I wake, the light in the room has softened. The alarm clock says quarter past three in the afternoon. I lie on my back and look out of the skylight. I think about what Ellie might have packed that day I lingered outside her room – her laptop, her phone, some clothes, her keys. Those are the things someone else might have access to now, and anyone with the key, I reason, and something to hide, would have been through all of this paperwork before. The only reason I found her passport was because it had been hidden, wedged behind the drawers.

On the desk, there's the Christmas card I'd given her just before she left: 'To Ellie and Rose. I can't wait to meet you.' How Ellie had cried at those presents – the card, the framed scan. I get to my feet with the urge to see it: the last true image of Rose I ever saw. Ellie left it behind. I still have it, locked up in my cupboard along with my Charles collection. I thank Juliet for teaching me about privacy all those years ago.

In my bedroom, I sit cross-legged on the floor staring at the kidney-bean swell of Rose's developing body: her plump head; a tendril curling away from it like a tadpole's tail.

'Is that her hair?' I'd teased Ellie. 'A little top-knot?'

She'd shaken her head. 'No, just a smudge on the image, I think. I'll check with the doctor.'

I didn't ask again when I gave her the scan on Christmas Day. She was too upset.

Magic Eye posters were all the rage in the Nineties when we were young – there were galleries dedicated to them. A couple of girls pinned them up in their cubicles. Yet, try as I might, I could never see the other world – the second image – I could never relax my eyes in quite the right way. Another club I couldn't join.

But I haven't looked at the scan for so long that it's as if my eyes have finally relaxed in the interim and I can see clearly at last.

Viewed again, the tendril curling from Rose's head doesn't look so much like a smudge: it looks like a tiny, threadlike arm in a place where you wouldn't expect an arm to be. Unless . . .

I turn the frame around and examine it from another angle.

I can't believe I have been so stupid.

There's another baby beside the kidney bean, cuddled up so close that the separate bodies look like one – as if the head of the first baby belongs to the body of the other.

All this time I've been looking for Rose. A single child. When there were always two. Twins.

There's only one family I know with twins. A family with a nursery upstairs, far away from prying eyes. Who

320

usher their children away from me at every given opportunity. Who never post their faces on the internet.

'You discover a hatred you didn't know you had,' Brenda had said. 'Your friend understood.'

But she hadn't meant Caroline. She'd meant Fiona. How could I have forgotten the cosy chat between them when she'd popped into the shop? Fiona leaning on the counter, Brenda desperate to confide in anyone who would listen.

And what had Fiona said? *I was so sick I couldn't leave the house.* Maybe that wasn't why she couldn't go out, after all. Maybe it was because she was never pregnant in the first place.

My hand goes to my belly, where there's a deep wrenching pain, and the framed scan slips to the floor.

Ellie, what happened to you?

The impact cracks the glass in two, shattering it into dagger-like pieces.

58

I don't know how long I sit on the floor staring at the smashed glass, trying to think, to work it out – is it possible Fiona could have taken Ellie's children without Charles knowing?

Charles in English, his finger running under the text in Mrs Fyson's class, showing me where to go when I got lost. His same hands lifting Ellie from the pool after Dickie had run to get him. I fish out the old rugby photo from my tuckbox and stare at his face, his golden hair. His eyes looking straight forward, ignoring Juliet while the other boys leered at her.

Charles. My rescuer. The one person who had made Chesterfield bearable for me. Whom I'd loved my whole life. He wouldn't hurt me, would he?

When I switch on my mobile, I have twenty-three missed calls from Caroline.

The phone begins to flash as she rings again.

'I've been trying to get hold of you all day,' she says breathlessly. 'I was just about to come over.'

'Caroline,' I try to stop her, picking at the edge of a carpet tile on the floor.

'Ellie's Facebook account,' she pushes on regardless. 'It's disappeared.'

'What do you mean?'

'Someone's deleted it – not just hers – Yasmina, Roberto. All of them. I've been beside myself trying to get hold of you . . . And then, I found something. A photograph Dickie saved. It was in a folder on his desktop. It sounds stupid. It's just called "Ellie's feet" – I think it might be something he downloaded from Facebook. It's a photo Ellie appears to have taken of her feet – at the end of a sunbed. The second and third toes are webbed slightly, aren't they?'

'Yes,' I say. 'That's right. Like our dad. It was one of those weird family traits . . .'

'The thing is,' says Caroline, cutting me off, 'Dickie noticed one of Charles's children had webbed feet on our holiday to Oman. They were messing around by the pool, him and his god-daughter, and he said, "Look at your toes – they must make you swim faster." And then he went very quiet.'

I remember the sketchbook, the strange aquatic creatures. My belly tightens like a fist. 'They're Ellie's,' I whisper. 'The twins.'

A neighbour's door slams, Caroline is quiet for a moment. 'What do you mean? What about Rose?'

I lick my lips, try to swallow. 'Ellie was expecting twins, but she never said, and then she disappeared before she gave birth. I never met Rose – I never saw her.'

323

Caroline is silent for so long I wonder if she's still there. 'Maybe Dickie guessed. Maybe he made the connection,' she says thickly. 'Why didn't he tell me?'

I hated Dickie, God knows I hated him, for what he did to me, to my sister, but the truth is the truth all the same. *Snitches get stitches,* quips his chirpy voice in my head.

'He was loyal,' I say. 'He had so much history with Charles. They knew each other's secrets. Like the cat.'

'The cat?'

'In the washing machine. The one Dickie killed.'

'No,' says Caroline. 'That wasn't Dickie. He told me about it – that was Charles.'

'Charles?' I have the dizzying feeling of being tipped upside down.

'Did he say it was Dickie?'

'I . . .' I hesitate. 'Unless I misunderstood.'

'Dickie was so traumatised by that – he told me about it when we first got together. The only way he could justify it was as a childish prank. An accident, even. But it was something he could never forget.'

We're both drawn into our thoughts. Hers of Dickie; mine of Ellie. I need to know what happened to my sister. I need to know where she is. I get to my feet, begin to look for my handbag.

Caroline's voice is so quiet I can barely make out the words. 'Do you think they did something to him?'

Dickie's face hazy with drink on the tube platform. Charles would have known when they were going to be there. It would have been so easy for him to text Fiona; for her to slip in with that group of women. Dickie's face,

324

unsure whether to be pleased or frightened at spotting his friend standing just behind him.

I pull on my coat as I talk, push my feet into my shoes.

'We should go to see them,' says Caroline as if she can hear my preparations to leave.

'Shall we tell the police?' I ask, playing for time as I put some dry food out for Branwell.

'Maybe later,' she says. 'I'll call the babysitter and we can go from here. We can go together.'

I'm sorry, I think, *but I can't wait.*

'Fine,' I say. 'See you shortly.'

'Great.' She pauses. 'You promise you'll come here first? That you won't do anything silly?'

'Like what?' I ask, pulling the smallest, sharpest knife out of the block in my kitchen and pushing it into my pocket.

On Great Western Road, I flag down a taxi and tell him the address. His eyes widen slightly but at least I can pay by credit card.

The ghosts of former journeys accompany me on my way. Times when I travelled to the Cotswolds to sit and watch the house from a distance. I try not to think about that. About how much I just wanted a glimpse of him.

I'd pinned so much onto him I didn't know what I was looking at.

I sit forward in the cab, my hands clenched between my thighs. The taxi driver is quiet as he drives and I'm grateful for that. My phone rings. Caroline. I don't answer. Instead, I have an idea. I call Kat and, at first slowly, then all in a rush, I tell her everything we know. I give her Caroline's phone number and tell Kat to call her in three hours if she hasn't heard from me.

'You should make peace with Juliet,' Kat tells me. 'You're fighting for the same side now. She knew something was up with Dickie. We talked about it; she told me he wasn't himself before he died – and then, when his death was so sudden, it made her feel uneasy. Suspicious. But she didn't know of what exactly – or whom. After Tom drowned, she got in touch to tell me everything. She wanted it all off her chest, in case she was next.' She sighs. 'Chesterfield damaged her too, you know.'

I think of Juliet before I left Chesterfield. Thin and strained, drained of all her powers. Despite myself, I feel sad for that Juliet. I want to go back and tell her it will be OK. That she will go on to be a successful television star with a perma-tan and more than a hundred thousand followers on Instagram, but I know, even as I have the thought, that all those things don't matter, really. That the teenage version of Juliet is still inside her, hungry-eyed, needy, desperate to impress the boys at any cost. That that version of Juliet stays with her as much as my teenage self – with chewing gum in my hair, weeping in the bathroom – is with me. We don't shed our former selves like snake skins. It doesn't work like that.

I don't commit to Kat one way or the other. We'll see where we are after this trip, I decide. And then I put my phone on silent.

My promise to my mother propels me on – I didn't look after my sister when I should have done. But I will find her now. During the journey, I check off, in my mind, all the places Ellie is not – not in France, not on Facebook, not in London delivering flowers. She is nowhere –

nowhere she said she would be, nowhere anyone knows her. My thoughts hare ahead in the darkness, circling around on themselves, always back to the same place, but I can't go there. I can't accept it. Every time, I shy away.

It's dark by the time the cab reaches Honeybourne. I ask him to drop me off at the end of the drive so I can approach on foot.

I don't have a plan, I realise. I don't know how to begin, so I begin by walking towards the house. More than anything, I want to see the children. I keep my hand in my coat pocket, close my fingers around the handle of the knife.

As I reach the house, the floodlights snap on.

Run away, Fran, says Ellie's voice, clear as a bell. *Get out of here. Run.*

But my feet are glued to the ground.

The front door swings open and Fiona stands, beaming, in a rectangle of light, their Labrador hovering benignly at her heels.

'Fran,' she says warmly. 'Come in – you're just in time for a gin and tonic.'

59

I don't know what I was expecting. Suspicion. Guardedness, perhaps. At the very least, surprise. But her warmth knocks me off balance. It's the strangest thing. It's as if she knew I was coming.

'Where's Charles?' I ask, glancing around the hallway, noticing for the first time that all the framed prints are of birds you'd hunt – pheasants, partridges, a red grouse.

'Upstairs in the games room,' she says. 'We'll join him in a moment.'

She shuts the door behind us and pulls the bolt across.

I reach for the knife again, just to touch it, to check it's there, but I follow her mutely to the kitchen. The longer she believes I don't suspect anything, the better that is for me. There's a Jo Malone candle burning on the kitchen table, a MacBook open on the counter, murmured voices coming from the Roberts radio on the windowsill.

'What an unexpected surprise, Fran,' Fiona calls over her shoulder. She heads for their corner fridge, as big as a spaceship. 'Will you join us for a gin?'

'I'd better not.' I need to keep a clear head.

'Go on. You'll make us feel bad.' She smiles at me winningly. 'Slimline tonic?'

'No,' I say. 'I like full-fat.'

Fiona laughs throatily then. 'Yes, of course.'

My eyes follow her as she makes our drinks, moving from the fridge to the chopping board. Fiona has never made me a gin and tonic before, so why would she say that? *Yes, of course.* Unless someone has told her. Someone I *have* gone for drinks with. Someone, it occurs to me now, I don't really know at all.

There's the clink of ice in the tumblers, her fingers curling around a knife as she slices the lime. 'It's the oddest thing, isn't it?' Fiona nods at the laptop on the counter. 'About Ellie's Facebook being faked.'

'Yes.' It's warm in the kitchen. My face feels flushed and hot.

'You know, when we looked it up, the account wasn't there.'

'Is that right?'

If Fiona hears the edge in my voice, she doesn't let on. 'What do you think is going on?' She pauses, still holding the knife as she looks over at me.

I swallow. 'What do *you* think?' I repeat back at her, looking down at the floor where Fiona's slim feet are neatly pedicured, as usual. Her toenails a surprising shade of blue.

'Perhaps someone hacked her account.' She squeezes

lime into our drinks. 'Deleting everything. Or it could be . . .' She hesitates.

'Could be – what?'

'I don't know.' She glances at me. 'Perhaps it had something to do with Tom.' She passes me my glass. 'What he did to Ellie.'

'What are you saying?'

Fiona gives me a meaningful look. 'I think you know what I'm saying.'

'That Ellie could have hurt him?'

Fiona shrugs. 'It's possible. And then gone into hiding. It's what people are suggesting,' she adds quietly. 'On Facebook. Old Chesterfield alumni.'

'Just gossip,' I say.

She tilts her head sympathetically, neither agreeing, nor disagreeing.

'We've all had thoughts like that, haven't we? About revenge.'

'Only thoughts,' I repeat. 'That's very different from doing something like that.'

'Maybe,' Fiona says, maddeningly agreeable still.

'She wouldn't,' I say. 'Ellie wouldn't. I know her better than anyone.'

There's so much I don't know, though.

Why do you have Ellie's children? The question hums between us. I have to ask, but I don't know how to begin.

'Where are the twins?' I say instead, slipping my hand into my coat pocket.

'In bed,' she says. 'Hence the gin.'

I'm quiet for a second, as if I could hear the girls from

330

here, but I can't make anything out over the murmur of Radio 4, the hum of the fridge.

'Let's go up,' says Fiona. 'The fire's lit – it's nice and warm. But first, let me take your coat.'

'It's fine. I'm quite cold.'

'I promise you – it's *very* warm up there.'

Before I can stop her, Fiona is on me, tugging the coat off my shoulders. I try to resist, but it seems a good idea to keep things calm for now. She marches out to the hall to hang it up and then she's back in the room tipping olives into a bowl. She places two glasses and the olives onto a tray.

'Right,' she says. 'I think we're ready.'

She begins to climb the staircase that sweeps up from the front hall. The Christmas tree is still up. It's a giant – stretching between floors.

On the landing, perhaps hearing our footsteps, a child cries, 'Mummy?'

My eyes dart to the closed door of the nursery. I have the strong urge to open it, to examine their faces closely. I've never had the chance before.

'Just a minute, darling,' Fiona calls back crisply.

Distracted, she picks up her pace and leads me past the master bedroom on our left and up to another cooler floor, with three closed doors on the landing, and then another flight of stairs. Behind her, I fish my phone out of my pocket and text Caroline, I'm here. Will ring you asap. As an afterthought, I tap on the voice memo app and press record, then shove my phone back in my pocket.

The last flight is the steepest. We must be climbing up into the turret. Fiona pushes the door open to a space like the billiards room in Cluedo. It's dominated by a snooker table in the centre, with a crackling fire in a nook in the wall opposite, with two leather armchairs in front of it and a gilt mirror hanging above. There's a drinks trolley tucked in the corner. To our right, Charles stands on the thin lip of a balcony, smoking a cigarette.

'His man den,' Fiona quips over her shoulder. 'Look who I found outside,' she exclaims. Her voice is bright and brittle.

'Fran,' Charles says, coming over and kissing me on the cheek. 'What a surprise.'

He seems as unflustered by my arrival as Fiona.

'She's worried about Ellie,' she tells him. 'About what's going on.'

'Of course.' He nods.

I glance from him to her. They're so smooth, so calm, so unruffled. I think again: *why do you have my sister's children?*

My gaze darts around the room to see if it can offer some kind of clue. Did Ellie ever come here? Ever catch a flash of her reflection in the mirror above the fireplace? All I can see is my own pale face staring back. What was I hoping? That a glimpse of her might have endured?

'I'm just going to check on the girls,' Fiona says.

It's the first time Charles and I have been alone since we lay on his bed together, but so much has changed since then. I stare at his face as if I'll be able to discern some trace of his deception, but he looks just the same. He could always act – he never needed my stupid *Henry IV* tutorial – he always knew how. He stubs out his cigarette in an ashtray and closes the balcony door.

332

'You look worried.' He gestures at one of the chairs in front of the fire. 'What's up?'

I perch on the edge of the armchair, cradling my drink. I don't know how to begin. For just a second, I hope that Charles will be able to explain everything away and life can go back to normal. It's a wild hope, like a flare in the sky.

'Where do you think Ellie is?' I ask him.

He stares at me unblinkingly. 'In France, I would guess.'

'But her account is a fake. Her photos are from libraries – or stolen from elsewhere. Even her friends aren't real.'

He looks at me gently. 'Maybe she doesn't want to be found.'

I think of Ellie. Her small hand in mine as a child; reading her stories; helping her with forms when she was older. She was the only person who ever looked up to me. The only person, once Mother was gone, who tried to protect me. Even the money she made had kept me in our home, allowed me to go on as normal.

'Ellie loved me,' I say, gazing at the fire. 'She wouldn't want me to be worried like this. That's why I find it difficult . . .'

'Of course it is,' he says soothingly.

But he's misunderstood my meaning. I don't mean difficult in general. I mean it's hard to believe Ellie would have done this to me. 'I don't even know what Rose looks like,' I push on.

My heart speeds up a little, but I keep my face as placid as I can. It's time to be brave. It's time to stick up for my sister, to protect her as I always should have done at school. I glance at the balcony, remembering how Dickie

333

and Tom fell to their deaths. I know this might not be safe for me but I need to ask anyway.

Holding the glass tightly in my hands, I picture it shattered into sharp shards. That wouldn't be so hard to do. If it came to it. If I needed to protect myself.

'Charles,' I say, 'why do you have my sister's children?'

60

His face doesn't change. He's clever like that. But the words hang between us – you can almost see them. We are quiet for so long that I begin to doubt myself: to wonder if I'd asked the question at all.

Fiona bustles back in. 'If you ever think the art of conversation has died,' she says chirpily, 'you should try and put a pair of two-year-olds to bed.' She looks from one of us to the other.

'I don't know what you mean,' Charles says to me as if we're still alone.

I don't break his gaze. I'm not scared any more. 'I think you do.'

'What's going on?' asks Fiona, stopping in her tracks, leaning, for a moment, against the snooker table.

Charles doesn't say anything. I can tell he's being purposefully cautious. Slow to react.

'Could one of you please tell me,' snaps Fiona.

Her silky voice has gone. I'm glad. It's a relief. No

more pretending. It's just that now the creeping sense of dread is impossible to ignore.

'I asked why you had Ellie's children,' I say.

Fiona picks up one of the snooker balls from the table and holds it in her hand.

Charles is silent, waiting for her lead.

'What an extraordinary thing to say, Fran,' Fiona begins. 'I can't imagine why . . .'

'I know they're Ellie's.' I glance from her to Charles and back again. Saying the words makes me feel powerful. 'I found an old scan. I know now that she was having twins.'

Fiona exhales. She gives me a sympathetic look. 'She may have lost one. There are lots of reasons . . .'

'Look,' I say, cutting her off again, getting to my feet, so I can level with her, eye to eye, 'please don't do this. I *know* they're Ellie's.' I take a breath. 'And I bet Dickie knew too.'

I think of Caroline again. I wonder if she is still planning to travel here tonight, and, if so, how far she is behind me. It occurs to me now that they must have told her about my presence the night Dickie died. How well they hid it when I came here last. How well they've hidden everything.

Fiona folds her arms. She catches Charles's eye. Something unspoken passes between them.

'Ellie was our surrogate,' says Charles.

'So, it was a legal agreement?' I rest a hand on the back of the armchair to steady myself. 'There was paperwork? A parental order?'

'Not exactly.' Fiona shakes her head. 'It's a delicate matter.'

'Delicate,' I repeat.

'It was a gentleman's agreement between old school friends.' Fiona lets out a long sigh. 'It's complicated. Surrogacy agreements aren't enforceable by law. There's so much hoop-jumping,' she says bitterly. 'You can't pay the surrogate or, at least, not officially – just cover their expenses – and the money you spend is subject to scrutiny. After all that, they can walk away with your baby in the end anyway. They hold all the power. It made sense to ask a friend.'

I stay quiet, waiting for her to say more.

'We tried for years,' Fiona says wearily. 'Since not long after we got together – we knew it might be difficult. Then we did IVF, like everyone does. It cost a lot but we could afford it. Charles was in the City back then. We tried so many times. I hadn't realised quite how dreadful it would be – injecting yourself, the nausea, mood swings from the hormones. It put our marriage under such pressure. It was my fault, you see, that we couldn't. We knew that.' She laughs darkly. 'But Charles stood by me, didn't you?'

She looks over at him; he's standing now, his expression tender. He loves her, I realise. He always did.

'Eventually, after nine years, we decided to give up, started to talk about adoption – but that process is so long. Arduous. All the phases. The forms and the counselling and the waiting. And what do you get at the end? Somebody else's problem child,' she sighs. 'We wanted one of our own. Someone fresh. Untainted. And if it couldn't be both of ours, at least it could be his. Then, not long after we'd made that decision, he bumped into Ellie. The timing was perfect.'

'It was Ellie's idea,' Charles says softly. 'I ran into her in a bar in South Kensington. I was there with some colleagues. We'd had a few drinks. Ellie was working there and we got chatting at the end of her shift. Fi and I had been trying for years by then, and I told Ellie all about it, how stuck we were. And she offered. She said she was healthy and fit – and that she could do with the money.'

The dealer's words come back to me: *Money. That's all it takes for most people to do most things.* My sister holding my hand as I wept about the mortgage. Passing over the envelope on Christmas Day, waiting for my reaction. I was right to be worried about where that money came from.

'Where is Ellie now?' I ask.

Another silence; another look between them. I hold on to the back of the chair, staring at the marks and runnels on the leather. I run my finger along them and wonder again how well Ellie knew this room. If she ever came close to telling me about any of this. My thoughts are circling again around the thing I don't want to face.

'She's travelling,' Charles says. 'Like she always wanted to.' He smiles at me sadly. 'You know she wasn't happy – that she wanted to get away.'

'I need to see her. How can I get hold of her?'

'Look, Fran,' he says, taking a gulp of his drink, 'we're not in touch with her ourselves. She gave birth to the twins and then she left. That was it.'

It still doesn't add up, though. All those fake photos – the effort someone went to in order to mislead.

'I need to see her,' I say again.

338

He tries to catch Fiona's eye. 'I might have an email address somewhere.'

'No.' I shake my head. 'No more technology. No more smoke and mirrors. I need to see her. I need to hug her. To talk to her. Where is she, Fiona?'

Fiona has gone very quiet. She walks to the balcony and opens the door. A breeze whips in, lifting her hair, making her pull her cardigan around her. She picks up the packet of cigarettes Charles left in the ashtray and lights one.

'Do you want one?' she asks.

I shake my head.

'I don't usually,' she says. 'But . . .' She takes a drag and exhales. 'You shouldn't have come tonight, Fran. You should have just left us alone.'

I realise, now that Fiona is close to telling me, I don't want to know. The brief moment of power I experienced is replaced by something desperate.

'Whitby,' I say. 'She could be in Whitby. That's what I keep thinking. That was our safe place. Our happy place. She could be there, couldn't she? Nothing bad would happen to her there.'

Fiona takes another drag of her cigarette. A gust of wind blows the smoke into the room.

Charles gets to his feet, blustering. 'I'll get that email address for you.'

Fiona raises a tired hand to stop him. 'Don't. There's no point.'

Panic claws at me. I don't want her to continue. 'She's probably in Whitby, isn't she?'

Something seems to crumble in Fiona's bony frame.

It's like watching a puppet become detached from its strings, the way her shoulders droop, her face falls. Releasing the tension that has been holding her together for so long. She puts her hand on the balcony rail to steady herself. There is a moment of compassion then, gentleness even, in her eyes.

'You don't have to,' Charles says. He makes his way to her. It's not clear what he intends – I imagine him covering her mouth with his hand. Forcibly preventing the words from escaping. But it's already too late. She's given herself away.

A heaviness takes over me then, pushing down on my shoulders, making my legs long to fold beneath me. I'm glad I'm holding on to something to steady me.

'You know,' she says quietly. 'You know she never left this house.'

61

Ellie was so brave as a little girl. She was the kind of child who didn't cry or make a fuss when she fell over. I never thought of her as someone who needed protecting. I failed her, I think. And I failed Mother.

Charles has joined Fiona on the balcony. He takes one of her hands in his. I stare at them both: the golden couple in this golden house. Underneath all the glossy beauty is something rotten.

'Did you plan it?' I say at last.

'No,' says Fiona. 'God, no. We were desperate.' She looks at me. 'Have you ever wanted something that badly it blinded you?' She is quiet. 'I think you have, you know.'

It occurs to me with a wave of nausea that they will have read all of my emails to Ellie. Everything I ever wrote about Charles.

Fiona gives his hand a squeeze. I think of how I loved him. All that love piled up like dust. How difficult it is to square up that Charles with the person standing in front of me.

'It all went so wrong,' Charles says. 'You have to believe us. We never intended . . .'

'You trapped her,' I say. 'You hurt her.'

I can't say the words. The finality of what they did to my sister.

'She knew what she was getting into,' Charles says.

'She didn't know she was going to die.' I put a hand to my throat. My skin is wet with tears.

Charles and Fiona are quiet. They can't say anything to that.

'And you kept her alive on social media just to protect yourselves,' I say, with quiet fury. 'To hide what you'd done from the world. You had her laptop, didn't you? Her mobile? You could have just got rid of it all.'

'We did, eventually, after we'd changed the passwords,' Fiona says. 'And it's true that we didn't want to raise the alarm about Ellie, that we came up with an alternative story. But we also thought it would be easier for you. To keep her going in that way. And it was easier, wasn't it? To hate her than to miss her?'

I glare at her, the glass tight in my hand. She can't dress this up as something she did for me. 'I never hated her. I never stopped missing her.'

But Fiona doesn't have siblings, so perhaps she doesn't understand how it works. How even when I felt jealous of Ellie, how even when I wanted the things she had, I would still have been the first to defend her against the world.

'Even when you saw her with Charles?' asks Fiona quietly.

'You knew about that?'

'We planned it.'

'And Ellie knew too? No,' I answer my own question. 'She wouldn't do it to me.'

Perhaps, she wanted you to know, Fran, says Dickie's voice, of all people. *Perhaps she wanted to show you what was going on. That something wasn't right.*

'It wasn't what you thought,' Fiona says. 'He wasn't kissing her – he was kissing the bump. They're his babies, after all. Biologically his and hers – created in this house, with an insemination kit I bought myself. We don't have secrets, Charles and I.' She touches his cheek gently. 'I know about your meetings with him too. Your little *dates*,' she says. 'After your emails to Ellie about witnessing Dickie's death, we decided Charles should find out how much you knew. If there was any way you'd seen me there on the platform that night.' She draws a hand over her eyes. 'I don't think you did, though, did you? You didn't know as much as you thought.'

I stare at her.

'Dear Dickie.' Fiona lights another cigarette and glances at Charles. 'He thought he was being so subtle with his questions. If only he hadn't seen Alex's toes. We'd already booked the operation to separate them. If the timing had been different, if he hadn't noticed, it would never have . . . It was only later that we heard about his drawings and, of course, something had to be done about them too.'

'Dickie. That was hard.' Charles shakes his head.

'It was just an idea at first. We thought we'd just try,' Fiona says, almost apologetically. 'To see if it could be done. He was drinking again by then, which made it easier. And we knew about that Seventies concert and timed it so Charles and Dickie would leave the bar as it ended. It was easy enough to squeeze myself into the crowd. He spotted me, though . . .' She pauses. 'Before it happened. I reached out as if to pull him back and then . . .'

'You pushed instead,' I say.

'It was messy – you suspecting something. Telling Ellie. Talking to Caroline too. We wanted to find out what you knew – and Charles was the ideal man for the job.'

Fiona glances at her husband proudly and my eyes follow hers. His handsome face was the perfect disguise. It's always harder to think ill of the beautiful – I've known that since Chesterfield, so why did I forget?

'Of course, you completely lost it,' says Fiona. 'And started talking about the police – we never thought it would come to that. You had too much to lose yourself, being there on the night. We couldn't have them digging into things, so we had to make it look worse for Ellie, make her seem more suspicious. After that, she could come off social media, disappear completely. Charles thought of Tom – what he'd done to Ellie. And let's face it, the world is a better place without him.'

'How?' I say weakly.

'That was Charles. Tom had been shouting all over Facebook about his trip to Paris. He'd even tag the bars he was in, so it was easy enough to find him, to follow him home. And Tom was plastered, of course.'

Charles is still quiet, letting Fiona explain.

'He got an early-morning train back from Paris on

Christmas Eve and the news broke the next day,' she continues. 'It worked. People started connecting the cases the way we thought they would. Journalists started looking into what happened at Chesterfield. With *both* of them dead, Ellie became the prime suspect. No one dreamed we'd had anything to do with it, good friends that we were, sheltering Dickie's wife under our roof.'

Briefly, they seem pleased with their cleverness – or relieved perhaps to be able to tell their secrets, not to have to hold them so close to themselves. I think of everything I'd told Kat. It's a relief to remember her and Caroline – I'm not the only one who knows.

'You wouldn't leave it alone, would you, Fran?' Fiona says again. 'You should have.'

'What did you do to her?'

Fiona pulls a garden chair from the balcony and perches on it. 'We took such good care of her. I want you to know that. She had the best private healthcare – we didn't send her to our GP, we sent her to see an obstetrician on Wimpole Street who'd never met me. She went with my ID – all my papers, so that the babies were always mine on the system. We were the same sort of weight, luckily, the same blood type. Ellie knew all my history and Charles went with her to appointments, so he could help her out. She was meant to give birth there and come back here to recover, but the twins had other ideas – they arrived early while she was here, not long after her fight with you.'

Hovering outside her bedroom, trying to think of the right words. I should have burst in; I should have said whatever it took to make her stay.

345

'She came to see us.' Fiona takes a gulp of her drink. 'But the problem was she'd started to change her mind. She seemed less sure about our arrangement in the weeks before, but especially after Christmas. She'd bring up the presents you'd given her – the books and so on – and how excited you were about the baby. Ellie was such a pragmatist, as you know, but she started to talk about family and compromises. Things like that. At one stage, a couple of weeks before the birth, she even came up with the hare-brained idea of us taking one child each – splitting the twins up. We should have realised then . . .'

I want to ask, *Realised what?* But the words get stuck in my throat.

'It could have worked perfectly,' says Fiona. 'It was such a beautiful plan. So simple. I pretended to be house-bound during pregnancy – so ill I couldn't go anywhere or see anyone – and after she had them, Ellie should have simply moved abroad with the money we'd given her. Disappeared. And we'd pick up the little red book from our consultant and present them at the registry office as our own.'

My hand is tight around the glass. 'What did you do to her?'

'The birth was barbaric. Beautiful but barbaric. The twins came early, like I said, when Ellie was staying with us. I think she was planning to bolt, even then. She was so upset about her fight with you. She wanted to make it better. She kept saying, "Do you think I should tell her?" She was sitting in that chair.' Fiona looks over to where I'd been sitting. 'We said: no, that she should calm down. That it would all be all right. And then her waters broke. Thank God she was with me,' Fiona says without irony. 'I helped deliver them. I was the first to hold them. It was a painful birth – Ellie tore herself, but she was brave. I stitched her up. I've never felt closer to a person. We were friends, you see, before it all went wrong. But then, as the days went by, she got agitated again.'

'What do you mean?'

'She started talking about keeping them. She was desperate to tell you, so we had to hide her phone, but she got more and more upset. I started to sedate her a little, with her medication for postpartum pain. Just a low dose at first, to calm her down, but her mood swings got worse. We caught her outside – trying to escape with one of them. In January. The dead of winter. With a newborn.' She shakes her head. Another slug of gin. 'A wicked thing to do. So we restrained her after that, kept her locked in the room, and I increased her dose, added it to her water. Her tea. Any way I could. I increased it quite a lot actually.'

The silence between us hardens like ice.

'She was unbalanced, you see. It's the same with race-horses. There comes a point – if they're damaged – when it's crueller to keep them alive. Beautiful creatures, but then . . .' Fiona gazes out from the balcony. 'It's actually not the worst way to go.'

347

62

Ellie's last days were spent in this house, drugged and restrained. I can't bear to think about it, about how long she would have lain like that, drifting in and out of consciousness. About how they might have forced the pills down her if she refused to take them. I shiver, though I'm still standing next to the fire. I look at the door; try to calculate how long it'll take me to get out of the room.

'Join us on the balcony,' Fiona says. 'It's a beautiful night.'

Fear pins me to the ground.

'You gave us a heart attack that day we found you in the water,' she says. The wind lifting her hair. 'We thought you knew. Christ, we couldn't have you *both* in there.'

It takes a couple of moments for the realisation to sink in. The lake. Where I always used to sit. Ellie has been there all this time.

'How?' I'm still holding on to my glass. It's the closest thing I have to a weapon.

'In Charles's trunk,' Fiona says. 'Weighed down with stones.'

I can picture it – CM Fry. I shake my head.

Charles lets go of Fiona's hand and comes towards me. 'It won't hurt,' he says. 'There won't be time.'

I take a step back.

'Our girls have a good life. The best life. Everything money could buy. Ellie couldn't give them that; you couldn't either. Please don't make this hard for me.' He pulls a pained expression, still acting, giving it his best performance, though there's no need now. 'You wanted to die, didn't you? When we found you in the water? You wanted to go.'

The smack my tumbler makes against the fireplace makes us both jump. I look at it, as surprised as Charles. I'm left with the glass's jagged remains still in my hand.

'Other people know,' I tell him, without shaking, without breaking eye contact. 'Caroline. The press. I've spoken to a journalist. You can't kill all of us.'

I notice how calm I sound, how in control.

Charles stops for a moment; he's made it around the table. He's only a few paces from me now. 'You're bluffing.'

'No,' I say, still clutching the glass. 'I never could. That's what *you* do.'

He hesitates, making up his mind.

'Charlie,' says Fiona.

We both turn back to her. She's climbed up on the balcony rail, sitting on the edge.

'It's over,' she says to him gently. 'We're done.' She sounds tired. Like someone wearily waiting for a bus.

'We can't keep going; we can't keep getting rid of people. It has to stop.'

'No,' murmurs Charles. An exhalation so quiet I don't know if she can hear him.

'I wanted them so much,' she says. 'More than anything. But they were never mine. Not really. And now they'll be taken away.'

Charles starts to move towards her, but the table is in the way. He's not going to make it in time.

'It's all been too hard,' Fiona says. 'Whatever happens next, it's going to get worse. It's only going to get worse.'

I want to tell her that I'll love them, that I'll give them all the love Ellie never could – not for Fiona's sake, but for my sister's, so it's the last thing Fiona hears. So that my words follow her like Furies.

But Fiona, being Fiona, doesn't let me finish.

63

Cleanly, neatly, she tips herself back as if she is on a swing. The last I see of her is a flash of her pedicured feet.

The house is silent in the moment afterwards. There's a depth to the quiet – a stillness, like the bottom of a well. Then, quickly, things change. Downstairs, a child shouts. Charles cranes his neck over the balcony to see and makes a noise like nothing I've heard. Worse than how we cried over Mother. How Ellie shrieked. Even more broken than me. You wouldn't think it would be that way around.

I need to block out the sound of him, to go somewhere else. Under the water with Ellie. Where I want to be. But then he's on me. Not the Charles I knew, but a roaring creature with an unrecognisable face, his hands warm and tight around my neck.

'She's gone. Isn't that what you always wanted?' he hisses. 'It's just you and me now.'

I can't move. My breath is rasping, reedy. Very quickly everything is yellow, just as Ellie said. My mind is as blank as a sheet of paper.

He tightens his fingers around my neck and the yellow turns red. Just like that. I try to remember that day in the prep room. How my heart leapt at the proximity of him. How I'd explained the difference between the types of acting. But he never needed my help. I always thought he was more noble than the rest of them, more restrained, but that wasn't it at all. He was just a better actor.

'You're a big fake.' My words are strangled and slow. 'Using other people,' I croak. 'Throwing them away.'

'Shut up, Freaky Fran.' He laughs nastily.

Dark red turns to purple. I'm struggling to speak now. It won't be long.

'It's OK.' His voice is softer. 'You'll be with her soon. We should have left you in the lake with her that day . . . Such a gorgeous little thing, your sister. So fit and strong. I liked watching her. I always did.'

My breath is so thin now, I'm struggling to hear him, to focus on the words. I don't want this to be the end. I'm not ready. I think of my mother stroking my hair. Ellie's small hand in mine. The bonfire smell of my father's jumpers. Branwell curled up next to me in the morning. Tiny snatched fragments of what I have loved.

'I'm like you,' Charles says. 'I enjoy watching too – that's why I was so early on the scene – that's how the boys got into the pool. I gave them the code – not Juliet – but I didn't tell them I'd be up in the gallery, watching. And then, just as I was leaving, I bumped into Dickie fleeing for help. I think he always had his suspicions.'

352

One more breath, as thin as a thread. Then another. I think of Daisy tilting her head back, the way her soft blonde hair falls over her forehead.

Focus on your hand, Fran: what you have in your hand. He has your neck, but your right arm could do it.

Charles is nearly done. As the grip becomes tighter, his rambling grows looser, like something unspooling.

'But Dickie was loyal. The most loyal person I ever knew. So he never said, never let on that I was there: that I watched what Tom did to her.'

Women don't fight to kill – that was what our self-defence teacher said. But he didn't know what I was made of. That I might have it in me to act, after all.

'I didn't tell her until the end,' he says. 'When she was delirious. Drug-addled. On her way out. I thought it'd give her something to think about. Sometimes it can be fun to find out just how bad you can be, when everybody thinks you're so bloody good.'

The colours are changing again. I don't have long. If I'm going to do it, I need to do it soon.

The name of the artery appears in my head: carotid. A word so like carrots. Which give me hiccups. As they did to Mother. And Ellie. One of the things that run through us all like Whitby rock.

Ellie, I think. *I love you.* And I stab him in the neck with the glass.

353

64

Two little girls. One in her bed, one on her feet. Both petite and blonde. Hair like candyfloss. Skinny legs. They move as lightly as birds as they jump up and down to greet a night-time visitor. No wonder they were rushed away from me every time I got close. Perhaps it occurred to Dickie even before he spotted the webbed toes. It would have become clear to anyone who knew and loved Ellie. The truth is pushing its way through – weaving itself into their hair, on their faces.

I look at my nieces. My eyes drink them in. I have missed them every day of their lives.

Rose. A pair of Roses.

The one on her feet wrinkles her nose. 'Where's Mumma?'

I have locked the door to the games room in anticipation of this question. I've also called the police, washed my face in the kitchen sink and put my coat over my blood-soaked clothes. I'm grateful now that I recorded everything on my phone. I'm not sure how much it picked up, but hopefully it will make explaining everything easier.

When I called Caroline, she was on her way, frantic. She should be here soon. I can tell her everything then.

I suppose I could have left the children in their nursery until the police arrived. I could have waited to see them.

No, I couldn't.

'Who are you?' asks the braver Rose. The one on her feet.

'I'm your mummy's sister.'

She looks unsure, glancing at her twin for confirmation.

I reach out to touch her hair. Golden wisps like smoke. Like something that could disappear. I'm not greedy; I just want to stroke one curl – to know the feel of it beneath my fingertips, as soft and light as Ellie's hair was. There is so much I want to ask them; there is so much I want to know.

Do they have any memory of her at all, buried deep? Her smell? The sound of her voice? When did she leave them? When was she erased? Is there ever a day, sitting on Fiona's lap, when they remember another mother?

I spot *The Velveteen Rabbit* on the bookshelf and go to get it. 'Do you want to read this?' I ask them. 'It's a story about real love.'

I don't know why, but, as we wait for the police, I think of the power of three. That's what we had – Mother, Ellie and me. Three makes a shape in the way that one never can. Or even two. But three – that's a story.

I should learn to be wary of such things. In my desperation for them, I missed everything important. Charles was my favourite story. My happy ending. But I was so

355

set on him that I missed who the heroes and villains were. I got everything upside down.

They are such good girls, Ellie. You would be so proud of them. They sit either side of me as I read the book. I think they enjoy it. They are so young still – not quite three. Young enough to start again, I hope.

As I read, I remember the patch under the weeping willow, where it's always been warmer, where it never ices over. Was that your way of telling me? Was that what I was swimming towards?

'I'm sorry I failed you,' I say out loud, and I start to cry.

The braver Rose puts her hand in mine. 'Everybody's scared today,' she says.

I think I can hear a car at the end of the drive and imagine for a second that it's Charles coming home. But not Charles now – not the man upstairs, lying still – but Charles as a teenager, running along the rugby pitch. Charles saying, 'You're a legend, Fran.' Charles leaping out of the car to tell us there has been a mistake.

But my ears are playing tricks on me – it's just the sound of traffic in the distance. The police will be here soon.

I look at the children next to me and make a promise – this time one I can keep – that no one will ever hurt them. That I will keep them safe.

'What are we doing?' asks the quieter twin.

'We're going to sit here,' I say to the girls who are not Rose, but also are. 'And we're going to wait.'

Acknowledgements

The idea for this book – and the birth of Fran – came from a conversation with one of my favourite people, Jeanie Cordy-Simpson. Jeanie and I were at boarding school together (very different from Chesterfield) and spent our teenage years with ill-advised crushes on boys who were completely unsuitable for us. These usually ended with us in tears in the loo at parties (not so different from Chesterfield). In the years since, I've thought a lot about the delusions and disappointments of obsessive romantic love – how we can get it so wrong and how much more the infatuation tends to say about the subject than the object of affection.

Conversations with other friends, old and new, formed the backbone of my research for this novel. I'm hugely grateful to the following for their patience and time: Emily and Sophie Hughes, Carole Mattock and Charlotte Rogerson. Thank you too to the wonderful team at Waterstones Abergavenny, in particular Cicely and Sol, who let me come in for a day of work-shadowing to jog my memory of my bookselling days. Thank you to Pete Small for answering lots of questions at what should have been a relaxing family gathering. To Dr John Carr and Miss Samantha Steele MRCOG for replying to endless messages (some during a pandemic, I might add) about birth registration, twins and scans. To Alison Thompson MBE, former coroner for west London, for responding to my queries about inquests so promptly and helpfully. And to Angus Cordy-Simpson for supplying detailed answers about the workings of a school rugby team. Any inaccuracies or wild leaps in imagination are entirely my responsibility.

Of course, none of it would have come to fruition without the team at Avon. What a wonderful, warm and supportive lot you are – and in the most difficult conditions on the run-up to publication. I was lucky enough to have not one but two incredible editors – my heartfelt thanks to Rachel Faulkner-Willcocks, who believed in *You and Me* from the beginning, and to Tilda McDonald, who worked tirelessly with me on the novel while Rachel was on maternity leave. Thank you too to the fabulous Sabah Khan – the best PR in publishing – and to Ellie Pilcher, Bethany Wickington, Helena Newton and every single person who has supported me in this project. Thank you also to Hannah Schofield, Alison Bonomi and the team at LBA Books, everyone at the Intercontinental Literary Agency and Emily Hayward-Whitlock at the Artists Partnership.

Huge thanks, as always, to my writing group: Saneh Arora, Conrad Stephenson and Adam Lively. Thank you, Sophie Rouhaud, for proofreading my French. And enormous thanks, too, to my early readers Nancy Alsop and Emma Bamford.